He Wanted [obscured] Where Her Softness and Strength Had Come From,

to know if he could ever love as she did, with sweetness and fire and courage. But he couldn't ask that. So he asked the only question he could, and Angel heard the other question beneath it, the one Hawk couldn't ask.

"Are these wild raspberries?" asked Hawk.

"No. They're like a house cat that has gone feral," Angel said. "Created and bred by man and then abandoned. Most things treated like that wither and die. Some survive . . . and in the right season the strongest survivors bear a sweet, wild fruit that is the most beautiful thing on earth. Like you, Hawk."

ELIZABETH LOWELL

writes in several fields. When friends ask her why she decided to write "romances, of all things," she just smiles. She has been married for sixteen years to the only man she has ever loved. How can she help but write novels that celebrate love and life?

Dear Reader:

There is an electricity between two people in love that makes everything they do magic, larger than life. This is what we bring you in SILHOUETTE INTIMATE MOMENTS.

SILHOUETTE INTIMATE MOMENTS are longer, more sensuous romance novels filled with adventure, suspense, glamor or melodrama. These books have an element no one else has tapped: excitement.

We are proud to present the very best romance has to offer from the very best romance writers. In the coming months look for some of your favorite authors such as Elizabeth Lowell, Nora Roberts, Erin St. Claire and Brooke Hastings.

SILHOUETTE INTIMATE MOMENTS are for the woman who wants more than she has ever had before. These books are for you.

Karen Solem
Editor-in-Chief
Silhouette Books

A Woman Without Lies

Elizabeth Lowell

Silhouette Intimate Moments

Published by Silhouette Books New York

America's Publisher of Contemporary Romance

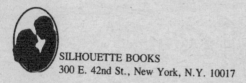
SILHOUETTE BOOKS
300 E. 42nd St., New York, N.Y. 10017

Copyright © 1985 by Two of a Kind, Inc.
Cover artwork copyright © 1985 George Jones

Distributed by Pocket Books

ISBN: 0-373-07000-4

First Silhouette Books printing February, 1985

10 9 8 7 6 5 4 3 2 1

America's Publisher of Contemporary Romance

Printed in the U.S.A.

Books by Elizabeth Lowell

Silhouette Desires

Summer Thunder #77

Silhouette Intimate Moments

To those who have risked love—
win, lose or draw

Chapter 1

ANGELINA LANGE STOOD QUIETLY AMID THE RAINBOW blaze of her stained glass creations. Some panels brooded in shades of green and blue, forest and ocean and sky, mountains falling away into the distance. Other panels radiated the iridescent beauty of Tiffany glass touched by shafts of gold, evoking British Columbia's cloud-swept summers. Several panels shimmered with drifts of flowers. A handful of panels were impressionistic swirls of color and movement, a sensual richness that was as compelling as a lover's whispered invitation.

The panels came in all sizes and shapes. Most were set in wooden frames and hung against the gallery's huge transparent wall. A few panels were suspended from the high ceiling. Light from both natural and artificial sources struck rich colors out of pieces of glass, making the room quiver with shadows of every hue.

A summer cloud came and went, concealing and then revealing the sun. Murmurs of pleasure rose from the people inside the room as Vancouver's clear sunlight poured through the gallery's transparent wall, making the stained glass art scintillate with brilliant colors. Unconsciously, Angel tipped her face toward the cataract of light, letting it wash over her. Her pale, curling hair glowed molten gold, a color as pure and compelling as any she had used in her stained glass. For a moment she simply stood, filling herself with light.

"Angelina?"

Angel opened her haunted, sea-colored eyes and turned toward the diffident voice. Bill Northrup, the gallery owner, stood nearby, quietly waiting for her attention. At one point in their relationship, he had wanted considerably more than her attention. Now, however, he settled for what she would give him, her friendship and her art.

Angel smiled at Bill, but her eyes were still haunted by the sadness that was as much a part of her as her long legs and slender body.

"I always feel that I should sign my pieces 'Angelina and Sun,' because without that incredible light, my stained glass is nothing," said Angel.

Bill shook his head. "You're too modest. Look around. You're selling very well, especially for a first show."

Angel looked, but she had eyes only for the brilliant shards of light and shadow, the shifting play of colors, the feeling of being in the center of a fantastic, slowly turning jewel. She was pleased that she was selling her creations, because that was how she earned her living. Money as such didn't give her any particular joy, however. Colors did. That, and knowing that other people enjoyed her rainbow visions.

"I'm glad," she said simply. "Beauty should be shared."

Bill sighed. "You're not hard enough for this life."

"A hardcase angel?" she asked, laughing lightly, turning aside the old argument. "Not very likely, is it?"

"So I'll be the hardcase and you be the angel," retorted Bill.

"That was our agreement," she murmured. Her lips curved in a tiny, teasing smile. "You've held up your end very well."

"The guy waiting for you could give me lessons."

Angel's honey eyebrows arched in silent question.

"On the phone," explained Bill. "Miles Hawkins."

She shook her head in a gesture of bafflement that made her breast-length hair shimmer and run with light. "I don't know him."

"He knows you. Said it was something about Derry and he had to see you immediately. I explained that the show won't be over for an hour, but the man wouldn't listen to reason." Bill shrugged. "I'll tell him to—"

"No. If it's about Derry, I'll take the call."

"I thought so. Derry's the only male you care about."

Angel gave Bill a swift, blue-green look, sensing the beginning of another old argument. "Derry is like a brother to me. Nothing more. And certainly nothing less."

Bill sighed and muttered to Angel's retreating back, "Yeah, and he's one handsome kid who isn't related to you in any way."

Angel heard and was momentarily surprised. She didn't think of Derry as physically handsome, although she had to agree that he was. Derry's blond looks and muscular body had turned more than one feminine head. But when Angel thought of Derry, she thought of his dedication to becoming a doctor, the ruthless discipline that kept him studying even in the summer, his anguish and rage the night he had dragged her clear of the wrecked car.

If anyone, even an utter stranger, wanted to talk to her about Derry, Angel would listen.

She walked into Bill's private office, punched in the lighted button on the front of the phone, and put the receiver to her ear. "Mr. Hawkins?" she said quietly, but her question and hesitation were clear. "I'm afraid I don't remember you."

"I suppose Derry spoke of me as Hawk," said the deep male voice at the other end of the line.

"Oh . . . *that* Mr. Hawkins. Derry's letters have been full of 'Hawk this' and 'Hawk that' for weeks. I didn't recognize your full name."

There was a pause before the deep voice resumed. Angel wondered for a moment if she had insulted him. She hoped not. Hawk was crucial to Derry's hopes of becoming a doctor.

"Derry said you'd be up to your blond curls in admirers," continued Hawk curtly, "but that you'd meet me in the Golden Stein if he asked you to."

Angel smiled to herself. "Derry is a tease, Mr. Hawkins. The people are admiring stained glass, not me. But he was right about the rest. If he wants me to meet you, I will."

"Just like that?" murmured Hawk. "You'd meet a stranger?"

The words sent shivers of uncertainty over Angel's skin. Hawk wasn't teasing or really questioning her. His voice was hard, disdainful, the tone both dark and cold.

"Just like that," agreed Angel quietly. "I'll be at the Golden Stein in ninety minutes."

"No. Now."

"What?" said Angel, not believing that she had heard correctly.

"Now, Angel." Then, sardonically, "Your Derry needs you."

"But—"

The line was dead. Angel stared at the phone, confused and more than a little irritated. Hawk had been rude, demanding, and abrupt. There was also the fact that nobody called her Angel, not even Derry. Angelina, yes. Angie, yes. Angel? Never. Only in the privacy of her own mind did she acknowledge that name, the name she had begun to call herself when she woke up in the hospital after surviving a wreck she'd had no right to survive. A wreck she hadn't really wanted to survive. Not at first. Not alone.

"Trouble?" asked Bill, standing at Angel's elbow.

Angel looked up from the receiver. She replaced it very gently. "I don't know." Decisively, Angel turned away. She bent over to remove her purse and lightweight black shawl from a desk drawer. "Make my apologies, Bill."

"Angelina, you can't just walk out on your own show," began Bill in a voice that tried to be reasonable.

"Derry needs me."

"Your career needs you more!"

Angel looked out into the full gallery. "They're buying my stained glass, not me."

Bill swore, started to argue, then gave up. Angel was immovable on two subjects. Her art was one of them. Derry Ramsey was the other.

Angel pulled the silk shawl over her black dress as she stepped out the back door of the gallery. Even in midsummer, Vancouver could be cool, especially when clouds and sun played tag across the afternoon sky.

She wasn't surprised to find the Golden Stein crowded. It

was a favorite watering hole with tourists and natives alike. Normally she would have avoided the noisy, smoky, exuberant bar. This afternoon, however, wasn't normal. This afternoon Derry had asked her to meet a rude man called Hawk, even though Derry knew that she was in the midst of her first stained glass show in the Northrup Gallery. In a way, she was almost grateful to Hawk for his rudeness. It kept her from dwelling on all the unhappy reasons Derry might have for needing her.

Dressed in black silk, her fringed black shawl thrown carelessly over her shoulders, her pale hair seeming to gather and concentrate light, Angel stood just inside the Stein's door, waiting for her eyes to adjust to the dim carmine light favored by the bar's habitués.

Hawk watched her intently from a nearby table. The Stein's front door opened again, bathing Angel in light, making her long, bright hair shimmer and float in the breeze. Derry's description—tall, blond, and skinny— barely skimmed the reality of the slender, self-contained woman standing by the door. Yet Hawk was sure that she was Derry's Angie. No one else could have eyes like that, too large for her face, too haunted to belong to a woman her age.

Hawk's mouth formed a cynical, downward-curving line as he realized how young Angie—no, *Angel*—was. Any woman who looked like that wasn't an Angie. She undoubtedly wasn't an Angel, either, no matter how ethereal she appeared. Hawk's lips thinned as he remembered the last innocent-looking blond he'd taken for a while, an actress with nothing beneath her soft exterior but emptiness and lies.

The actress was, in short, like every other woman Hawk had known. Like Angel standing so quietly, staring at him. Angel. A three-dimensional lie. But a beautiful one.

Damned beautiful. The worst ones always were. So he would call her Angel, and each time he used the name, it would remind him that she was anything but.

Angel looked back at the man who was watching her from only a few feet away. Instinctively she knew that the man was Hawk. In the atmosphere of forced bonhomie that pervaded the Stein, Hawk was like a rocky island at sunset, darkness condensed amid color, immovable certainty anchored in an aimlessly shifting sea. Then the front door opened again, spearing the man with light, and Angel knew why he was called Hawk. It wasn't the blunt angles of his face or his thick, black hair and upswept eyebrows. It wasn't his hard, lean body. It wasn't even his predatory grace as he walked toward her. It was his eyes, the eyes of a hawk, a crystalline brown that was clear and deep, lonely and wild.

"Hawk," she said.

"Angel." His voice was deep, gritty, as essentially uncivilized as his eyes.

"People call me Angie."

There was a moment of uncanny stillness as Hawk measured her. "People call me Mr. Hawkins to my face. Even friendly puppies like Derry Ramsey."

Angel hesitated, wondering at the abrasive description of Derry, for Derry thought that Hawk all but walked on water. "What do people call you to your back?" she asked, curious to know more about the man who had earned Derry's unqualified hero worship.

Hawk's eyes narrowed. "A lot of names that angels wouldn't know about." His clear, hard eyes measured her impersonally, lingering on the nimbus of light that was her hair. "Angel. It suits your looks."

Hawk's tone said that her name was Angel so far as he was concerned, and Angel was what he would call her. She bridled at his arrogance, then forced herself to relax. Hawk couldn't know the meaning of the name Angel to her, something alive that once had died.

"Then I will call you Hawk," she said, her voice soft, "and we both will be unhappy with our names."

Hawk's left eyebrow lifted, emphasizing the ruthless lines of his face, but all he said was, "What do you drink, Angel?" As he spoke he turned away from her, returning to his table.

"Sunlight."

Hawk turned back so suddenly that Angel couldn't suppress a startled sound. She had never seen such quickness in a man. Yet for all his speed, his motions were smooth, utterly controlled.

"Sunlight," he said, gesturing to the smoky room, "is in short supply here."

"I didn't come here to drink, Hawk. I came because Derry needs me." Though Angel's voice was soft, there was the same determination in it that had warned Bill that she wasn't prepared to be reasonable on the subject. "What does Derry need?"

Hawk hadn't missed the changed quality of Angel's voice. "A new leg," he said bluntly. "He had an accident."

The room swirled darkly around Angel, sound spinning into cries of pain, carmine light splintering into broken glass silvered by moonlight, the smell of raw gas choking her, fear and pain clawing in her throat. She tried to say something, to ask questions, to reassure herself that Derry was all right, that this wasn't a return to the horrible car wreck three years ago when her mother, her father, and her fiancé had died, and she had been broken almost beyond healing. But Angel could say nothing, do nothing, except tremble and fight for breath. Derry had saved her life three years ago. She could not bear to think that he was hurt, needing her, and she wasn't there.

Even in the Stein's dim light, Angel's sudden loss of color was obvious. Hawk heard her harsh intake of breath, saw her sway, felt the coldness of her skin as he grabbed her, steadying her.

"D-Derry?" asked Angel, forcing the word between trembling lips.

"It's just a broken leg," said Hawk harshly, shaking Angel to make sure that he had her attention. Then he saw the fear and pain in the depths of her eyes and his hands instinctively gentled. "He's all right, Angel." Hawk's voice was soft, reassuring, a surprising sound from a man who looked so ruthless. "Just a broken leg."

"Car wreck," she said hoarsely. "All that glittering broken glass and twisted metal . . . screams."

Hawk's eyes narrowed as a chill moved over him. Angel sounded so certain that Derry had hurt himself in a car wreck. The certainty was there in her eyes, and the horror.

"Soccer, not a car wreck," said Hawk, his hands tightening on Angel. "Derry and some friends were playing soccer. He went up to deflect the ball, came down wrong, and broke his ankle in two places."

For an instant Angel sagged against Hawk. Then her head came up and her legs straightened. She looked up at him with eyes that were too large and too dark for her face, wondering if he had meant to be cruel with his first, brutal words describing Derry's injury. *A new leg.* She searched the uncompromising lines of Hawk's face for long moments before she realized that he could have had no way of knowing the impact his words would have on her.

"Angel?" Hawk's fingertips found the pulse beating erratically in her throat. "Did you hear me?"

"Yes. . . ."

Angel's voice was so soft that Hawk had to lean close to understand. His fingers slid around her throat and lost themselves in her smoothly curling hair, but his thumb remained on her pulse. He pulled her close, cradling her against his chest, rocking her slowly. The gestures were instinctive, surprising him as much as they surprised her. Yet what he did was natural, what he wished someone had done for him when he was young, or even when he was not. He had seen horror-shadowed eyes before, seen broken glass and wrecked cars and death. The horror and some of the wrecks had been his, but nobody had comforted him. Perhaps that was why he comforted her now. And perhaps it was simply that she was soft and smelled like sunshine and her skin was warming beneath his touch.

When Hawk's lips brushed Angel's temple, her closed eyes, the sensitive corner of her mouth, he felt the sudden surge of her heartbeat beneath his thumb. She moved subtly, clinging to his comforting touch without holding him, and her breath came out in a ragged sigh. Hawk's expression changed, cynical again. Angel was indeed like other women he had known. When she wasn't with the man she loved, she loved the man she was with.

Angel sensed the sudden coldness in Hawk's touch. She looked up at him, confused. She hadn't expected comfort from him. Nor had she expected to find herself suddenly adrift from his warmth while he watched her with eyes that were calculating, as cold as the line of his mouth.

"Save those big haunted eyes for Derry," said Hawk. "He's young enough to believe anything."

Abruptly, Angel became aware of the noisy bar, the amused glances from nearby patrons, the dense carmine light giving a satanic cast to Hawk's already harsh features. She didn't know what kind of game Hawk was playing with her. She didn't want to know. It was bad enough that her skin was warm everywhere he had touched her, a warmth that had begun with his comforting touch and then had subtly altered into a heat that she had not felt in three years.

Angel turned and walked toward the door, leaving Hawk holding her silk shawl, all that had remained behind when his hands had tightened to prevent her from leaving. He looked at the black silk draped like broken wings in his hands. Then he swore.

The sun blinded Angel as she stepped outside. She clutched her purse and walked quickly to the street, looking for a taxi. When her vision cleared, she spotted one. She raised her arm, only to have her wrist caught by lean, brown fingers. She didn't have to turn around to know that she was in the grip of Hawk. She didn't bother to struggle against his grasp, knowing it was futile. His fingers were like . . . talons. Turning, she confronted Hawk with her silence and sea-green eyes.

"Going somewhere?" asked Hawk.

"To Derry."

"Lucky Derry," said Hawk, sarcasm making his voice into a whip.

For an instant Angel looked as though she had been struck. Her eyes narrowed with anger. Then her expression changed as she remembered two simple truths: Hawk was important to Derry's future; Derry was important to her. For Derry's sake she would hold her tongue and her temper. And for her own sake. Unbridled emotions would destroy her.

Hawk saw the change in Angel. Where there had been emotions and color, now there was nothing. She waited to be released with a stillness and controlled patience that was more infuriating than any struggle would have been. He was holding on to her, but she was utterly removed from him.

"Nothing to say?" challenged Hawk. "No pretty-pleases and practiced sighs and enticing little struggles?"

Angel waited, controlling her anger. She had had a lot of practice at that since the wreck. The rage she had felt at her parents' deaths, at Grant's death, had nearly destroyed what Derry managed to salvage from the wreck. She hadn't begun to live again until she had learned to control her savage fury at the unfairness of life and death. Like the ability to walk again, serenity had been won at appalling cost. She wouldn't surrender to anger now.

Angel thought of sunlight and colors in more hues than she had words to describe. She gathered the colors in her mind like a miser hoarding gold. She stood beneath them like summer rain, colors bathing her, washing away destructive emotions. Colors, beautiful colors. Cerulean and ruby, topaz and umber, sapphire and wine and jade . . . but most of all, she sought the crimson perfection of a rose climbing toward dawn, soft petals triumphant and serene in their unfolding.

Angel opened her eyes. They were clear, as deep as the sea. "What do you want, Mr. Hawkins?"

Hawk took a swift, silent breath. In the brief time that he had been with Angel, he had seen her shocked and afraid, had seen relief and the first stirrings of passion darken her eyes, had seen her hurt and enraged. This eerie calm was unexpected. He had seen nothing like it except in his own mirror, when he had been young enough to still feel emotions and old enough to know that he had to conceal what he felt or be destroyed. Now he was simply controlled.

It angered him that Angel seemed so controlled. She was too young to have such discipline, and too shallow to need it. She flitted from man to man and feeling to feeling like the pretty, mindless little butterfly she was.

But she was one hell of an actress. He'd give her that. It

was the most convincing appearance of real emotion and real control that he had seen in years.

"Derry will tell you what I want," said Hawk curtly, not releasing Angel's wrist.

Hawk walked quickly toward a waiting limousine. Angel followed, because she had no choice. She got in for the same reason. Hawk dumped her shawl in her lap as the limousine pulled out into traffic.

"Where are we going?" asked Angel calmly.

"To your one true love," retorted Hawk.

Angel simply looked at him, waiting.

"That's what I thought," said Hawk in his caustic voice. "Women like you have so many true loves that they can't tell the players without a scorecard."

She looked at him with wide, calm eyes. "I don't know what you're talking about. And," she added coolly, "neither do you. You know nothing about me, and you prove it every time you open your mouth."

Hawk's lips took a downward, sardonic curve. "I know one thing. I'm going to do Derry a favor this summer."

"Buying Eagle Head isn't a favor, Mr. Hawkins. It's a shrewd business decision."

Hawk shrugged. "I didn't mean the land." He looked at the woman beside him, remembering how she had softened against his body when he held her. The clean summer smell of her hair caressed his senses, making him take a deep, involuntary breath. It rankled that she should look so aloof, so untouched, when she was just like every other woman— emptiness and lies.

In silence Hawk watched Angel's coolness and reserve, and remembered her softness and sighs. He decided then that he was going to have her. And when he was finished, he would strip her of her bright facade. He would be sure that Derry knew his Angie was no angel. Derry was far too young to cope with a woman like Angel Lange. He would be hurt as Hawk had once been hurt; but unlike Hawk, Derry was too soft to survive that kind of lesson.

Hawk was not. He had known about women like Angel since the night of his eighteenth birthday—women who took and took and took, giving only the casual use of their bodies in return. Hawk didn't mind that. Not anymore. He'd become a taker too. Once Angel got used to the idea that he saw through her, they would get along just fine. Users, both of them. Using each other.

Angel looked out the window but all she really saw was the image of Hawk as she had first seen him in the dark bar. If he hadn't been gentle with her for those few instants, she would have decided that he was merely cruel, and avoided him. Yet her first impression of his loneliness had been oddly reinforced by his comforting touch. She knew that loneliness could give a person both a capacity for cruelty and, eventually, a capacity for empathy.

Empathy took longer to develop than cruelty, however. First you had to heal. Once she had raged at Derry for dragging her out of the wreck, for forcing her to live when the man she loved had died. Derry had been appalled. Then he had wept and she had held him, hating herself for hurting him, hating herself for being alive, hating everything except Derry. He was as alone as she, yet he wasn't cruel. That realization had been the turning point in her long climb out of agony and despair. From that instant she had cherished Derry. In time she had even thanked him for dragging her out of the wreckage of her past into an uncertain future.

She wondered what Hawk's turning point would be. Then she remembered his strength and harshness and wondered if there was anything powerful enough to penetrate the ruthless chill that surrounded him as deeply as sky surrounded a hunting hawk. Or perhaps, like a hawk, he preferred the lonely, icy reaches of the sky to anything human.

Yet Hawk had been so warm for just a moment, so close.

The motion of the limousine changed as it turned toward Vancouver harbor. Angel swayed slightly, caught herself, and recognized her surroundings. Island Taxi's bright sign poked above the calm water. Just beyond the sign a pontoon plane floated. She turned quickly to Hawk. He was watching her. She sensed that he had been watching her the whole time. With a shock, she noticed that he had a mustache, a smooth band of midnight just above his hard mouth, black hair shifting and gleaming subtly as he moved his head. She hadn't noticed the mustache before, not with those hard, dark eyes watching her.

"Hawk—Mr. Hawkins—"

"Hawk," he said, watching for her reaction as he spoke. "Call me Hawk, Angel. It will help both of us to remember what we really are."

"What does that mean?"

"That I'm a hawk and you're an angel." He laughed briefly, a sound without humor or warmth. "Well, that's half the truth, anyway. One of us is just what he seems."

"Are we flying to Vancouver Island?" asked Angel, irritated with the enigmatic conversation.

"Don't tell me an angel is afraid to fly?" he asked softly.

"No more than a hawk," she retorted, then frowned. He had a devastating effect on her temper. "My car is at the gallery. I'd planned to take the ferry over."

Hawk pulled a small leatherbound book and a gold pen from his pocket. He handed both to her. "Write down the gallery's address, the car's license number, and a description of the car. You'll have it by tomorrow."

Angel hesitated, then accepted. The pen was warm to her touch, radiating the heat of the man who sat so close. She wrote quickly, feeling as though the pen were burning her skin. Hawk took the keys she pulled out of her purse, the book, and the pen. His fingertips caressed the smooth length of the gold metal. Angel knew that he was feeling her heat as surely as she had felt his. The knowledge shortened her breath.

Then Hawk looked quickly at her, catching the sensual knowledge in her eyes. The corner of his mouth tilted sardonically. He replaced the pen in his pocket. The sound of paper tearing was very loud in the silence as he removed the page she had written on and handed it and the keys to the chauffeur.

"When—when did Derry hurt himself?" asked Angel, hating the breathless quality of her voice yet unable to change it.

"Two days ago. I didn't know about it until he got out of surgery."

"Surgery!" Instantly Angel forgot about everything, including her reaction to Hawk. "But you said he just broke his leg!"

Hawk saw the fear darkening Angel's eyes again. She was a natural actress, able to control her body on command. Hawk was surprised, but only for a moment. The best actresses were always like that. While they were playing the part, they believed. Change the scenes and the lines, and they believed in that part, too, and the next and the next. Beautiful, shallow creatures living on lies. He had been like that for a time, believing the soft words and softer kisses, until he had learned to see through the light to the darkness beneath.

"He broke his ankle, to be precise," said Hawk. "Clean through. The surgery was to put in a pin until everything grew together again."

"Oh, my God," breathed Angel, fighting nausea. "I

should have been with him. To come out of anesthesia alone, in pain and confusion, no one there to touch you, comfort you. . . ."

Dark brown eyes narrowed, searching Angel's face. Hawk knew what it was to wake up in a hospital, disoriented and in pain, the horrible moments until memory came and told you what had happened. It surprised him that Angel, too, seemed to know how it felt.

"You sound like you've been there," said Hawk.

For a moment Angel didn't answer. Then, softly, "I have." Before Hawk could ask another question, she turned on him, her voice cold and controlled. "Is there anything else you haven't told me about Derry?"

"He refuses the painkillers."

"Why?"

"He says that pain has a purpose."

Angel closed her eyes, remembering the months after the wreck when she had thrown away her painkillers and her cane and forced herself to walk again. Derry had wept with her, supporting her for those first few steps. Then she had made him leave, telling him that it was all right, that pain had a purpose. It told her that she was alive.

Hawk started to ask another question when the limousine eased to a stop in the Island Taxi parking lot. Automatically Angel groped for the door handle, not wanting to face the curiosity in Hawk's eyes. Before the chauffeur could get out to open Angel's door, Hawk was out and standing beside the car, extending his hand to Angel across the seat. She hesitated, then put her hand in his. The male heat and power of him shocked her, but it was too late to retreat.

With the same easy strength that he did everything, Hawk pulled Angel out of the limousine. As he released her hand, he let his fingertips glide from her wrist to the sensitive pads of her fingers, stroking her as he had stroked the gold pen. He felt the sudden surge in her pulse, saw the delicate bloom of color beneath her pale cheeks. She looked up at him, confusion in her startled, blue-green eyes. His black eyebrow lifted.

"Is something wrong?" he asked mildly.

Angel's flush deepened. She felt like a fool for being so physically aware of this hard stranger. With a quiet breath, she recalled serenity to herself. At times it almost seemed that Hawk wanted her; yet more often it seemed that he disliked or resented her. His emotions were complex, quick, and very intense beneath his utterly controlled exterior. He was unlike any man she had ever known. She had no way to measure him. She could only respond to his searching intelligence, and the loneliness and male sensuality she had glimpsed beneath his cold exterior.

Silently Angel looked at Hawk, nearly afraid of him, and of herself.

Hawk watched Angel, measuring the emotions that were conveyed so clearly on her face. With a sense of triumph, he realized that he had found Angel's weakness. A gentle touch would unravel her. Hawk almost smiled. Like a raptor soaring on the wind, he had caught the flash of movement, of vulnerability, far below. The prey had revealed itself. Now would come the swift darts and turns, sudden shifts of direction, a chase to heat the blood.

And then she would be his, an angel brought down by a hawk, an angel shivering and crying in his arms.

Chapter 2

PERCHED ON THE EDGE OF A SLATE-GRAY CLIFF, THE
Ramsey house faced east, toward the island-dotted Inside
Passage. Between the blue-black mainland and Vancouver
Island itself, the ocean was a smooth, burning gold, a
molten contrast to the nearly black, ragged rise of tiny
islands. Small boats circled favored islands, dancing on the
choppy sea while fishermen trolled in search of elusive
silver salmon. To the right of the house lay the small city of
Campbell River, its boundaries determined by saltwater and
the jade-green river rolling powerfully to the sea. The late
afternoon air was clear, surreal, as though diamond dust
hung suspended, quivering with light.

Angel barely spared a glance for the magnificent view.
The closer she got to the Ramsey house, the more she was
afraid that Hawk hadn't told her the truth about the extent of
Derry's injuries. It had taken all of her discipline not to
question Hawk during the flight and the short drive from the

Island Taxi terminus on Vancouver Island. Angel had said
nothing to Hawk, though. Some instinct warned her that she
had already revealed too much of herself to him.

The instant Hawk's powerful BMW stopped in front of
the house, Angel was out and running to the front door. She
went through without calling out or knocking. She and
Derry had shared the house for three years. Initially the
arrangement had been necessary; she hadn't been able to
care for herself in those first months after the accident.
Later she and Derry had continued to share the house
during the summer, for she had sold her own family's
Campbell River vacation home in order to help Derry pay
the inheritance taxes on Eagle Head. Technically, one
quarter of this house and the surrounding twelve hundred
acres belonged to her. It was something Angel rarely
thought about. So far as she was concerned, the Ramsey
house and Eagle Head still belonged wholly to the surviving
Ramsey.

"Derry?" called Angel, moving quickly through the
entry and living room, searching for Derry. "Derry, where
are you?"

"Back here," replied Derry.

Hawk came in the front door just in time to see Angel run
toward the back of the house, her pale blond hair rippling
and lifting with each step. He stood without moving for an
instant, riveted by her grace and the smooth curves of her
legs. He wondered how it would feel when she wrapped
those long legs around him, holding him tightly to her.

With an impatient curse, Hawk shut the door and stalked
across the living room. The fair-haired Angel was getting
under his skin. He knew of only one way to exorcise that
type of obsession. In bed. That was where the lies always
showed for what they were, no matter how beautiful the lips
that uttered them. Practiced passions and movements chore-

ographed by lies rather than love. Using and taking and discarding with a check and a smile. Then back to the cold, transparent sky, back to circling and gliding and waiting for that flash of vulnerability far below, the instant when adrenaline raced and the chase began, making him alive again. Years ago he had stopped believing that he would ever capture a woman who had no lies. He didn't even know he was looking for one. He only knew the hunt, and the kill.

Impassively, Hawk caught up to Angel as she raced through the kitchen and family room to the enormous, cantilevered cedar deck that flared like bronzed wings over the rocks and sea. Derry was stretched out on a chaise lounge. From his left thigh to his big toe was a swath of bright white plaster, immobilizing his normally active body. Angel caught her breath at the paleness of Derry's skin, the purple smudges beneath his eyes, the full mouth drawn thin and bracketed by pain. Soundlessly she went to her knees beside him, cradling his head against her breasts. When she spoke, her voice was low, crooning, as though he were a sleepless baby.

"Take the pills, Derry," she murmured, threading her fingers through his blond curls, kneading neck and scalp muscles that had knotted against the agony that spread through him in waves with each incautious movement. "Pain has nothing new to teach you. Take the pills for a few days. Just until you can move without feeling as though a knife is turning in your ankle." She leaned back, searching Derry's blue eyes. "Promise me?" she asked in a husky voice.

"Hey," said Derry, his supple tenor voice at odds with the muscular breadth of his shoulders and chest. "I'm all right, Angie. Really."

"The only thing you 'really' are is pale," retorted Angel.

Derry smiled and hugged her close. "I'm fine. Or I will be as soon as my back teeth stop floating."

Angel smiled despite her worry and looked around for his crutches. "That bad, is it?" She spotted the crutches, grabbed them, and put her arm around Derry, helping him into a sitting position. "Come on, ox. Use those muscles for something besides impressing the pretty tourists."

Hawk realized that Angie was going to help Derry to his feet. She looked absurdly fragile next to Derry's bulk. Yet before Hawk could object, she had begun to lever Derry to his feet. Instantly Hawk moved closer, taking Derry's weight from Angel's slim shoulders.

"What the hell do you think you're doing?" snapped Hawk.

"Helping Derry to the bathroom," said Angel, surprised by the harshness of Hawk's voice, and by his strength. He had literally lifted Derry off the chaise. "Thanks," she said, smiling at Hawk. "Getting up is the hard part. The rest is just awkward." She positioned Derry's crutches. "Ready?"

"I was ready an hour ago," said Derry sheepishly. "I just didn't feel like struggling to get up."

"You should have called me sooner."

"Oh, hell, Angie. I can take care of myself. And I didn't want to take you away from the opening." He looked at Hawk, then back at Angel. "I still don't think I should have. I know what your art means to you."

"There will be other shows," Angel said, firmly tucking the crutches under Derry's arms. "There's only one *you*."

Hawk watched Angel admiringly. She had it all down, all the caring little gestures, the worried glances, the determined smile, the words. A flawless performance of love. Hawk might have begun to believe it himself, if she hadn't softened and flowed over him like honey at his first touch in a smoky bar. She didn't love Derry or anyone else. She could play the part, though. But so could Hawk. It was a necessary aspect of the chase, of the hunt. He could appear to be whatever the prey wanted him to be, until it no longer mattered.

Angel paced alongside Derry, not touching him despite her need to reassure herself that he was all right. He moved awkwardly at first, then with more confidence.

"You haven't been on these crutches much, have you?" she asked.

Derry shook his head, not wanting to talk. He knew that the pain that was sweeping up in waves from his ankle would change the quality of his voice, telling Angel just how much his ankle hurt.

"Where are the pain pills," Angel said flatly.

Derry drew a deep breath. "You didn't take them three years ago."

"I did at first," she said. "Too many and too often. This is different, Derry. You're different than I was. Try one pill. Please. I'll stay right by you. If you get groggy and forget which year it is, I'll be there."

Angel looked up at Derry with wide, haunted eyes. He started to argue, then sagged against the crutches. "How did you know what I was afraid of?" he asked.

"I've been there," she said simply, standing on tiptoe to kiss his cheek.

Derry closed his eyes. "It's good to have you home again, Angie. The pills are on the kitchen counter."

"Do you need any help in the bathroom?" asked Angel as she turned away to get the pills.

"If I get stuck, I'll holler for you," said Derry, grinning crookedly. "Almost like old times, huh?"

Angel laughed sadly and shook her head. "Some homecoming."

Smiling, Derry swung his body between the crutches, heading for the downstairs bathroom.

"Watch the loose tile in the hall," Angel called after him.

"I know, I know. I've lived here longer than you, remember?"

Hawk walked closer as Angel went to the kitchen cupboard and got a glass. She filled it with water and turned around. Hawk was so close that he startled her.

"You live with Derry?" asked Hawk, his voice bland.

"Only in the summers," said Angel, setting aside the glass in order to wrestle with the cap on the pill bottle. "The rest of the year I live in Seattle. I come up whenever I can, though. Especially on Christmas."

Her hands paused as she remembered the first Christmas without her family, without Grant. That holiday was the worst time for memories and regret and rage. She and Derry spent Christmases together, knowing that the other would understand if tears rather than smiles came in response to Christmas carols and presents. But she wouldn't think about that now. Tears couldn't bring back the dead.

Beneath Angel's white-knuckled grip, the cap popped off the bottle and fell to the floor. Hawk retrieved the cap with a smooth, rapid motion. He had seen both the sadness and the . . . courage . . . in Angel's face. He wondered what thoughts had caused her such deep unhappiness. Or was she simply pretending to sadness and determination? Had she found his Achilles heel where other women had failed? Had she somehow sensed that there was nothing on earth he respected except the guts it took to climb out of the deep holes life dropped you into?

"Thank you," said Angel, her voice tight as she took the cap from Hawk's lean fingers.

"Have you lived with Derry long?"

"Three years," said Angel, shaking out a pill into her palm.

"During summers and holidays," murmured Hawk.

"Yes." Something in the tone of Hawk's voice brought up Angel's head sharply. Drifts of pale, soft hair curled around her breasts in sensual contrast to black silk. "Didn't Derry tell you? We were all but raised together."

"Yes, he told me. Very convenient."

Angel shrugged. "Our families lived next door to each other during the summers, and our fathers were brothers in all but blood."

"Yet you live in Seattle most of the time?"

"I'm a U.S. citizen."

"When you marry him, that will change."

"Marry who?" said Angel, startled.

"Derry," said Hawk, watching her with cold brown eyes.

Angel's response was just what he had expected, a denial of involvement with Derry. As she moved her head in a reflexive, negative gesture, a subtle fragrance drifted up from her hair to Hawk's nostrils. They flared, drinking her scent. Desire ripped through him, but he did not show it. A man who showed need to a woman was a fool. Hawk hadn't been a fool since his eighteenth birthday.

"I'm like a sister to Derry," said Angel.

"In all but blood," Hawk added blandly, repeating Angel's previous words, not believing her.

"Exactly," agreed Angel. "Derry and I are family."

She turned away and set the pain pill next to the glass of water on the counter. Uneasily, she turned and glanced up the hallway.

"He's all right," said Hawk. "Besides, how much trouble can he get into in the bathroom?"

"You'd be surprised," Angel said, smiling wryly at the

memory of her own clumsiness when she had first asserted her independence and hobbled into the bathroom on crutches. Derry had had to come in and untangle her. She had always been grateful that it was concern rather than laughter that had shown on Derry's face when he had found her and her crutches wrapped improbably around the toilet and wash basin. Fortunately nothing had been hurt but her pride, and Derry had salved even that by his matter-of-fact help.

Hawk saw Angel's small, private smile and wondered how many times she and Derry had played in the shower or the bathtub. Yes, there were lots of amusing ways to get into trouble in a bathroom, now that Hawk thought about it. But thinking about it would make his desire obvious, so he turned his thoughts elsewhere with the same discipline that had once made him a top race car driver and now made him a ruthless businessman.

"Want me to check on Derry?" asked Hawk, his voice casual, his eyes so dark they were almost black.

Angel hesitated. Then, "Would you mind?" she asked softly. "Crutches can be the very devil to use the first few times out."

Hawk turned and went down the hall, silently agreeing with Angel about crutches. He'd been forced to use them twice, after each major racing crash. Once it had been only for a few days. The second time, though, it had been nineteen weeks. Except for the months following his eighteenth birthday, Hawk couldn't think of a more unpleasant period in his life than the time he'd spent on crutches.

He met Derry coming up the hall. The younger man looked surprised, then resigned.

"Did I take that long?" asked Derry.

"Not for me. Angel was a bit nervous, though."

"Angel? Oh, Angie." Derry looked uncertain, then said quietly, "She doesn't like being called Angel."

"I know."

"Then why—"

"She'll get used to it," Hawk said, turning his back on Derry, "just like I got used to Hawk."

In silence the two men went back to the kitchen where Angel waited. When Derry appeared, relief was clear on Angel's face. She held out the pill and the glass of water.

"Bottoms up," she said.

Derry grimaced but took the pill.

"Have you eaten?" asked Angel.

"Sure. I'm not exactly helpless, you know."

She put her slim fingers against his cheek. As fair as her skin was, it was darker than Derry's right now. "You're so pale," she whispered.

Derry pressed his cheek lightly against her hand. "I'm fine, Angie. Really."

"You'll do better lying down," said Hawk, more an order than a suggestion.

Hawk followed Derry back to the lounge and waited while the younger man lowered himself down. Other than taking the crutches, Hawk didn't help in any way.

"He isn't an invalid," said Hawk coolly, restraining Angel when she would have helped.

"But—"

"Don't tell me you're one of those frustrated mother types," said Hawk, his voice teasing and his eyes hard as cut crystal. "Fussing and fidgeting around men, trying to reduce them to the status of babies. Or does Derry like being babied?"

Anger thinned Angel's mouth, but before she could tell Hawk what she thought of his unfeeling abrasiveness, she heard Derry laughing.

"Mr. Hawkins," said Derry, struggling to straighten a pillow behind his head, "you don't know—"

"Call me Hawk," he said, bending over and shifting the pillow so that it would be centered beneath Derry's head. The gesture was so swift that it almost passed unnoticed. "I'm told the name suits me."

Derry looked surprised. "It does, you know. Suit you. Except I've never known a hawk with a sense of humor." Derry smiled and settled back onto the pillow. "You'll never meet anyone less likely to fuss and fidget than Angie. She's the most serene person I know."

Hawk lifted one black eyebrow and looked at Angel as though he'd never seen her before. "Really?"

"Really. She should be the one studying to be a surgeon, not me. Nothing, but nothing, flaps her anymore."

Angel tried to look serene under Hawk's skeptical regard, knowing that he was remembering her flush of response to him, her temper and her fear for Derry. "I'm afraid I flapped but good when Hawk told me that you'd been hurt," said Angel. "And then I took it out on Hawk." She smiled slightly. "So much for serenity and angels."

Hawk's dark gaze lingered over Angel's lips, the grace of her neck rising out of black silk, and the soft tendrils of hair curling around her breasts. Angel felt her breath shorten in a combination of surprise and sensual response. She wished that she had never sensed vulnerability beneath this man's hard surface. She wished that Hawk were as unfeeling as he seemed to be, for then she simply could have ignored him, letting his probing glances and touches slide off the serenity she had worked so hard to develop. Yet she kept sensing flashes of warmth and gentleness in Hawk, like the simple straightening of the pillow beneath Derry's head. The contrasts and complexities that made up Hawk both fascinated and unnerved her, keeping her off balance.

Serene? Hardly. Not so long as Hawk was in sight.

Angel stepped around Hawk and smoothed back the curls from Derry's forehead. "Ready to sleep yet?"

Derry shook his head, then sighed. "That feels good."

Angel smiled and continued to stroke Derry's hair.

Derry returned the smile, then looked up at the tall, dark man whose quick intelligence and blunt manner had drawn Derry from their first meeting several weeks ago. "You have a point, Hawk. Some men just love to be babied."

"Shall I hire you a nanny?" asked Hawk.

"Only if she's young and pretty," retorted Derry.

"They don't call them nannies if they're young and pretty," Hawk pointed out. "They call them—"

"Never mind," interrupted Derry. "I couldn't do much about it anyway, not until I'm out of these concrete overalls."

Derry shifted uneasily, trying to get comfortable. Hawk went to one of the cushioned patio chairs, took a pillow, and came back to the lounge. With a few swift, careful motions, Hawk had the cushion tucked under Derry's cast, relieving the strain on his back.

Derry sighed. "Thanks. Damn thing weighs as much as I do."

Angel glanced up at Hawk, surprised again by the contrast between his unsympathetic words and his caring actions. Hawk looked back at her coolly.

"Go ahead and pet him," said Hawk. "It will keep his mind off his ankle."

Derry laughed aloud, his blue eyes dark with pleasure. "That's what I like about you, Hawk. Everyone else tiptoes around being nice and you don't. As a doctor-to-be, I believe there's a place in this world for astringents."

"Yes," agreed Angel curtly. "In bottles. Tightly capped."

For an instant Derry looked shocked; then he gave way to laughter again. Lines of strain melted away from his face, making him look barely eighteen instead of the twenty-one he was. He took Angel's hand, squeezed it, and put it back on his forehead.

"Pet me," he said complacently. "You're good for me. Both of you. I was feeling pretty sorry for myself before you came."

Angel's irritation disappeared at Derry's admission. She resumed stroking his forehead, smoothing away tension, all the while sensing Hawk's dark, enigmatic glance on her. Closing his eyes, Derry sighed deeply, relaxing beneath her touch.

"Your hands are like you, Angie," he murmured. "Kind. Generous. Calm. Will you help me?"

"Of course," she said quietly.

"Are you sure? I know how busy you are."

"It's summer, Derry. During the summer all I do is absorb the patterns of color and sunlight."

Derry's eyes opened. Relief showed clearly in their blue depths. "Thanks," he said, his voice husky, slow. The pain pill was obviously taking effect. He looked past Angel to Hawk. "When do you want . . . to start your . . . grand tour?"

For an instant Hawk almost felt sorry for Angel, neatly trapped by a young blond charmer. Then the corner of Hawk's mouth lifted in a curve well short of a smile. Derry's charm was a real force, a radiance like the sun that encouraged people to come and warm themselves. But Hawk hadn't seen any sign that Derry was a liar or a cheat. Derry could no more help his easy charm than he could help the fact that he had ten fingers and toes. Derry was unspoiled by women and lies. Hawk would see that Derry stayed that way.

"Tomorrow is soon enough," said Hawk. "Until Angel is sure that you can take care of yourself, her heart won't be in her work."

Angel's head came up. "What are you two talking about?"

Derry looked back at Angel. He squinted, trying to focus through the effects of the pill. "Taking Hawk . . . around. I . . . can't."

Angel looked up at Hawk, surprise clear in the eyes that were too large for her face. "Do you know what Derry's talking about?"

Through the pain pill's haze, Derry heard Angel's words fade in and out of his consciousness. He knew that he had to make her understand how important it was that she help Hawk, but Derry's tongue just wouldn't form the words. Suddenly he realized how much of his strength had drained away, how weak he had become. He began to fight the effects of the pill, something close to panic in his body and voice. "Angie?"

Angel felt the bunching of Derry's muscles beneath her hand and spoke quickly, remembering her own feeling of helplessness in the hospital three years ago, the shots that whirled her down into darkness, taking away even the power to scream. Except in her mind. She had screamed there, endlessly, caught in barbiturate chains.

"Don't fight the pill," said Angel urgently. "Do you hear me, Derry? Don't fight it. Let go, Derry. Let go. It's all right."

"Can't . . . Hawk."

"I'll take care of Hawk," she said, stroking Derry's forehead and his cheek, focusing only on him, willing him to be calm. "It's all right, Derry," she said quietly, her voice like a benediction. "Sleep."

Derry's eyes focused on Angel for an instant. He took a

ragged breath, nodded slowly, and stopped struggling. Only then did Angel realize that Hawk had come to her side, helping her by holding Derry's shoulders in a powerful vise. Without Hawk, she wouldn't have been able to contain Derry's struggle to sit up.

"Thank you," said Angel, her voice soft. "He'll be all right now. He just had a bad moment when he realized that the pill was stronger than he was. The helplessness is frightening."

Angel's fingers clenched as she remembered three years ago, pain and helplessness and rage. Hawk saw. Without stopping to think, he took her hand between his and gently pried her fingers open. He stroked her fingers, surprised by their chill.

"Derry's as strong as he is charming," said Hawk, warming Angel's hands between his. "He'll be fine."

With an effort, Angel forced her hands to relax. The heat of Hawk's skin was almost shocking. She looked up suddenly and found herself reflected in the hard clarity of Hawk's eyes. Reflected and . . . measured. His eyes were not nearly so soothing as the slow rhythm of his hands rubbing warmth into hers. Suddenly Angel felt wholly vulnerable, as though she were naked and an ice-tipped wind was sweeping down out of the dark sky to claim her.

Angel eased her hands free of Hawk's. She returned to stroking Derry's hair, but this time the soothing contact was more for herself than for him. Silently Hawk watched, following every movement of her hands, her eyes, the light sliding like a caress over her pale hair, and the slow rise and fall of her breasts beneath midnight silk. The fact that he wanted Angel didn't surprise him. The fact that he had wanted to comfort her did. The sooner he got her into bed, the better. He'd never seen an actress who portrayed both strength and vulnerability so easily, so convincingly. Only in bed would the act fall apart, freeing him from her soft fascinations and lies.

"What was Derry talking about?" asked Angel after a few minutes of silence.

"The grand tour?" asked Hawk.

Without looking away from Derry, Angel nodded her head, signaling her understanding. The motion sent strands of her hair whispering over each other. Hawk wanted to wrap a curling tendril around his finger and then slowly release it, letting the silk and radiance of her hair caress the sensitive skin between his fingers.

"I've never spent any time in the Pacific Northwest," continued Hawk. "I frankly don't know a damn thing about the country. Before I build an enclave of exclusive homes, I want to be sure that I have more to offer buyers than high-priced houses and an expensive resort complex."

Angel waited, her hands still, her fingers relaxed due to an act of will that made her ache. The thought of selling Eagle Head made her want to cry or scream or plead with Hawk not to buy. Yet selling Eagle Head was the only way Derry could afford the eight years of advanced education and training that being a surgeon would require. She would not stand in the way of that. No matter how much she loved Eagle Head, she loved Derry more.

"That's where you come in," Hawk said, his voice as expressionless as his eyes. "You're my tour guide."

"What?" said Angel, not quite believing she had heard Hawk correctly.

"Derry would have a hell of a time getting in and out of a car, much less a boat," Hawk said, his voice matter-of-fact. "Beach walking would be impossible, especially down these cliff trails. He said you could do it, though. In fact, he said you were a better fisherman than he was. Better at clamming, too. He also pointed out that you could cook like a European chef and knew all the best places to be for a hundred miles in all directions.''

"He exaggerates."

Hawk shrugged. "It's up to you." Then, coolly, "You do understand that I won't buy a pig in a poke. No tour, no sale. Sorry, but that's the way life is. There's no such thing as a free lunch.''

He watched the realization sink into Angel. No tour. No sale. And no money for her 25 percent of the land. Derry had told Hawk about that—Angel and a quarter of Eagle Head. Hawk assumed that it was payment for services rendered. How else could she afford to laze away three months of the year and her holidays, too? Somebody had to pay for the privilege of her company. A quarter interest in Eagle Head wasn't bad wages for three years of "work."

Angel didn't see Hawk's cynical appraisal of her. She was watching Derry, seeing the shadows of pain and sleeplessness beneath his tanned skin. He looked very young, but she knew that he wasn't. Not really. No one who had lived through the wreck three years ago would ever be young again. Inexperienced, yes. Young, no.

Angel sighed. Derry must like Hawk very much to have promised Angel as a tour guide. Derry, too, must have sensed the loneliness beneath Hawk's proud surface. As lonely as a hawk riding a cold wind. And as compelling. Power and grace and darkness, eyes that saw all the way through to the core.

Angel's hand hesitated over Derry's hair, then resumed stroking him almost absently. There was no reason not to show Hawk the leisure possibilities of the Pacific Northwest. She would spend her summer roaming the island and the Inside Passage anyway. It was hardly too much to ask that she take Hawk along, and in so doing help Derry fulfill a dream.

Angel looked up at Hawk, not surprised to find that he had been watching her. She met his hard, enigmatic eyes without flinching. "How long will you need me?"

A corner of Hawk's mouth turned down in a cynical curve. *Not more than a night or two, I'll bet.* But the thought went no further than his narrowed eyes. When he spoke, his voice was smooth, without emotion of any kind.

"Six weeks at most. That's all the time I can afford. I have several other land deals coming together." Hawk frowned faintly. He had an intricate, interlocking network of stock and land sales that should culminate within six weeks. Then he would either be a great deal richer or he would get to start all over again. Either way, it would be exciting.

That was what mattered to Hawk. Not the money, but the adrenaline. He had made and lost several fortunes since he had quit racing. As in racing, he preferred winning in business to losing or crashing. But win or lose, the adrenaline flowed. The discovery, the pursuit, the kill. The endless cycle, endlessly exciting, telling him that he was alive.

"Six weeks," repeated Angel, keeping her voice level with an effort.

"On and off. I'll be flying in and out." Hawk gave her a dark-eyed glance. "We can hammer out a tentative schedule. You tell me what's available to see and do, and we'll figure out the best times for both of us." Hawk paused. "No promises, Angel. I may not like what I see. If I don't," he added, shrugging, "no sale."

Angel looked at Derry. Despite the barbiturate's embrace, he stirred restively and made a small sound. His pain had merely been put at a greater distance, not vanquished. Angel's hand hesitated in its soothing journey as she realized how many times Derry had sat by her bed, watched her restless sleep, and heard her whimper as unconsciousness released the harsh guard she kept on her emotions. So many times she had awakened to his affectionate smile and encouraging "You look better today."

There was really no question about helping Derry. If Hawk needed Angel as a guide for six weeks or six years, she would be there.

Gently, Angel's hand resumed smoothing back Derry's springy blond hair. "Fine," she said quietly, not looking up at Hawk again. "Whatever is necessary."

Chapter 3

IT WAS STILL DARK OUTSIDE, ALMOST AN HOUR UNTIL dawn. Angel worked quietly in the kitchen, putting food into grocery bags, wrapping sandwiches, and turning strips of bacon in the pan. When she heard the unrhythmic thump of crutches in the hallway, she peeled off another handful of bacon and put the strips into the pan to fry.

"You're up early," said Angel, turning to smile at Derry. "Did I wake you?"

"No."

Derry grimaced as he shifted his weight. Normally he was cheerful—maddeningly so—in the morning. His present state told Angel that his ankle was throbbing. "How did you sleep?" she asked, searching his face.

Derry glowered. Between that and his tousled blond curls, he looked a surly sixteen. "Lousy. I feel hung over."

"You look it, too. Orange juice?"

Yawning, ruffling his hair with one hand, Derry nodded.
"Please. Coffee?"

"Sit down. I'll bring it to you."

While Derry went to the little breakfast nook that had a
view of the strait, Angel fixed up a tray with coffee, juice,
toast, and homemade jams. The latter were courtesy of
Mrs. Carey, a neighbor who made the best jams on
Vancouver Island. Two months ago she had tripped over her
cat and broken her hip. The cast was off now, but Angel
still shopped for her, as well as for two other temporary
shut-ins.

"Where's Hawk?" asked Derry as Angel set the tray on
the table.

"Telephone."

Derry shook his head. "He works too hard. The sun isn't
even up."

"It is in London. He's talking to Lord Someone-or-
other."

"Must be the island he's trying to buy."

"A whole island?" asked Angel.

"Yeah. He wants to turn it into a cracking plant for North
Sea oil."

Angel hesitated, then went back to the stove. "He must
be very rich."

"I guess. When I asked the bank to check him out as a
potential buyer for Eagle Head, I got no further than the
name Miles Hawkins. Old man Johnston's eyes lit up like a
Christmas tree. Hawk has quite a reputation in what
Johnston refers to as 'the international financial communi-
ty.' A bona fide high roller." Derry paused, sipping at the
fragrant coffee. "Odd, though. He doesn't act rich."

"How," said Angel, turning bacon, "does someone 'act
rich'?"

"You know. Throwing money everywhere. Dropping

the names of the right resorts, the right people. Private jets and cars faster than the speed of sound.''

''Like Clarissa?''

Derry paused, then sighed. ''Yeah. She was something else, wasn't she?''

Angel suppressed a smile. ''I'd tell you what that something was, but I'm not supposed to know the word. Thank God you saw through her, Derry. She was gorgeous, sure, but she had the intelligence of a clam.''

''You're slandering clams,'' said Derry dryly.

Smiling, Angel set strips of bacon out to drain on paper towels. ''How many eggs?''

''Five.''

''Hungry, aren't you?'' murmured Angel.

''I slept through dinner, remember?''

''Ummm,'' she said, wielding a chopper over the crisp bacon.

Angel remembered dinner very well. She and Hawk had spent an hour working on a schedule. She had made up a list of things to do and the approximate times involved in doing them right. Hawk had scanned the list very quickly and set it aside. Then he had questioned her in detail, missing none of the thirty-seven items on the list that he had looked at for less than a minute. His questions had been concise and incisive. At the end of the hour Angel had felt wrung out. When he had all the information he required, Hawk— without looking at the list again—had written out a tentative schedule, handed Angel several thousand dollars for expenses, and excused himself. He had spent the next hour talking to Tokyo's equivalent of the stock exchange.

The beaten eggs hissed as they slid into the hot omelette pan. Angel swirled the pan deftly, adding ingredients as the omelette formed.

''Mushrooms?'' she asked, her hand hovering over the

mounds of freshly prepared ingredients heaped on the breadboard by the stove.

"The works," said Derry hungrily.

The omelette thickened, glistening with melting cheese. Just as she folded it in half, a timer went off. She slid Derry's omelette onto a warm plate, then pulled a pan of croissants out of the oven and put them into a napkin-lined bun warmer. The marvelous fragrance of the croissants and omelette preceded her to the table.

Derry smiled up at her. "Thanks, Angie," he said softly. "This beats hell out of peanut butter and toast."

"Anything beats that," said Angel.

"Creamed liverwurst?" he asked innocently.

She shuddered.

Derry took a bite of the omelette and sighed. "Clarissa was right about one thing," he said.

"Oh?"

"You're gonna spoil me for any other woman."

Angel laughed and ruffled Derry's hair affectionately. She turned to go back to the stove, and nearly walked into Hawk.

"Oh!" She stepped back, her eyes wide and startled. "Good Lord, but you're light on your feet!"

Hawk simply looked down at Angel with a cold expression. The planes of his face seemed unusually harsh, his eyes black in the artificial light. Angel would have backed away even farther but Derry's outthrust, plaster-encased leg prevented it.

"Didn't you sleep well?" asked Angel, searching Hawk's face.

"As well as I ever do." Hawk's voice was clipped, as cold as his eyes raking over her.

He turned and picked up a mug from the counter. Then he grabbed the coffee pot and poured a dark stream into the mug. As he took a sip of coffee, he eyed the omelette ingredients heaped colorfully on the counter.

"Sit down, Hawk," said Angel quickly. "How many eggs do you want in your omelette?"

"Don't bother." He gave her a dark glance. "I'd hate like hell to be spoiled for other women."

Derry made a choking sound that rapidly escalated into laughter. Angel's lips flattened in the instant before her normal control asserted itself. She wished she could find Hawk's caustic comments as entertaining as Derry did. Instead, she forever seemed to take them personally.

"Don't be ridiculous," said Angel, crossing quickly to the stove. "How many eggs?"

"Six."

Angel looked startled. She glanced covertly at Hawk and realized that he was even bigger than she had remembered. He had to be at least six foot three, lean, hard, very male. Somehow the casual clothing Hawk wore now revealed his size more than the civilized three-piece suit he had worn yesterday. The black pullover that fitted his chest so well was patterned after Irish fishermen's sweaters. Just standing there, he looked unreasonably large, his shoulders wide enough to block out the light. He seemed taller, too, than yesterday, more . . . primal. Faded jeans fit snugly across his thighs and hinted at the muscular calves beneath. Soft-soled suede moccasins wrapped neatly around his feet. But it was the power of his body that drew Angel's eyes, the deceptively slender line of his hips and waist blending into the male wedge of his shoulders.

"Everything zipped?" asked Hawk, too softly for Derry to hear.

Angel flushed. "Everything except your mouth," she retorted. But she was careful not to let Derry overhear.

A corner of Hawk's mouth turned up. "You aren't," he murmured.

"What?"

"Zipped."

Angel looked down and discovered that Hawk was right. In her haste to get dressed, she had overlooked the zipper on her jeans. A ribbon of silky tangerine briefs showed through the narrow opening. The reversal of the usual unzipped roles made her irritation evaporate into a laugh. Maybe Derry had the right outlook. Hawk's abrasive, unexpected humor could grow on you. Still smiling, Angel matter-of-factly zipped up her jeans as she turned to the counter and began cracking eggs into a bowl.

Hawk watched as Angel made his omelette with the casual skill that came only from experience. It didn't surprise him that she was an accomplished cook. Men liked being cooked for, and Angel was obviously a woman who had made a career out of pleasing men. As he sipped the rich coffee, he wondered how else she had learned to please men. The thought made desire ripple darkly through him. Smoothly, he changed the focus of his thoughts, knowing that his curiosity wouldn't be satisfied today. Probably not for several days. Like a doe that enjoyed running the hounds, Angel would twist and turn and double back, tantalizing him by staying just beyond reach. Hawk didn't mind. It only made the inevitable end of the chase sweeter, hotter. Easy prey wasn't worth the trouble it took to reach out and pick it up.

In silence Hawk ate the tender, succulent omelette. The croissants were flaky, steaming as he pulled them apart, so rich with butter that his fingertips glistened. The jams were unique, tasting of fruit rather than sugar, and as colorful as jewels. Out over the strait, the first hint of predawn light slowly transformed night into luminous shades of black and gray. Around Hawk were the small, companionable sounds of silver clicking lightly against plates, the gentle thump of a coffee mug returning to the tabletop, the creak of a chair as Derry shifted his weight, Angel's soft footsteps as she joined them at the table.

The peace of the moment seeped past Hawk's barriers, spreading through him as silently and inexorably as dawn itself. It had been a long, long time since he had eaten breakfast like this. Usually he was alone. When he wasn't, there was a woman trying to talk to him, words and more words pouring out as she tried to fill the emptiness that came the morning after the end of the chase. That kind of desperate chatter left Hawk cold. To be with people who demanded nothing of him was as unusual as it was soothing.

And then Hawk heard his own thoughts. His lips flattened and he pushed away his empty plate. Who was he trying to kid? Of course Derry and Angel wanted something from him. Money. Angel wasn't showing him Vancouver Island out of the goodness of her gold-digging little heart. If he bought Eagle Head, she would be well paid for her trouble. Even if he didn't, she should be able to make a tidy profit by padding the expenses. The same was true for Derry. Nor did Hawk mind particularly. It was how the game was played, and he'd known it since his eighteenth birthday, the day he learned that to be an emotionally honest man in a world of lies is to be a fool.

Angel finished her small omelette, stood, and began to clear the table. Derry looked out at the strait. Tiny lights bobbed about, marking the sport-fishing boats pouring out of the Campbell River marina into the strait.

"Leave the dishes," said Derry. "You'll miss the tide."

"We've already missed it," Angel sighed.

Hawk heard the wistfulness in Angel's voice. "You actually like fishing?" he asked, surprised.

"No, I'm actually crazy about it," she said.

"She's good at it too. Better than I am," said Derry. "She knows just where to go, how deep to fish, what lure to use, which little coves and bays and headlands—"

"Enough," interrupted Angel dryly. "Hawk obviously isn't a fisherman."

"Why do you say that?" asked Hawk.

"You were on the phone when we should have been on the water."

"That was business."

"Like I said, not a fisherman. Nothing, but nothing, gets in the way of a dawn salmon raid if you're a fisherman."

Derry chuckled. "Give the man a break, Angie. He's never caught a salmon, so he doesn't know what he's missing."

Angel looked at Hawk. In the oddly gloaming predawn light, her eyes were dark green, very brilliant against the pale nimbus of her hair. "Have you ever fished at all?" she asked as she bent over to take Hawk's plate.

Hawk remembered the small reservoir on the farm where he had grown up. Whenever his father could steal a few minutes from the endless demands of a marginal farm, the two of them would go to the reservoir. One of the few times he could ever remember his father laughing was when he had pulled a ten-pound catfish out of the opaque water.

"I've fished once or twice," said Hawk, his voice husky, almost yearning.

The changed quality of Hawk's voice made Angel's throat tighten. She saw the poignant shadow of memories cross his face, softening for a moment the harsh lines around his mouth. Absurdly, she felt tears burn behind her eyelids. She sensed that Hawk's memories were like he was, bittersweet and lonely, complex and sometimes cruel. She wanted to ease the bitterness, enhance the sweetness, enrich the complexity with all the colors of emotion. As for his occasional cruelty, it didn't frighten her. For a time after the accident she had been unspeakably cruel to those around her. Finally the time of cruelty had passed, leaving her purged.

Angel looked up into the dark eyes that were so close to her. Her fingers curled around a fork that still retained the heat of Hawk's body. "You'll catch a dawn salmon this summer," she said softly. "I promise you."

Before Hawk could answer, Angel straightened and turned, removing Hawk's plate and silverware. In silence she stacked dishes into the dishwasher, moving quickly. Even though they had missed the tide, she was eager to be out on the water.

"Ready?" she asked, looking up.

He was watching her, had been watching her since she had promised him a dawn salmon in a voice vibrant with emotion. Without making a sound, he set down his empty mug.

"I've been ready since I was eighteen," said Hawk.

Then he heard his own words. His face settled into its normal enigmatic lines, concealing thoughts and emotions behind a mahogany mask. Silently Hawk helped Angel carry everything out to the car. Groceries, a lot of fishing gear, jackets, and a sketchbook Angel had thrown in at the last instant.

"Are we going to Alaska?" asked Hawk dryly, looking at the gear heaped up in his BMW.

"What a wonderful idea," said Angel in a wistful voice. "I've always wanted to sail the Inside Passage." She didn't see Hawk's quick, assessing look. "But that's not on our list this summer," Angel continued, shifting the bags around until she could close the trunk.

Hawk started to help, then stopped, riveted by the high, wild whistle of an eagle calling to the dawn. He searched the sky with dark, fierce eyes, looking for the bird. A black shape plummeted down, wings flared, talons outstretched. The prey was hidden from Hawk's sight in the tall grass, but the raptor had no such problem. The bird struck and mantled its dying prey with half-spread wings, protecting it from view. Then the eagle's uncanny eyes spotted the two people standing so quietly. With a high, angry cry, the eagle took flight, carrying its prey to the treetops.

Predawn grays had faded as the sky flushed with the delicate, transparent colors of true dawn. Across the strait the serrated ranks of mountains loomed like fragments of night, black and yet strangely radiant. Overhead a few tufted clouds burned scarlet, then molten gold. A feeling of exhilaration speared through Hawk. He lifted his face to the sky, letting sunrise wash over him. He had spent too much time indoors since he had left the farm. He hadn't known how much he had missed the sky until this moment.

From the thrusting rock summit of Eagle Head came again the untamed cry of a bird of prey.

Angel looked up, saw the fierce pleasure on Hawk's face, and felt desire shiver through her. The feeling shocked her in the instant before she accepted it. She shouldn't be surprised by passion. She had chosen to live after Grant had died in the wreck. Love and desire were a natural part of life. Just because she hadn't wanted any man for three years didn't mean that she would never want a man again.

Even as Angel admitted the intensity of her attraction to Hawk, she knew that she could be hurt badly by him. Hawk was as hard a man as she had ever met. Yet beneath that hardness was a yearning for beauty, for warmth, for . . . love. Without that, she wouldn't have been attracted to him. But there was no guarantee that she would be the one to touch Hawk's yearning. There was no guarantee that anyone could touch it, even Hawk himself. He was strong. He had lived a long time alone.

So had she. Was she ready to risk her hard-won serenity for a man who might no longer believe in love?

Angel closed the trunk with a sharp, metallic sound that brought Hawk's attention back from the sky. He watched as Angel got into the car. After a moment's hesitation he slid behind the wheel, reluctant to break the luminous silence of the British Columbia dawn. Angel said nothing during the drive, however, apparently as pleased as he was by the quiet and the colors radiating through the sky.

They parked at the marina and stepped out to the keening of gulls and the smell of the sea. As one, Angel and Hawk began to carry supplies down the wooden dock to the slips. When Angel saw Hawk's boat, she stopped in the middle of the dock and stared. The boat was almost forty feet long and had the sleek lines that were the hallmark of Italian powerboats. Angel knew that the boat would handle beautifully, riding the often rough water with the ease of a hawk soaring on troubled currents of air.

"She's beautiful," breathed Angel, turning toward Hawk. "What's her name?"

"I haven't given her one."

Angel realized then that the boat was as new as it looked, polished and shining like the sun rising over the sea. "Don't name her too quickly," she murmured. "A boat gets only one name. This one deserves the best."

"Because it's pretty?" asked Hawk casually, stepping onto the boat's shifting deck without hesitation.

"This boat isn't pretty," said Angel, looking at its lines

with appreciative eyes. "It's magnificent. Form and function perfectly married. Nothing unnecessary. Nothing missing."

Hawk turned and looked back over his shoulder at Angel. She didn't notice. She had eyes only for the glistening white boat. His lips curved sardonically.

"Expensive, too," he said.

Angel looked at the boat for another long moment before she sighed. "Yeah, I'll bet. The Italians aren't bashful about pricing their works of art." She glanced at Hawk. "Can you, er, handle this boat?"

"I used to race powerboats."

"I thought Derry said you'd raced cars."

"I did both. There was more money in cars, though."

"And more danger?" asked Angel.

Hawk's eyes narrowed. "Does the idea of danger turn you on?"

"No," she said simply.

"It turns on a lot of women."

"Does it?" asked Angel. "Why?"

Hawk made a harsh sound. "Adrenaline, honey. It tells them that they're alive."

"Or that someone else is dead," said Angel, her eyes too dark, too large, as memories rose, threatening to choke her.

Hawk saw the haunted expression shadow Angel's face, her eyes. Then she shifted the bags in her arms and stepped onto the boat as though nothing had happened. And, Hawk realized, nothing had. Whatever ghosts haunted Angel weren't new. They were an accepted part of her life, just as his ghosts were part of his. Or else the haunted look was simply an act, as seamless as the night.

With a mental shrug, Hawk dismissed the subject. Act or reality, it didn't change what Angel was. Even animals twitched in their dreams, haunted by whatever ghosts their limited minds could conjure.

"I'll show you how to handle the boat when we're out in the strait," said Hawk. "If you want."

"Of course I do. Besides, that's the only way you'll get to fish."

Hawk lifted a black eyebrow in silent query.

"It's almost impossible to fish alone in a boat this size," explained Angel. "Someone has to be at the helm, especially if you hook up with a big salmon when the water is crowded with other boats and the tide is running."

Together they finished loading the supplies aboard. The sun was well over the mainland mountains by the time Hawk eased the boat out of the marina and into the grip of the Campbell River current. To the left were evergreen trees and flatlands, then a forested headland rose powerfully out of the sea. To the right a spit of land thrust out, dividing the sea from the intertidal waters. A small plane taxied out over the water. The engines revved hard, pushing pontoons through the water faster and faster until the plane lifted into the pale blue sky.

As soon as the last speed limit buoy fell astern, Hawk smoothly fed power to the twin diesels. The boat lifted slightly, splitting the blue-green water into silver foam. Hawk kept the speed well below the boat's capability, for small craft were thickly clustered to the right, beyond the spit of land. As though there were invisible markers, all the boats circled within a defined area. Rods sprouted from the sides and stern of the boats, rods curved like whips against the clean sky.

"Must be God's own fishing hole," commented Hawk.

Angel smiled. "That's Frenchman's Pool," she said, her voice pitched to rise above the potent mutter of the diesels.

"Before the dam was built, Campbell River used to flood in the spring. The floods dug out a huge hole in the ocean floor. Salmon coming in from the ocean school up there. Some people say the fish are adjusting to fresh water after years at sea. Others say they lie up there waiting for just the right sensory signals to lure them into the river itself."

"Which do you believe?" asked Hawk, looking at Angel's profile.

For a long moment Angel didn't answer. Against the sun, the tendrils of hair that escaped from her single French braid burned like pale flames licking over her clear skin. There was an unusual purity of line in her profile, a harmony of forehead and nose and chin that was very strong without being in the least unfeminine. When she turned to face Hawk, her eyes were as transparent and deep as river pools.

"I think," said Angel slowly, her eyes unfocused, looking inward rather than at Hawk or the restless sea, "that the salmon school up in Frenchman's Pool to come to terms with themselves and the fresh water that will be both their summation and their death."

"You make them sound almost human."

"Do I?" murmured Angel, smiling sadly. "Most people aren't that brave. They look no further into the future than their next meal. The salmon look at death and beyond."

"Beyond?"

"Birth. The eternal cycle, death and renewal blending together like Campbell River and the sea."

A shout came across the water, followed by an excited babble of French. Angel leaned over the rail, peering into the brilliant light.

"Look!" she said, pointing toward a small rowboat that appeared to be pinned to the iridescent surface of the sea. "He's got one on!" Impatiently, Angel slid open the cabin window beside the boat's helm. Her fingers fastened onto

Hawk's arm. "Can you see? The rowboat next to the yellow inboard. Oh, they've got a dandy! Look at that rod bend!"

Hawk looked past Angel's glowing hair. For a moment he was aware only of her nearness, her sweet scent, her fingers pressed against the muscles of his upper arm. Then he followed her pointing finger until he saw the small boat being towed against the current by an invisible force. There was no engine on the boat, nothing but a broad-shouldered man rowing steadily and another man straining against the coiled rod.

"What happened to their engine?"

"The boat is from the Tyee Club," said Angel. "No engines allowed. The whole idea is to hunt the salmon as the first Englishmen did, wooden oars and wooden lures, nothing but your strength and the power of the salmon. People come from all over the world just to try to catch a thirty-pound salmon from a hand-rowed boat. If they succeed, they become members of the Tyee Club."

"Are you a member?" asked Hawk softly.

"Yes."

"Who rowed for you? Derry?"

The question ripped through Angel, leaving memories welling in its wake like blood from a fresh wound. Grant had rowed for her. They had laughed and exulted together, making a pact to smoke the salmon and serve it at their wedding reception. Ten days later Grant was dead.

"On weekend mornings," said Angel, her voice husky, ignoring Hawk's question, "Frenchman's Pool is so crowded you can almost walk from boat to boat across it."

Hawk had missed neither the instant of anguish written on Angel's features nor the unanswered question. "I'd like to try my hand at rowboat fishing," he said. "Is the man who rowed you still available?"

"No." Angel's voice was soft, final. "I'm not strong

enough to row for more than an hour or so against the current. That's not long enough to give you a fair chance of a fish. Carlson would row you if I asked him to. Carlson is strong enough to row for days against the tide."

"Carlson?"

"A friend. A very old friend."

The corner of Hawk's mouth lifted. He wondered how many other "very old friends" Angel had up and down the strait.

"Would you like me to ask Carlson to row for you?" said Angel, looking toward Hawk again.

"I'll think about it," he said, turning away.

The smooth shift of Hawk's muscles beneath Angel's fingers made her realize that her hand was still pressed against his upper arm. She lifted her fingers quickly.

"Do you want to wait while they land that fish?" asked Hawk, adjusting the boat's throttles.

"No. It could be hours. Salmon are very strong. Unless you want to wait?"

"I'd rather get out of this crowd and teach you how to handle the boat. Which direction?"

"North. The farther you go, the less people there are."

"Sounds like my kind of direction."

Hawk sat in the cockpit and gunned the engines, letting them lift the boat's gleaming white prow above the waves. As the boat picked up speed, Angel braced herself against the cockpit seat and stared through the windshield to the sea ahead.

"Have you been warned about deadheads?" asked Angel, looking at the water in front of the boat with intent, narrowed eyes.

"What are deadheads?" asked Hawk, answering her question and asking one of his own.

"Logs that have broken loose from a towing raft. When they get waterlogged, they ride just below the surface until they finally sink."

"Sounds lethal," said Hawk, immediately cutting back on the throttles.

"Sometimes. Most often you just get a cold swim and a bashed boat."

A powerboat came up on their left, passing them in a brilliant cloud of spray.

"Looks like no one told him about deadheads either," said Hawk.

"You get used to them," said Angel, "like wind storms and fifteen knot currents. Comes with the territory."

"Like car wrecks."

Angel flinched in the instant before she controlled herself. "Yes. Like car wrecks. We keep driving anyway."

Hawk had seen Angel's ghost reappear, pain written for a second across the smooth skin of her face. "What do you consider a safe speed?" he asked.

"Right now?" Angel turned slowly, measuring the sea surrounding the boat. "There's good visibility. The wind is down. The tide is running but not boiling." She gestured toward the powerboat surging away from them. "About what he's doing."

A black eyebrow lifted, but Hawk said nothing as he brought the boat up to speed again.

"There aren't that many deadheads," explained Angel. "And most of them are flagged as soon as they're found."

"Is that what those are for?" asked Hawk, gesturing toward a handful of meter-length rods with a sharp point on one end and a bright triangular flag on the other.

Angel nodded. "If we spot a deadhead, we flag it. Usually a log scavenger will pick it up. With the price of lumber so high, a log is worth several hundred dollars. If no one picks up the deadhead, the flag makes it easy to spot and avoid, even at twice this speed.''

''Be nice if all of life's little trouble spots were so neatly posted,'' said Hawk, his voice sardonic.

''The flags only work if you have the sense to heed them,'' Angel said, her tone as sardonic as his.

Angel's words were directed at herself, not at Hawk. There were flags sticking out all over Hawk, but she kept seeing past them to the man beneath, hunger and intelligence, heat and strength, all that made life valuable.

And danger.

Angel hadn't forgotten the danger inherent in Hawk. But danger always existed, as much a part of life as love. To have the one you must accept the other. Grant Ramsey had taught her that, love and death. The learning had nearly destroyed her.

She didn't know if she was strong enough to risk learning again.

Chapter 4

ANGEL DIRECTED HAWK TOWARD A QUIET STRETCH OF water by touching his arm and pointing to the right. Neither of them had attempted to talk over the unleashed thunder of diesels. Smoothly, Hawk brought the boat into calm water in the lee of a gray headland. He put the engines in neutral and waited, testing the amount of drift. There was very little. With an easy motion, Hawk slid out from behind the helm.

When he stood up, he was so close to Angel that she could smell the clean scent of his after-shave. His eyes were a clear, crystal brown with surprising flecks of gold. His mustache was as black as the center of his eyes. Angel wondered what it would feel like to have that mustache against her skin. Would it be rough or soft or a tantalizing combination of the two? Would it be cool beneath her fingertips, or would it have the same heat that the rest of

Hawk's body had, a heat that touched her even though she wasn't touching him.

The intensity of Angel's silence and speculations froze her, overriding even the need to breathe. Then she saw Hawk's pupils dilate suddenly as he became aware of her appraisal. She retreated, looking away from the hard, sensual line of Hawk's lips. She wanted to say something, anything, because she sensed that he was looking at her as completely as she had looked at him. No words came to her. With downcast eyes, she brushed past him and sat behind the helm of the powerful boat.

Hawk bent over Angel and the boat's controls, knowing from her quickly indrawn breath that his presence disturbed her. He didn't touch her, though. He had seen her retreat as clearly as he had seen the consuming sensuality of her appraisal. Though he controlled his desire to stroke the rapid pulse beating visibly in Angel's throat, he couldn't help the sudden coursing of blood through his veins, the adrenaline and heat as the chase began. None of what he felt showed in his voice or his body. Like the prey, the predator was capable of measured retreat, knowing always that retreat was temporary.

"Have you ever handled anything as powerful as this?" asked Hawk, his voice low, almost intimate.

Angel kept her eyes on the gauges in front of her. "No," she said. The word sounded ragged to her ears. "No," she repeated, breathing deeply, evenly, calming the erratic race of her pulse. "Derry's boat was about half this size and a quarter the power."

"Was?"

"He sold it a few months ago." What Angel didn't say was that it had been sold without her knowledge in order to pay off debts that had piled up in the last year of Derry's undergraduate education. She would have given him the money if she had known he needed it. At least, she would have tried. But Derry was determined not to take any more from her, even though she could think of nothing she would rather spend money on than his future.

"You didn't approve," said Hawk flatly.

"Of what?"

"Derry selling his boat."

"It was his to sell," Angel said, her voice calm. She was in control again.

"But you loved taking it out on the water."

Angel looked up, caught by the harsh current of emotion in Hawk's voice. "Yes."

"Lucky for you I came along," said Hawk, straightening. "Otherwise you might have had to sell your pretty little . . . smile . . . to get a ride."

"The people who take me out pay for more than a smile," said Angel, deliberately giving Hawk an opening.

"I'll bet." Hawk's voice was laced with contempt.

"You'd lose." She watched his face impassively. "I'm a licensed fishing guide."

Other than the rakish tilt of an eyebrow, Hawk made no reply.

"As I told you once, Hawk. You don't know a damn thing about me."

"You'd be surprised, honey," said Hawk, his voice flat but for the slight, sardonic lilt that was as much a part of him as his thick black hair.

For an instant Angel wondered what woman had so embittered Hawk that he assumed all women were shallow and unfeeling. But speculating about the woman or women in Hawk's life splintered Angel's calm into a thousand sharp pieces. She had no control over Hawk, his women, or the conclusions that he drew from his past and then applied to the present, to her. All she could control was herself, her own reactions and conclusions.

Deliberately, as she had learned to do in the terrible months following Grant's death, Angel re-created in her mind a vision of the most beautiful thing she had ever seen. A single rose unfolding in the summer dawn. The petals were crimson, luminous, serene. The possibility of beauty that had endured through the cruel winter and uncertain spring had been consummated in radiant silence.

A simple thing. A single rose, victorious and serene.

Calmness spread visibly through Angel as the rose unfolded in her mind. Confidently she put her hands on the boat's controls, her body and mind united in a sensitive appraisal of the unnamed boat.

Fascinated by the change that had swept over Angel, Hawk watched her every move with narrowed, measuring eyes. He sensed that she had retreated. No, not retreated. She had simply gathered herself into an inner place, a quiet place. A place where he could not go.

Angel slid the throttles up, increasing the revolutions on the twin diesels. She watched the gauges carefully. The engines were beautifully balanced, performing in exact synchronization with each other. With a sound of approval, she decreased the revs, shifted the engines into gear, and began to put the boat through its paces under Hawk's intense and finally approving scrutiny. The boat responded eagerly to Angel's touch, the prow curving and recurving through green water, sending chaotic wakes slapping across the shifting surface of the sea.

Angel flipped on the sonar and watched the changing pattern as the boat roved up and down the strait.

"Ever use a fish finder before?" asked Angel, aware of Hawk's curious glances at the plate-sized sonar screen.

"No."

"Right now," said Angel, pointing toward the lower part of the screen, then indicating the depth scale alongside, "the bottom is about twenty fathoms. There's nothing between us and the bottom but—wait." Without looking away from the screen, Angel cut back on the throttles and turned the boat, retracing her path slowly. "There," she said, pointing to a bright, shifting series of lines that had appeared at about ten fathoms on the scale. "A school of fish. Herring, probably."

"How can you tell?"

Angel shrugged slightly, a graceful movement that caught Hawk's eye. "Experience," she said simply. "Herring are erratic yet dense. See how quickly the lines shift?"

Hawk watched the screen, but much of his attention was on the slender hands that had so quickly learned how to handle the powerboat. Whatever else Angel was, she had the confidence and coordination of a race driver.

"What do salmon look like on the screen?" asked Hawk in a quiet, deep voice. He bent over as though to see the screen more clearly, but it was the woman that filled his senses. His nostrils flared as he smelled the delicate perfume he had come to associate with Angel, a blend of sunshine and wind and hidden flowers.

"Salmon look less well-defined, unless you happen onto a good school." Angel closed her eyes for an instant, sensing the heat radiating from Hawk's body. "They're rarely on the bottom. If you see a school just above the bottom, you've found cod, not salmon." *Why did he have to stand so close?* "Are you near-sighted?" asked Angel finally, feeling caged by Hawk's heat, serenity burning away with each breath she took, bringing his male scent deeply into her body.

"Near-sighted?" asked Hawk, surprise in his voice.

"As in not able to see things unless you're right on top of them," explained Angel dryly.

Hawk glanced sideways. His face was only inches from hers. In the slanting morning light her eyes were as green as matched emeralds. "Sorry," he murmured. Then, "Am I crowding you?"

"No more than I'm crowding you," retorted Angel.

"Good," he said huskily, "because I don't feel a bit crowded."

Angel turned the wheel suddenly and gunned the engines. The motion forced Hawk to step back in order to keep his balance. She took the boat closer to the cliffs looming on the east side of the passage. Hawk watched the cliffs approach at an alarming speed. He glanced at the sonar; the bottom was thirty-three fathoms and getting deeper every moment. He measured the cliff with narrow eyes. One hundred feet at least. Closer to two hundred. Huge evergreens clung to cracks in the cliff's face, but the trees looked no bigger than weeds against the immense expanse of rock.

With a sideways glance, Angel measured Hawk's response to the cliff. To someone unaccustomed to the Inside Passage, it would seem like insanity to approach the shore at such speed because of the danger of running aground. But Angel knew the land and the sea.

"Geologists call this land the drowned coast," said Angel, pitching her voice automatically to carry above the sound of the engines. "During the last ice age the sea level was several hundred feet lower. Then all the ice melted, flooding the land. That cliff"—she gestured ahead—"goes straight down about three hundred feet below the sea. There's no way to run aground here unless I ram the cliff itself."

"Like Norway," murmured Hawk, looking at the land with new eyes.

"That's what one of my fishing clients said. He had been born in Norway. Said that all these fjords made him homesick. It was the first time I'd realized that a fjord is nothing but a valley drowned in saltwater."

Amused, Hawk glanced sideways at Angel. She didn't notice. She was easing back on the throttles and turning the boat so that they paralleled the cliff face at a distance of about twenty feet. Then she put the engines in neutral and left them idling while she estimated the amount of drift that would be caused by wind and currents. The boat moved slowly away from the cliff.

"How much do you trust these engines?" asked Angel matter-of-factly.

"To do what?"

"Start the first time."

"I wouldn't bet my life on it. But then, I don't bet my life on anything anymore." Hawk shrugged. "They'll start ninety-nine times out of a hundred."

"Good enough. I wouldn't mind a little silence."

Angel cut the engines, then restarted them. They caught immediately. She turned them off again, giving the boat to the subtle movements of wind and water. Silence flowed over her like a benediction. Unconsciously she closed her eyes and smiled with pleasure.

Hawk saw Angel's pleasure and was tempted to run first his fingertip and then his lips over her smile. He did neither. For the first part of the chase he was content to let the prey set the course and the speed. That didn't mean he wouldn't crowd Angel from time to time, just to watch sensuality deepen the color of her eyes and soften her mouth. But the crowding would be gentle, would seem utterly natural, and would give her no excuse to retreat too far. He sensed that she was not nearly so aggressive as many of the women he had taken. With those women, the sport had been to twist and dodge away from them, watching their frustration grow at his elusiveness. With Angel, the sport would be to let her come to him.

Either way, the end was the same. Satiation and then dissatisfaction, tears and Hawk flying away, spreading his dark wings until he hung poised in the sky, waiting for the next chase to begin. Hawk's mouth turned down in a cruel curve aimed as much at himself as it was at the women he had brought down and then flown from. He was beginning to tire of it, the chase and the kill; and most of all he was tired of the restlessness that consumed him the morning after. The adrenaline was no longer enough.

But adrenaline was all there was.

Hawk had known that since he was eighteen. He'd never accepted it, though. Not completely. Hope was why he flew again, searched again, chased again. Hope kept telling him that there was more to life than betrayal and lies and the hollowness that came in the aftermath of adrenaline.

He had learned to hate hope, but he hadn't learned how to kill it. Yet.

"Hawk?"

He blinked, returning to the present and to the beautiful actress who promised to lead him on a fascinating chase—for a time. "Yes?"

"If you'll move, I'll start putting the fishing gear together."

Hawk stepped back just enough so that Angel could get out of the cockpit seat, but not enough so that she could avoid touching him as she got to her feet. Angel hesitated, then brushed quickly by Hawk, leaving behind her scent and a hint of warmth. Hawk absorbed both with a hot thrill of pleasure. Nothing showed on his face, though. He was as impassive as the cliff rising out of the sea.

Angel rigged the fishing rods quickly, explaining as she worked. The rods she chose were eight feet long and as flexible as fly rods. The boat rocked idly, drifting almost imperceptibly toward the shallow end of the tiny bay.

"I won't try trolling for salmon. They aren't here yet."

"How can you tell?" asked Hawk.

Angel's lips curved in a small smile. "Carlson isn't here. That man's uncanny. If there are salmon around, he knows it. Must be his Tlingit heritage."

"An old gray shaman?" asked Hawk with an amused tilt of his eyebrow.

Angel laughed as she bent over the tackle box and pulled out a spinning reel. "Hardly. His hair is as black and thick as yours. Handsome as sin and hard as that cliff. Like you." She began threading line through the guides on the rod.

Angel's voice had been so matter-of-fact that it took Hawk a moment to understand what she said.

"Thank you," he murmured, watching her narrowly.

"Thank your parents," said Angel, pulling a wicked-looking jig out of its slot in the tray. The hook gleamed cruelly in the sun. "I had nothing to do with it."

For a moment Hawk was off balance. Women had told him he was handsome before. Often. He was tired of hearing it, just as he was tired of so many things. But Angel's offhand summation of his appearance was . . . pleasing. She expected nothing in return, not a touch, not even words. It was as though she had pointed out that he had ten fingers. Nothing remarkable. Everyone had ten fingers.

A feeling of quiet exhilaration rippled through Hawk. First Angel retreated, then she returned, but she returned so delicately that he had all but missed her reappearance.

Never before had his prey moved so gracefully, so unexpectedly. He had been right to let her set the pace. He would continue to do so, until desire overcame his predator's patience and he swooped down, ending it.

"What if I said you were beautiful?" asked Hawk, real curiosity in his voice.

"I'd say you had good manners and bad eyesight," answered Angel, fastening the round-headed jig to the fishing line by means of a bronze safety pin that was already tied to the line. "My forehead is too high, my cheekbones are too prominent, my hair is too thick, my body is too thin, and my skin is too pale." She touched the tip of the hook with an experimental fingertip as she spoke. "On the plus side, my eyes are a nice color and everything else works better than it has any right to. There's nothing wrong with my mind, either—most of the time," she amended wryly.

While she spoke, Angel had pulled out a small whetstone and begun sharpening the jig's hook. Hawk watched, intrigued by both her words and her casual inventory of herself. What she had said was true in the strict factual sense. She wasn't beautiful in a conventional way. She was fascinating. Like a kaleidoscope, changing with each breath, never the same, always subtly shifting, brilliant. She must know how unusual she was, yet she had sounded absolutely certain of her lack of appeal to men.

"You're an astonishing actress," murmured Hawk, meaning every word of the ambiguous compliment. "Quite the best I've ever seen."

Startled, Angel looked up. The hook slipped, piercing the skin on the ball of her thumb. She snatched her hand away from the hook and frowned at the single bright drop of blood rising on her thumb. "What do you mean?"

Hawk shook his head admiringly. "Just that, *Angel*." He

took her hand and brought it to his mouth. He sucked lightly on her thumb. "Your blood is real, though," he murmured, releasing her with a final, flicking caress from his tongue.

Hawk had moved very quickly, capturing and releasing Angel before she could realize what had happened. Her body knew, however. Even now she could feel the soft rasp of his tongue, the quick pressure and heat of his mouth. Her breath was wedged tightly in her throat.

"I think the hook is sharp enough now, don't you?" asked Hawk softly, taking the rod from Angel's hands as though nothing had happened.

"Yes," said Angel, looking away from Hawk.

She walked quickly back into the cockpit and checked the sonar. They had drifted past the cliff face. Now the bottom was shelving up steeply. No more than eighty feet of water lay beneath the boat. With a quick glance at the land, she estimated where they were in relation to the rock reef that lay beneath the lower portion of the tiny bay.

Absently Angel sucked her stinging thumb. When she realized that her skin tasted of Hawk, her pulse hesitated, then accelerated raggedly. She took several steadying breaths, recalling the tranquil rose to her mind. It was the way she had discovered to gather and steel herself against the pain of learning how to walk again, how to live again.

Oddly, she hadn't realized until now that her special rose was the exact color of blood, the color of life itself.

Angel let the understanding radiate through her like light through stained glass, bringing color to everything it touched. When she returned to the open stern of the boat, her breath was easy, her voice and body relaxed.

"Have you ever jigged for cod?" she asked Hawk calmly, taking the rod from his hands.

"No. Is it difficult?"

"For you? I doubt it. You're very quick."

"Another compliment? You'll turn my head."

Angel gave Hawk a cool sideways look. "Another *fact*. And it would take a bulldozer to turn your head."

The left corner of Hawk's mouth turned up. It was as close to a smile as Angel had seen from him. Maybe it was as close to a smile as he ever got.

"Have you used a spinning reel before?" asked Angel, turning away from the intent brown eyes watching her.

"Yes. And I was soundly whipped for taking it without permission."

Angel looked at the tall, powerful man standing so close to her. "That must have been when you were a lot smaller. Either that, or they ganged up on you."

"I was six."

Shadows of memory changed Hawk's eyes. Angel watched, wondering what had caused the instant of grief and . . . rage? Yes, it had been rage. She had felt both those emotions, knew how viciously they could tear at you. Suddenly Angel was certain that Hawk's childhood had not been a happy one. She wondered if he had ever laughed as a boy, and if he ever laughed now, as a man.

"No matter how many bird's nests you make in my line," said Angel quietly, "I promise I won't beat you."

Hawk's dark eyes focused on Angel, startled by the intensity that seethed beneath her calm voice. His fingertip lightly traced the straight line of her nose. "Wise of you," he murmured. "In case you hadn't noticed, I'm bigger than you are. Much bigger."

"Harder, too," agreed Angel, but her eyes were luminous, reflecting Hawk's closeness. "Much harder."

Hawk's eyes changed, darkening as his pupils dilated. The temptation to taste the rosy softness of Angel's mouth

was almost overwhelming. Just as he had decided to accept
the ripe invitation of her lips, she turned away. For a few
moments she stood with her back to him. When she turned
around again, she was as tranquil as a flower unfolding into
the dawn. In a calm, professional voice she described the
theory and practice of jigging for cod.

"We'll be drifting over a rocky reef soon," said Angel.
"The reef is about six fathoms—thirty-six feet—down.
We're looking for black cod or ling cod, although I'm not
fussy. I learned to like rock cod when I was young because
Dad wouldn't let me keep anything I wouldn't eat."

Angel stepped back toward the cockpit, leaned in, and
looked quickly at the sonar screen. She thrust the rod into
Hawk's hands and gestured for him to go to the side of the
boat. A few inches below the wiggling tip of the rod, the
lead-weighted, hula-skirted jig danced and quivered as the
smallest movement of Hawk's body was transmitted up the
flexible length of the rod.

"This is the bale," said Angel, flipping aside the curved
piece of metal that kept fishing line from falling off the reel.
Immediately the heavy jig plopped into the water and sank,
dragging transparent line down into the blue-green sea.
"Let it sink until it bounces off the bottom. Then reel in
about six feet."

Hawk watched the line flip off the reel in graceful,
glistening curves until the jig touched bottom. The bale
clicked thickly in the silence as Hawk began to reel in.
When he estimated that he'd pulled in about six feet of line,
he turned to Angel and raised one black brow.

"The idea is to make the cod think that there's a
wounded herring fluttering down to the bottom," explained
Angel. "Pull up quickly, then let go, wait a few seconds,
and repeat. If a hungry cod is anywhere around, he'll come

'hunting. And then,'' said Angel, licking her lips delicately, "we'll have a leg up on dinner."

Hawk's clear brown eyes followed the tip of Angel's tongue as it left a thin shine of moisture over her lips. "Sneaky," he said, his voice deep. "What seems to be the prey turns and catches the predator."

Angel tipped her head to one side. "I never thought of it like that," she said. "Maybe it's only just. The cod is finally paying for a lifetime of free herring lunches."

The left corner of Hawk's mouth curled up. "What about you?" asked Hawk. "When do you pay?"

With a downward sweep of her lashes, Angel concealed the sadness that haunted her eyes. "I already have."

Hawk hesitated, wanting to ask what Angel meant. He waited, but she didn't look up. With a shrug, Hawk decided that her words had been one more graceful, elusive twist of the prey. He turned his attention back to the fishing rod, lifting it with quick, smooth power, then letting the line go slack again. Angel watched for a few moments, appreciating his deft handling of rod and line. In addition to Hawk's obvious male strength, he had superb reflexes.

"You're a natural," she said finally. Fact, not compliment, as her voice made clear.

Hawk glanced sideways but Angel was bent over the tackle box, selecting a lead-headed jig for herself. Within moments her rod was set up. She let down the lure over the stern. For a time there was only silence and the occasional high vibration of fishing line stretched taut and then released.

Hawk's rod tip dipped deeply, quivered, then dipped sharply again.

"You've got one," said Angel, reeling in quickly and setting her rod aside. "Keep your rod tip up!"

Silently Hawk glanced at the flexible rod. It was impossible to keep the tip up. As though Angel knew what he was thinking, she stepped to his side.

"Bring your elbows in against your hips," she said.

As soon as Hawk obeyed, the rod butt came nearly parallel to his body, forcing the tip up.

"Good," said Angel. "Now keep up the pressure as you reel in. Steady and slow. That cod isn't going anywhere but into our frying pan."

"Sure it's a cod?" asked Hawk, his eyebrow raised in a question or a challenge.

"Sure am," she said confidently. "It isn't fighting much."

Hawk looked at the lashing rod tip and felt the life of the fish quivering through his hands up to the muscles of his arms. "Not fighting?"

"Nope. Wait until you get a salmon on that tippy little rod," said Angel, her voice rich with memories. "Then you'll know what it's like to hold sunrise and lightning in your hands."

Angel didn't notice Hawk's quick look or the surprise that showed for an instant on his face. Her excitement and pleasure was as clear as the sunlight bouncing off the calm water. Whatever else might or might not be true about Angel, Hawk believed that she enjoyed fishing as few people enjoyed anything on earth. And then he wondered if she brought the same passionate honesty to bed that she brought to fishing.

The rod jumped and quivered in Hawk's hands.

"Keep the tip up!"

Angel leaned over the rail, straining for her first glimpse of Hawk's fish.

"The fish just gained ten pounds," said Hawk, startled. The rod bent in a tight, inverted U.

"That's a cod for you," laughed Angel. "He caught a

glimpse of the boat and spread his fins to make it harder for you to pull him up. Good-bye streamlining. It's like hauling up a cement slab, isn't it?''

Hawk grunted and kept reeling in until a long, surprisingly slender shape showed just beneath the surface. The lateral fins were widely flared.

Angel slid past Hawk to reach for the net that was in a rack beside the cockpit door. She leaned over the low railing, net in hand, and deftly scooped the sullen cod out of the sea. ''Hand me the cosh, would you?''

Hawk glanced just beyond Angel's reaching fingertips to what looked like a short axe handle. He pulled it out of its holder. Angel dispatched the fish with a single, quick blow. Her grimace told Hawk that this was one part of fishing that she didn't particularly enjoy.

''You could just throw it in the box and let it die,'' he pointed out.

''I can't stand to hear fish flopping around,'' she admitted.

''Soft-hearted, Angel?'' asked Hawk, his voice sardonic.

''I'm no more cruel than circumstances require,'' said Angel quietly. She pulled a pair of needle-nose pliers out of her hip pocket, fastened the pliers onto the cod's lower lip, and extracted the cod from the net.

''Teeth,'' she said succinctly.

A glance showed Hawk that the cod's jaws were lined with needle-like teeth. The fish was indeed a predator. Angel opened the fish box, dropped the cod in, and closed the lid. She tested the sharpness of Hawk's jig with a careful fingertip, nodded, and gestured for him to go back to fishing.

Silence returned, broken only by the soft nibbling of small waves along the boat's length. Angel caught the next fish, two pounds of fiercely ugly red rock cod. When Hawk reached for the net, Angel shook her head.

"No," she said, reeling in smoothly. "This one has spines that can rip apart a net. They're poisonous, too. Not lethal. Just painful."

She pulled the pliers out of her hip pocket again. Leaning low over the rail, rod held high in one hand and pliers in the other, Angel fastened onto the shank of the hook. She gave a quick shake, freeing the fish. It swam languidly back into the green darkness, more disgruntled than frightened.

"Not good to eat?" asked Hawk.

"They're fine. That one was a bit small. It would fillet out into about two bites per side."

"More trouble than it's worth."

"Unless you're hungry, yes."

As Hawk turned to resume fishing, the radio in the cockpit crackled to life.

"*—calling Angie Lange. Can you read me?* Black Moon *calling Angie Lange. Can you read me? Over.*"

Angel spun and reached the cockpit in two steps. She snatched the mike off its rack, punched in the button, and spoke quickly, her voice excited. "Carlson? This is Angie. Where are you?"

"*Heading up the passage for ten days.*"

"Oh." Angel's disappointment was as clear in her voice as it was in her face. "You're an elusive man, Carlson."

"*You're a bit hard to catch yourself. Must be those big white wings growing out of your back.*"

Angel smiled.

"*Derry's been trying to raise you on the radio for the last hour,*" continued Carlson. "*I figured you must be jigging behind one of the islands, so I offered to relay for him.*"

"He's all right, isn't he?" demanded Angel anxiously.

"He's doing okay. Grouchy as a spring bear, but okay otherwise. There's a message for a Mr. Hawkins. Your client?"

"Yes," said Angel, suddenly aware that Hawk was leaning against the frame of the open cockpit door, listening.

"Derry said that Lord Something-or-other called with a counter-counteroffer." Carlson's amusement was clear in the extraordinary precision of his words. *"Poor Angie. You always end up with the stuffiest shirts and the clumsiest white eyes ever to get a yen to go fishing."*

"Not this time," said Angel, smiling at the man in the doorway. "This time I've got a real live hawk."

Carlson's deep laugh seemed too big for the small speaker. *"Have fun, Angie, but watch your fingers. Hawks are the meanest birds ever to fly."*

"Take care of yourself, Carlson. I heard that there was a storm coming down out of the Aleutians."

"Yeah, I know. That's why I left without waiting to see you."

"Call me when you get back."

"Don't I always?" There was a pause, then, slowly, *"I may still be out on the twelfth."*

"That's okay," said Angie, her voice too even, too calm, belying the sudden paleness of her cheeks.

"Are you sure?"

"Derry will be here. I'll be fine." Her voice softened, revealing a hint of the emotion beneath. "Thanks, Carlson. It means—a lot."

"Save your best hug for me, Angel Eyes."

The faint hiss of static filled the cockpit. Suddenly Angel felt very much alone. The old nickname had brought back too much of the past with it. She loved Carlson in the same way that she loved Derry, but Carlson's voice inevitably reminded her of Grant, of love and death and loss. Yet she needed Carlson. His laughter and the memories that they shared created a bridge between the irretrievable past and the often lonely present.

"I take it that was the salmon shaman," said Hawk, his voice smooth and cold. He was irritated by the transparency of Angel's ploy in dangling her deep-voiced admirer in front of him.

"The salmon shaman? Oh." Angel smiled slightly. "Yes, that was Carlson. Did you hear the message?"

Hawk's mouth made a cynical downward curve. He'd heard the message all right. In case he hadn't, she was giving him a replay with her lonely, wistful look. Well, that was one type of chase he wouldn't participate in. If she wanted to play one man off against the other, she'd find herself without a game. When Hawk hunted, he hunted alone.

He pushed away from the cockpit door, turning his back on Angel. "Take me back to Eagle Head," he said curtly. "I have some calls to make."

Chapter 5

THAT WAS THE FIRST OF MANY TIMES THAT THE DEMANDS of Hawk's business interrupted Angel's guided tour of Vancouver Island and the waters around Campbell River. Hawk had flown to Vancouver three times, where he had met with lawyers and signed papers. When he stayed in the Ramsey house, he was often on the phone. In ten days Angel had managed to get Hawk out fishing only twice. Each time phone calls had made them miss the tide. Not that it really mattered; the run of silver salmon had not yet begun. Even the commercial fishermen were catching only a handful of fish for each day spent on the water.

In the end Angel settled for giving Hawk a slow-motion tour of rocky heads and tiny bays as she showed him how to troll for salmon. It was, to her, the least satisfactory method of catching salmon. The stiff rods required for trolling masked the energy and vibrancy of the fish. But trolling was the price of missing the tide changes, when the shifting balance of water and moon coaxed the salmon to feed closer to the surface.

Angel was determined that there would be no more missed tides. Word had come through the fishing grapevine that the first true run of summer salmon was sliding silently down the Inside Passage. Yesterday the catch had been up at the north end of the passage. If the fish followed past patterns, one of Angel's favorite stretches of coastline should be hosting the salmon for a while on their run south to the countless rivers that drained the mountainous land. By boat, it would take nearly six hours to get to Needle Bay, but Hawk had finally agreed that he could take time away from the phone for a five-day trip. In order to do so, though, he had worked steadily. Other than mealtimes Angel had seen very little of Hawk for three days.

Angel had been busy too. The used kiln she had bought and shipped up from Seattle for her summer use had finally arrived. With it had come a surprise, a large crate full of carefully packed cullet—scrap glass—sent by her Seattle gallery owner. The note on top of the box said only: "Incredible price. Glass factory collapsed. Larger pieces sent to your Seattle studio." The delivery men had just finished carting everything into the north wing of the Ramsey house. Under Derry's amused eyes, Angel was attacking the crate with a crowbar.

"Sure you don't want me to do it?" asked Derry lazily, perfectly content to lounge in an overstuffed chair and watch her handle the brilliant, incredibly sharp pieces of glass.

"You'd probably break every piece of glass in the crate," said Angel, smiling across the room at him.

"You're just going to make it all into little pieces anyway," Derry pointed out in a reasonable, teasing voice.

"But there's method in my madness," said Angel. "In yours there's just muscle."

The top came off to the accompaniment of high squeals from the nails used to secure the crate. Angel set aside the crowbar and pulled on a pair of thin, supple suede gloves. Scrap glass had edges sharper than any razor she had ever used.

"Careful," said Derry.

Angel gave him a long-suffering look. He smiled and shrugged lightly. Neither of them noticed that Hawk had come to stand just outside the doorway of the studio, drawn b · the sound of nails screaming against green wood.

"That stuff's lethal," persisted Derry, eyeing the glass.

"Only if you're careless."

"And who bandaged your hand the last time you slipped up?" asked Derry in a dry voice.

"I did," said Angel without looking up from the glass. "You were carousing in Vancouver with your friends." Angel set aside a mound of packing material. "Oh," she said, delighted, "Jess found me a batch of muff!"

Eagerly, but carefully, Angel drew out the layers of packing material and began to sort the biggest pieces of scrap glass into the rows of cubbyholes that lined one wall of her studio. Most of the cullet was muff glass, a special kind of glass that was treasured for its flaws rather than its perfection. A single sheet of muff had infinite variability in texture, thickness, and color. Muff glass added a depth to stained glass designs that never failed to excite Angel.

"That piece looks like hell," said Hawk.

Startled, Angel turned and looked over her shoulder at Hawk, then back at the tray-sized piece of muff she was putting away. Its purples varied from ultra-pale to nearly black. Swirls, ripples, and bubbles randomly distorted the surface of the glass. She pivoted gracefully, holding the piece up to the light streaming through the north window. Instantly the glass was transformed into something alive, light pooling and sliding, every tint and tone of purple the eye could see, glass haunted with radiant shadows and flashing possibilities.

"It's magnificent," Angel said, slowly lowering the glass.

"It's flawed," said Hawk.

"So is life. That's the most complex part of its beauty."

Hawk went very still for a moment, held as much by Angel's words as by the jeweled flash of color when she turned and carefully slid the unique glass into a cubby that held other shades of purple. Though he said nothing, he watched her with an intensity that made his narrowed eyes glitter like lines of clear brown crystal.

Angel didn't notice. She had just seen a shaft of unusual color. Packed in with the muff were several partial sheets of flashed glass. The dominant color of the two-layer glass was an amazingly clear, rich chestnut. Beneath the thin layer of luminous brown was a layer of bronze-toned glass. When the top layer of glass was etched with acid, the bronze would show through, giving depth and highlights to the brown.

"Like sunlight on a hawk's feathers," murmured Angel. *Or the gold lying beneath Hawk's eyes.*

But Angel didn't say that aloud, for she sensed Hawk walking toward her, closer with every second. A frisson of heat went through her, a tiny shiver of response that she couldn't control. The more she was around Hawk, the more she was drawn to him. She didn't know if it was the same for him, though. She could not read his silences.

Hawk stepped forward, drawn by the beauty of the glass

and the woman holding it. When he stopped, he was so close to Angel that he could feel her hair drift across his chest as she turned to look over her shoulder at him.

"Is this glass more to your taste?" asked Angel. She stepped slightly away from Hawk as she held the transparent, deep brown glass to the northern light. The glass blazed like a cinnamon diamond. She looked critically at the pattern of illumination. "Flawless."

Hawk simply looked at Angel's hair, thick with the same light that had transformed the glass. He was still consumed by the echoes of her earlier words about life and flaws and beauty. Then Hawk realized that he had softly wound a tendril of Angel's hair around his finger and was bringing it toward his lips. Instantly he let go, angry at himself for revealing the obsession that Angel had become to him. He planned to purge himself of it, and her, on their five-day trip.

Abruptly Hawk turned away from Angel and the light pouring incandescently through her hair. "I have a few more calls to make before we can leave," he said curtly.

Angel watched Hawk leave, her eyes dark. She had sensed a vague stirring in her hair, the warmth of Hawk's breath and his body, and then his withdrawal. She looked over at Derry and smiled crookedly.

"I seem to annoy your Mr. Hawkins," said Angel, her voice light. "All I have to do is breathe."

Derry, who had seen nothing but the broad line of Hawk's back as he stood near Angel, shrugged and hoisted himself onto his crutches. "It's just his manner, Angie. Nothing personal. And whatever business deal he's working on is rough. He's as busy as a one-legged soccer player." Derry went to the door. "I'd better get back to the books. If you cut yourself, holler."

"Don't trip over Mrs. Carey's stuff. I left it in the hall."

"Hawk loaded the bags in his car. He thought they were for the trip."

Angel watched Derry leave, but her mind was on Hawk. Even after ten days the man was as much of an enigma to her as he had been when they first met. Most of the time Hawk was cool and abrasive, making her subtly uneasy with his intense, dark brown eyes, eyes that watched each movement she made, each breath. He would touch her casually, impersonally, as they moved about his powerboat or went sightseeing in his car. The touches were invariably gentle, a simple brush of fingertips over her wrist or palm or, once, her cheek.

At first Angel had been startled by Hawk's touch. She had retreated, watching him narrowly. He had done nothing, neither pursued her nor sought to make the next touch more intimate. In time, Angel had decided that Hawk's touches were simply part of his complex nature, like his fierce eyes and unsmiling mouth. She no longer retreated when he touched her. She accepted him for what he was—if not a *gentle*man, at least a very controlled man.

In the hours they had spent together Hawk had never really crowded Angel, never said or done anything out of line. And he was easy to be with, despite his moments of startling intensity. Long silences didn't disturb him as they did most people. He didn't require chatter to cover the untamed murmur of wind and sea. Once, when they had been out on the water for several hours, relaxation had eased the harsh lines of his face. She had not been able to look away from him, held by the changed expression. It had been as though peace had dissolved away the darker surface color of him, revealing the warmer color beneath.

Yet sometimes Angel felt pursued. When she looked up and found Hawk watching her, her heart hesitated and then beat too quickly. He seemed to see right through her to the blood racing in her veins. Once, when he had touched her cheek with his hard fingertips, she had thought he was going to say something. Surely he had seen the rapid beat of her pulse beneath her throat. But he had said nothing, simply looked at her, and a feeling of longing had swept through her like sunlight through stained glass, transforming her. She had found herself holding her breath, anticipating the next time his fingers would brush over her skin. She had found herself watching him, wondering with strange urgency what it would take to make him smile.

For Hawk had never smiled in the time they were together. Not once.

Perhaps when he caught a salmon. Perhaps then he would smile. No one could resist the flashing beauty of the fish, the thrilling power vibrating up through the rod, the moment of capture when the net was bursting with rippling silver energy.

The phone rang, startling Angel. It didn't ring a second time. Hawk had picked it up before she could do more than look at the extension in her studio. She glanced at the wall clock. Nine thirty. A bit late for London. The call was probably from one of Hawk's limited partners in the United States. Later in the day Hawk would usually talk to Tokyo, long calls that left him irritable, restless, like a caged thing ready to lash out at whatever was within reach.

But not today. Today they were going fishing if Angel had to grab Hawk and drag him to the boat. First, though, she had to take care of her own obligations. She glanced at the partially unloaded box. The glass could wait. Mrs. Carey could not.

Angel pulled off her gloves, grabbed her purse, and left the room at a half-run, eager to have everything done so that she could be out on the water. She stopped long enough to poke her head into Hawk's suite of rooms. As she had expected, Hawk was on the phone. His head was resting against the back of the leather chair, his long legs sprawled across the beautiful Chinese rug. Tension and fatigue were clear on his face. Eyes closed, he was listening without speaking.

Angel knocked lightly on the door frame. Hawk's eyes opened. They were startlingly clear, as intense as focused sunlight.

"Go ahead and talk," said Hawk to Angel, his voice rough. "His damned secretary lost the last offer. They're looking for it right now."

"Can I have your car keys for a minute?"

Hawk looked surprised, then reached into his slacks for his key ring. As he shifted, the slacks pulled tightly across his lower body, revealing every masculine line of him. Angel closed her eyes, but it was too late. The image of Hawk was etched behind her eyelids as surely as if she had done the job herself with acid and flashed glass.

Keys jingled in front of Angel's face.

"Thanks," said Angel, her voice tight. "Your car is blocking mine. I'll give you back the keys as soon as I move it."

"Don't bother. Just take my car."

"What?" said Angel, barely hearing his words.

Hawk had unbuttoned his shirt when he sat down for the round of morning calls. Tanned, powerful, with a wedge of curling midnight hair, the lines and textures of Hawk's chest between the crisp white edges of his shirt appealed to both the woman and the artist in Angel. It was all she could do not to grab her sketch pad and go to work, capturing him. Or to lean over and tangle her fingers in the rough silk of his hair, capturing him in a different way.

"Take my car," said Hawk, his eyes roaming over Angel's face, lingering on her moist, slightly parted lips. "I won't be needing it." She was just within his reach. With very little effort he could pull her between his legs, hold her against the growing ache of his arousal, the ache that came whenever he was with her for more than a moment. Hell, it came whenever he thought about her soft mouth and haunted eyes, about what it would be like to hear and feel her passion surrounding him.

When Hawk spoke again, his expression was impassive —and his voice a caress. "Take it, Angel. It's easy to handle." Then Hawk's voice changed. "No, Jennings," he said into the phone, "I didn't mean you." His mouth curled up at the left corner. "I wouldn't give you a saucer of warm spit, and you know it."

Angel heard the blast of laughter that came from the phone. She took the keys from Hawk and hurried out of the room, wondering if he had noticed her staring at him; and if he had, what he thought about it. She was drawn to him as surely as waves were drawn to the shore. She wanted to be with him, to touch him, to talk with him, to enjoy his quick intelligence and even his abrasive wit. Yet she didn't know if he was attracted to her in the same way. There was no reason he should be. There was no lack of women for Hawk. Women wanted him. It was that simple. Every time Hawk walked down a street or into a restaurant, women looked, and then looked again, drawn by the maleness that radiated from him as inevitably as color radiated from stained glass.

But Hawk didn't look back at the women who looked at him. Either he didn't notice, or he didn't care.

Angel slid behind the wheel of Hawk's black BMW. A quick study of the dashboard told her everything she needed to know. She started the car and drove confidently, enjoying the responsiveness of the BMW. As Hawk had said, it was easy to handle. She wished that its owner were half so easily managed. He wasn't, though. All Angel could be sure of was that Hawk had made no unmistakable overtures toward her as a woman. Until he did, she could only assume that he wasn't interested. Despite her attraction to him, she would not chase him. It not only wasn't her style, but she had a deep feeling that Hawk had been too often chased and never caught. Not really. Not for more than a night or two.

That wasn't enough. Whatever Angel's feelings were toward the enigmatic Hawk, they were too complex to be satisfied in a few nights.

Angel parked in front of a small house that had been built forty years before. The other houses on the street were more recent, having been built after Mr. Carey died and his widow was forced to sell the small farm in order to pay death taxes. Angel retrieved the two bags of groceries from the trunk and walked carefully up the cracked sidewalk to the front porch. On either side of the walkway, once-elegant roses were going to seed. Angel made a note in her mind to make time to prune the roses the next time she was there.

Mail stuck out from the box by the doorbell. Angel pressed the button with her elbow, then braced a bag against the brick house long enough to grab the mail in the box.

"Mrs. Carey?" she called out. "It's Angie."

"Coming," came a faint voice from inside the house.

Angel waited without impatience, balancing the bags of groceries and the mail in her arms. After a few minutes the door to the small house opened. A tiny, gray-haired woman smiled up at Angel and retreated a few steps to allow her to enter. The woman's walker squeaked slightly on the flagstone entryway.

"Come in, Angie. My, you're looking lovely this morning. Such a pretty color you're wearing."

"Thank you," said Angel, smiling. The sea-green pullover sweater she wore matched her eyes exactly. The rest of

her outfit was strictly functional—faded black jeans and
sneakers, plus a rumpled black felt fishing hat that kept hair
and sun out of her eyes. She'd forgotten to put on the hat,
though. It hung rakishly out of her hip pocket. "You're
looking very nice too. How's it coming with the walker?"

Mrs. Carey made a small face as she rested against the
U-shaped steel support that had made walking possible
since the cast had been removed from her hip. More like
half of a cage than crutches, the walker offered a security
that crutches did not. Even so, it was obvious that Mrs.
Carey was less than pleased to be confined to a walker.

"Darn contraption hasn't thrown me yet," she said, both
proud and defiant.

Angel concealed her smile. Mrs. Carey was one of
Angel's favorite people. The old woman's astringent,
uncomplaining approach to hardship was refreshing.

"You go on ahead," continued Mrs. Carey. "I'll catch
up with you in the kitchen."

"Thanks. I'm running kind of late this morning."

Angel walked quickly to the kitchen and began to put
away the groceries she had bought for Mrs. Carey early that
morning. She noticed the tea service set out with a tin of
biscuits and knew that Mrs. Carey had hoped to spend some
time with her over a cup of tea. Angel glanced at the kitchen
clock, hesitated, and shrugged. A few minutes more or less
wouldn't matter. If she and Hawk left by ten thirty, they
would be anchored in Needle Bay well before dark.

The rubber stoppers on Mrs. Carey's walker squeaked on
the linoleum floor as she walked slowly over to Angel.

"I'll put away the rest, dear," said Mrs. Carey. "You've
done more than enough."

Angel looked at what remained to be unloaded. She could
do the work faster herself, but she knew how much being

dependent bothered the proud Mrs. Carey. Quickly Angel set on the counter a few items that she knew went into easily reached cupboards.

"If you take care of these," said Angel, gesturing to the pile of tins on the counter, "we'll have it under control in no time at all."

Angel finished with the second sack just as Mrs. Carey placed the last tin of biscuits in the cupboard.

"Teamwork," murmured Angel, folding the empty sack triumphantly. "That's all it takes."

"Do you have time for a cup of tea?" asked Mrs. Carey hesitantly. "I don't want to keep you if—"

"You're a lifesaver," said Angel, interrupting gently, smiling. "I was in such a rush this morning that I didn't even have tea."

Mrs. Carey walked slowly toward the breakfast table, shaking her head vigorously. "Nothing is more important than a cup of tea, young lady."

Discreetly Angel looked at the kitchen clock. Her impatience faded as she sat and drank tea, listening while Mrs. Carey talked about children and grandchildren, the crabapples that were almost ready to be made into jelly, and the berries that would come in later in the summer. Gently Angel refused a second cup of tea. She stood and carried her dishes to the sink.

"I'll call you in a few days to see what you're out of," said Angel, rinsing and setting aside her cup. "If you need anything before then, call Mrs. Schmidt." Angel bent over and hugged Mrs. Carey gently. "See you in a week."

"I don't want to bother you—" began Mrs. Carey.

"No bother," said Angel honestly. "I have to shop for me and Derry anyway."

"I feel like a clumsy idiot."

Angel smiled. "Just unlucky," she said, bending and giving Mrs. Carey another light hug. "You'll be back to shopping for yourself in a few weeks."

"Blasted cat."

The cat in question chose that moment to meow at the back door. Mrs. Carey went slowly to let in the old tom, muttering every step of the way about the stupidity of the cat that had tripped her and caused her to break her hip. Angel watched, struggling not to smile. She knew that so far as Mrs. Carey was concerned, the sun rose and set in that scruffy cat.

Angel gave another glance at the kitchen clock, then let herself out the front door. She made a concerted dash through the grocery store to get everything that she had missed that morning in her headlong rush to get back in time for the arrival of the glass. The unexpected delivery had disrupted her carefully planned morning. It was more than worth it, though. The glass was exquisite. Already designs were forming in her head, mountains and the sea and a man's hidden smile.

It was just a short drive to the Ramsey house. Angel hurried anyway, eager to get out on the water. Although she and Hawk had taken out his big powerboat several times before, this would be their first real fishing expedition. Up until today their trips had been more sightseeing excursions than anything else. Today, however, she was finally going to get to show Hawk what it was really like to go in quest of the silver salmon. Privately, she was sure that Hawk would succumb to the lure of the beautiful, powerful fish.

Angel grabbed three bags of groceries from the trunk and rushed up the front walk. Juggling bags, leaning against the door, she groped for the front door handle. The door opened suddenly, throwing Angel off balance. She grabbed at the bags desperately. Before she lost either the groceries or her balance, strong hands clamped around her arms, holding her upright until she was steady again. Angel knew it was Hawk who held her even before she looked up; his clean, male scent filled her nostrils. Suddenly she wondered if he would taste as good as he smelled. The intensity of her curiosity disturbed her. Since Grant's death, she hadn't wanted to touch or be touched by men. Not like this. Hawk had slid by her fears and defenses as easily as sunlight sliding through glass.

Yet Hawk didn't seem to know it, or care.

"I—thanks," said Angel, her voice strained, her thoughts chaotic.

"You wouldn't be any good to me in a cast," Hawk said, releasing her.

Though Hawk's words were indifferent, almost curt, his fingers slid all the way down to Angel's buffed nails before he let her go. Angel's breath caught again, pulled between Hawk's impassive exterior and the hunger she sensed beneath, a hunger like hers, a yearning toward the warmth and beauty that a man and a woman could give to each other. She had caught tantalizing glimpses of that feeling with Grant, sweet moments of passion before he pulled back and sat without touching her because he wanted to wait until they were married.

But Grant had died before they were married.

Angel wrenched her thoughts into the present as Hawk took the grocery bags from her arms. She followed him into the kitchen, admiring the silence and power of his movements.

"Where's Derry?" she asked as Hawk set the sacks on the counter and began unloading items.

"Studying."

"Organic chemistry?"

Hawk shrugged. "All I saw was a formula as long as my leg."

"Organic chemistry," confirmed Angel, putting away food as fast as Hawk unloaded the bags. "That's the course that separates the ones who will-be from those who might-have-been."

"Derry's intelligent and disciplined. If he wants to be a doctor badly enough, he'll be one."

Only if you buy Eagle Head. But the words went no further than Angel's mind. She looked toward the kitchen clock, wondering if they were going to miss the evening tide at Indian Head, which was just below Needle Bay. Even when she stood on her tiptoes, Hawk's shoulders blocked her view of the clock. Without thinking, Angel grabbed Hawk's wrist and looked at his watch.

"We're going to miss the tide unless we run," Angel said, leaning around Hawk's arm to see the face of his watch.

She glanced up to see if Hawk understood. His clear, dark eyes were watching her with unusual intensity. Suddenly Angel felt the heat of him reaching through his clothing, through her clothing, spreading through her in waves that made her dizzy. Her heart beat raggedly. Her breath caught in the back of her throat and stayed there. She was incredibly aware of her breast brushing against Hawk's arm, her nipple tightening until it ached. Her eyes darkened as her pupils expanded, all but eclipsing the blue-green iris.

Angel was too inexperienced to recognize the symptoms of sudden, passionate arousal. Hawk wasn't. Every one of his senses was fully alert, quivering with the signals that radiated from Angel. He wanted to put his hands on her, all of her, and then take her completely, finishing what her touch on his wrist had started. But Derry could come into the kitchen at any moment. Or in the next breath Angel could remember where she was, and draw back. Hawk had waited this long for the right moment, for the last sudden turn, the cry, the capture. He could wait longer. He could wait until she walked into the open, all pretense of innocence and retreat gone.

Slowly Hawk turned back to the counter. As he moved, his arm brushed lingeringly over Angel's breast. Angel's breath came in swiftly, brokenly. She stared at Hawk for an instant, wondering if he felt even a small part of what she was feeling. No expression showed beneath his dark features. For all that she could see, Hawk hadn't noticed her reaction to his closeness. Nor had he reacted to being close to her. The realization should have comforted her, but it did not. It made her feel lost, lonely, almost afraid. Sadness and passion ached in her.

Was Hawk so used to being alone that he couldn't respond to her? Or was it simply that she had survived Grant's death only to find herself wanting a man who neither needed nor wanted her?

Angel stood motionless in the kitchen, seeing nothing, not even Hawk. The thoughts turning in her mind consumed her. She realized that it was not merely eagerness to go fishing that had made her blood race when she had awakened today. It was the knowledge that she was going to have Hawk to herself. No Derry. No phone calls from New York and Texas and Tokyo to delay sightseeing trips and picnics. Nothing but Hawk and Angel and the restless, island-studded sea. Five days. Perhaps more.

Anything could happen in that time. Even love.

The thought shocked Angel for an instant. Then she accepted it the same way she had finally accepted the automobile accident that had so brutally changed her life. Running from the truth didn't alter anything, certainly not reality. Running just weakened you.

And she would have to be very strong with Hawk.

Quietly, standing in the kitchen not an arm's length from Hawk, Angel admitted to herself that if she spent much more time with him, she ran the risk of caring for him too much, being too drawn to the lonely reaches of his mind, the intelligence and power of him, the rare gentleness that spoke so movingly of the emotions hidden beneath his harshness. He was like a stained glass window in a black night, mystery and brooding hints of color. So much darkness, so little life. Yet when bathed in sunlight, the beauty inherent in the glass would leap into silent, over-whelming life, all the colors of love pouring forth where only darkness had been before.

Angel didn't know if she was strong enough to be the sunlight to Hawk's stained glass. She only knew she had to try.

Chapter 6

ANGEL LOOKED AT THE CLOCK ON THE CONTROL PANEL and swore silently. Everything seemed to conspire against getting Hawk out on the water at the best time for some decent fishing. It was five o'clock, and they had barely cleared Campbell River. For a moment Angel considered slowing and trolling along the floating rafts of logs waiting to be picked up by a towboat and hauled to Vancouver Bay. Some good-sized salmon had been known to school up under the rafts.

"Something wrong?" asked Hawk, his voice pitched above the sound of the engines. His eyes raked quickly over the gauges. He saw nothing to account for Angel's sudden frown.

"I'm tempted to fish here," she said, disgusted. Then, both wistful and heartfelt, "Damn it, I was looking forward to drift fishing off Indian Head."

A corner of Hawk's mouth turned up slightly. "Sorry. I didn't know the Honorable Mr. Yokagamo would have insomnia and decide to call me. I got rid of him as soon as I could without insulting him."

"And then London called."

"Paris, actually. London was the next call."

"Then Tokyo again," she sighed.

Angel shook her head. Having to look at a globe and have a clock that kept time in every world zone before you even answered the phone struck her as an unnerving way to do business. It seemed to come easily to Hawk, though. She could see his quick intelligence assessing every possibility and lining up arguments even as he reached for the phone. His concentration, memory, and patience were phenomenal. He would make an excellent fisherman if she ever got him out on the water long enough to teach him anything. As it was, they were only going to get a short distance up the coast before dark.

"Well, as long as we're late anyway, we might as well stop in at Brown's Bay," said Angel. "We'll top off the tanks, catch up on the fishing gossip, and then head over to Deepwater Bay for the night. If we're in luck, we might even get in some fishing. It's early for salmon to be there, but," Angel shrugged eloquently, "we have to get our lines wet somewhere."

"Or you'll go crazy."

"That," she said, "is a distinct possibility." She gave Hawk a sideways look out of green eyes. "Have you ever considered taking a vow of silence for a few days?"

The left corner of Hawk's mouth curled slightly. "Tired of my phone calls?"

"You could say that. And then you could say it again."

"I've been meaning to break this to you gently."

"What?"

"I have to check in with Tokyo tomorrow evening." Hawk saw the combination of disappointment and irritation that crossed Angel's features. "We don't have to go back to Campbell River," Hawk added. "I can patch through on the radio."

"Do you mind if I fish while you talk?" asked Angel, exasperated by the unending demands of Hawk's business.

"It's not always this bad," he said. Then the corner of his mouth lifted again. "Sometimes it's worse."

Angel shook her head in despair.

"Most of the time it's better," added Hawk, measuring Angel's disappointment and wishing he could be sure that it was his company rather than the chance to fish that she was missing. "The deal I'm working on is rather complex. Tomorrow's call should be the last major hump for a few weeks."

Angel made a neutral sound. She'd heard that before. Yesterday, to be exact. Automatically, she cut back the speed as she turned into Brown's Bay. The first thing she saw was the black, long-line troller tied at the dock. Her hand tightened on the throttle.

"Carlson!" breathed Angel.

As she guided the boat into a berth near the fuel pumps, Hawk watched her intently. Anger turned deep inside him when he saw the clear light of pleasure erase for a moment the haunting sadness that was so much a part of Angel's eyes. Hawk looked away from her, raking the marina with his dark glance until he spotted the battered troller tied opposite the pleasure boats. *Black Moon* was painted on the troller's side. Men were unloading fish from the ship's hold into wheelbarrows and pushing them up the dock to a scale. There the fish were weighed and put into a refrigerated truck to be hauled to market.

Quickly Angel shut down the engines and left the

cockpit. The manager of the station tied off the bow while Angel leaped out and tied off the stern, leaving Hawk standing in the boat.

"All the way to the top, Don," Angel called out, then she sprinted up the dock, turned, and ran down an intersecting dock toward the *Black Moon,* calling Carlson's name.

Hawk leaped lightly to the dock, following Angel with long strides. He was halfway down the intersecting dock when he saw a very big man descend from the *Black Moon* and stand waiting for Angel, his massive arms spread wide. She threw herself into them and was lifted and spun around and around like a leaf in a whirlwind. She laughed and held on, letting the colors of the world blur around her.

"How are you? Was the run good? When are you going back? Oh, Carlson, you look fantastic!" Angel said, questions and words tumbling out of her. "Was the storm bad? Did you get any smileys?"

Carlson's laugh was as big as the rest of him. "Slow down, Angie."

Angel threw her arms around Carlson's massive neck and hugged him with all her strength, burying her face in the rough, masculine textures of his workshirt. He smelled of sea and salmon and sweat. The combination brought a storm of memories sweeping over her. Shaking, she held on to Carlson until the storm passed.

Gently, Carlson let Angel down onto the dock, cradling her head against his chest. He knew that seeing him always brought Grant Ramsey back to her. Dead, Grant was between them as much as he had been when he was alive. Carlson accepted it as he accepted bad fishing and violent storms. Some things were not meant to be. For him, Angel was one of them.

"How's it been for you, Angie," said Carlson, tugging

gently on her thick French braid, remembering when her beautiful eyes had held a quality of incipient laughter rather than shadows. "How's the glass?"

"The Vancouver show was good," said Angie, smiling up into Carlson's brilliant black eyes. "I have so many new designs I want to do. One of them is the *Black Moon* and the sea and the salmon beneath like a silent silver storm. Would you like that?"

"I'd love it, but I can't afford it. Fishing's been real slow this year."

Angel looked shocked. "It's a gift!"

"Your smile is gift enough," said Carlson quietly. Then he glanced over the top of her head into a man's icy brown eyes. "You must be Hawk."

Hawk nodded once.

"I'm Carlson," said the Indian, holding out his hand.

Hawk took it. Both men measured each other with a strong handshake that stopped well short of the adolescent knuckle squeezing that some big men indulged in.

"How's fishing?" asked Carlson.

"Don't ask," retorted Angie in an exasperated voice before Hawk could say anything. "I'm going to have to surgically disconnect Hawk from the telephone if I want to catch any salmon this summer."

Carlson smiled, his teeth like a white half-moon against his dark face. "You haven't missed much yet. The run is just starting." He looked down into Angel's face. The lines and shadows of the past were there for him to read just beneath her smooth surface. "I'm glad you found me, Angie. I'm heading back out tomorrow morning. Derry said you were going to be gone for five days. Will he be alone tonight?"

Angel nodded slowly. "For a while. He said he didn't

mind. He was going to have some friends over later and play cards until he couldn't see straight.''

"Today is the twelfth, isn't it?'' said Hawk, catching the ripple of emotion beneath Angel's words. "Is there something special about that date?'' he continued, his voice sardonic and his eyes piercing. "This is the second time I've heard it mentioned in hushed tones.''

Carlson's eyes changed, opaque as the rocks lining the bay. Everything about the big Indian warned Hawk that he was trespassing. Hawk stood without flinching, waiting for his answer. He had fought big men before. And he was tired of watching Angel nestled within that thick arm.

"If you're going out right away," said Angel distinctly, ignoring Hawk, looking only at Carlson, "the fishing must be pretty good.''

"Not bad. I set aside a smiley to smoke for you and Derry.''

"What's a smiley?'' asked Hawk. "Or is that another private matter?''

Carlson gave Hawk a second black look. Hawk didn't budge. Grudgingly, Carlson realized that Hawk wasn't going to be intimidated short of a brawl, and probably not even then. Under other circumstances, Carlson would have enjoyed testing Hawk. But not today, with Angel fighting memories. Carlson suspected that Hawk was more than a little interested in the woman who was curled so trustingly against his own arm. The thought made Carlson's lips stretch into a smile that was neither welcoming nor cruel.

"A smiley," said Carlson, his voice so deep that it rumbled like water over rocks, "is a salmon that weighs more than thirty pounds. When you pull one of them off the long-line, you smile.''

The corner of Hawk's mouth curled up almost unwillingly. "I see.''

"You will when you catch one," said Carlson. "Or do you ever smile?"

"I'm smiling now."

Carlson laughed. "Come fishing with me, Hawk. By the end of the trip we'll be friends—or one of us will be dead."

For a moment Hawk simply looked at the massive man standing so confidently on the dock. Then Hawk held out his hand, liking the other man in spite of himself. "I'll hold you to that, Carlson."

Carlson took the offered hand. Just before he released it, he said easily, "One other thing, Hawk. If you touch Angie, I'll cut you into thin strips and use you for bait."

"Carlson—!" said Angel, angry and appalled.

Hawk was neither. "What if she wants me to touch her?" he asked softly.

Carlson looked from Angel's flushed face to Hawk's fiercely impassive expression. "Then I'd say you were the luckiest man alive." Carlson turned and kissed Angel's forehead. "Don's waving for you to get that fancy boat out of the way. See you in a few days, Angie. By then," he added, smiling, "maybe you'll be over your mad."

Shaking her head helplessly, Angel stood on tiptoe to kiss Carlson's black-stubbled cheek. "I can't ever stay mad at you," she said, then added crisply, "though God knows I should. You might consider apologizing to Hawk."

Carlson's black eyes were brilliant with suppressed laughter as he looked over Angel's head at Hawk. "I might, but I'm not going to. You understand, don't you, Hawk?"

"Perfectly." His mouth had a tiny, sardonic curl at the left corner.

Angel went back down the dock, hurried on her way by a friendly swat from Carlson's big hand. She glanced sideways at Hawk, still embarrassed by Carlson's warning. The slight upward tilt of Hawk's mouth told her that he had been amused rather than angered. But then, he had shown no signs of wanting to touch her, either. Not really. Not the way she wanted to be touched.

Quickly, grateful for the excuse to avoid talking to Hawk, Angel took the powerboat out of Brown's Bay and across the channel to work her way up to Deepwater Bay. She watched the ocean carefully. It was Saturday, and the water was alive with small craft.

"Hang on," said Angel calmly, spotting a slick ahead.

The slick's deceptively smooth surface concealed an enormous shift in the current. Some of the slicks were upwellings of water from below, where the ocean was squeezed between invisible rocky obstructions until water surged powerfully upward. Other slicks became whirlpools during the height of the tidal race. Small boats could be capsized and sucked down into the cold sea if the person at the helm was careless or inexperienced.

The helm bucked suddenly in Angel's hands. She was braced, expecting it. The stern of the boat drifted like the back end of a car on a patch of icy road. Angel turned the bow into the watery skid, controlling the motion of the boat. Within seconds they shot off the slick and back into the normally roiled water that came with changing tides.

Sensing Hawk's eyes on her, Angel turned and smiled. "Fun, wasn't it?"

A black eyebrow lifted, rewarding Angel's smile. "Looked like a rather nasty piece of water to me," said Hawk.

"That was just a baby. At some times of the year it gets rough, though."

"Storms?"

Angel shrugged. "Storms are bad any time of the year. So are the tides," she admitted, "if you don't know what to expect. The Inside Passage isn't for amateurs. Ask him,'' she added, gesturing toward a towboat and barge.

The towboat was straining northward up the narrowing channel. The thick, braided steel cable that connected the towboat to the heavily loaded barge was taut, humming with energy. Despite the obvious laboring of the heavy engines, the towboat was barely making one knot forward speed.

"Missed the tide," said Angel succinctly. "He'll spend the next few hours like that, going flat out and getting nowhere. Then the race will stop and he'll pop forward like a cork out of a bottle. Until then, though, he's stuck, working like the devil just to stay even and keep the tow cable straight against corkscrew tidal rips."

"Is that the voice of experience talking?" asked Hawk, realizing as he spoke that he wouldn't be surprised if Angel had handled one of the tugboats that dotted the Inside Passage. She was supremely at home on the water.

Angel hesitated, memories welling like blood. The summer she and Grant had fallen in love, he had piloted towboats up the Inside Passage. Even today the visceral, elemental pounding of diesel engines going flat out peeled away the years, leaving her naked and bleeding with memories.

"I've ridden on the towboats," said Angel, her voice even and her eyes too dark.

"With a man."

Angel didn't answer. It hadn't been a question.

"Wasn't it, Angel? A man?"

Hawk's persistence surprised her. She turned, only to find him very close. "Yes."

"The salmon shaman?"

"No." Her knuckles whitened as she clenched her hands

around the wheel. She didn't notice, though. She was impaled on Hawk's dark glance.

"Who was it?" asked Hawk lazily, his eyes as intent as those of a bird of prey. Then, "Maybe you could get me a ride."

"Derry's brother."

Angel caught the flash of surprise on Hawk's features. She knew what would come next. Turning away from Hawk, she prepared herself for it, calling up the dawn rose, pure color radiant with light, serene, softness triumphant over the worst that bitter winter ice could do.

"Derry never mentioned a brother," Hawk said, watching Angel closely. Her face gave away nothing. Whatever ghost had haunted her features for a moment had been chained again. "But that should make it easier to get a ride."

"Grant Ramsey is dead."

Hawk was silent for an instant, searching Angel's face for the emotion he sensed locked away inside her. "When?"

"A long time ago," said Angel, her voice tired and calm.

"He must have been much older than Derry."

"Yes."

Angel turned her attention to the sea again. Just short of Deepwater Bay, a cloud of gulls wheeled over the shifting water, gulls turning and crying like lost souls, hundreds of keening voices filling the air. Gulls dived and swooped, filling their beaks with herring and then flapping off heavily as other gulls dodged and darted, trying to steal herring from the overflowing beaks of the successful gulls. For a few minutes the water literally boiled with thousands upon thousands of herring, tiny fish hurling themselves into the air, shedding silver waterdrops that flashed brilliantly against the descending sun.

"Salmon," said Angel, automatically cutting the speed of the powerboat.

"Rather small," said Hawk dryly.

"Not those," she said, dismissing the frantic herring. "Beneath them, driving them to the surface. Salmon are feeding way down, where the sea is almost dark. The herring come up, trying to get away. Then the gulls feed on them from above and the salmon from below."

"Makes me glad I wasn't born a herring."

"To be alive is to eat," said Angel, her shadowed eyes searching the vibrant, seething water. "And, sooner or later, to die. Some die sooner rather than later."

"Not a very comforting philosophy," Hawk murmured, watching Angel with eyes like very dark topaz, hard and clear.

"Sometimes comfort doesn't get the job done," Angel said quietly, remembering the people who had tried to comfort her after the accident and had only made her more angry. Even Derry. It had taken Carlson's measured cruelty to shock her out of self-pity. Carlson, who had loved her as much as Grant had; but she hadn't known until it was too late. It would always be too late, now. They would never be lovers. They were friends, though, their friendship the kind that was as deep and enduring as the sea itself.

As mysteriously as the herring had appeared, they vanished. All that was left of them was a vague, metallic glitter deep within the green water, a glitter that faded as Angel watched. Abruptly she decided that it was time and past time to go fishing. Several hours of light remained, plus a tide change, and at least a few salmon were in the vicinity. What more could any fisherman ask?

Hawk read the decision in Angel. "Can I help?" he asked.

Angel had already rigged trolling rods. It wasn't her favorite method of fishing but it was better than being skunked. Besides, the salmon wouldn't be feeding on the surface until well into September. By then Hawk would be gone.

The thought went through Angel like a cutting wheel over glass. First just the thought, pressure and a faint trail of emotion behind it, followed by a spreading sadness. The idea that Hawk might leave Vancouver Island without catching a salmon, without knowing the island's rugged magic, without smiling. . . .

"Angel?" asked Hawk, wondering what new ghost had risen to trouble the blue-green depths of her eyes. "Is there something I can do?"

Angel blinked and focused on Hawk. The lashes fringing her eyes were long, surprisingly dark. They swept down suddenly, concealing her from his intense brown glance.

"Take the wheel," said Angel, her voice tight. "Point the bow at the headland and keep us moving slowly."

When she felt the motions of the boat change, Angel began letting out line into the water.

"How deep are you going?" called Hawk from the cockpit.

"Does the fish finder show anything?"

Hesitation, then, "Something at about four fathoms, maybe deeper. It shifts fast."

"Then I'll go down twenty-five feet on one line and about thirty-three on the other."

The planer attached to the line took it down quickly. When enough line was out, Angel set the reel's brake and slipped the butt of the rod into a holder along the side of the boat. For a moment she watched the tip of the rod. It moved subtly, rhythmically, responding to the boat sliding over the restless surface of the sea.

Within moments the second rod was set up on the starboard side. Angel paused, then shrugged. Nothing ventured, nothing gained. She grabbed one of the long, limber rods, dove into the tackle box, and came up with a bucktail fly half as big as her palm. She let the fly out over the stern, feeding line until the big, pale fly danced over the surface about thirty feet behind the boat. Even though it was weeks too soon for salmon to be feeding on the surface, there was such a thing as luck.

"I'll take it now," said Angel, coming into the cockpit.

Hawk slid out of the seat and past Angel. As they switched places, she smelled again the compound of soap and subtle after-shave, heat and man, that had come to be indelibly associated in her mind with Hawk. When she turned to lower herself into the seat, her body brushed over Hawk's. Though it only lasted for an instant, the contact sent shards of awareness splintering through her. Unconsciously she held her breath, freezing in place, unwilling to end the racing sensations.

"Watch the rod tips," Angel said, her voice too low, almost husky. "Get used to their motion. Then you'll know instantly if anything changes, if there's weed on the herring strip or if a salmon strikes or . . ." Her voice faded as she looked up at Hawk. Her eyes were as green and restless as the sea. "Do you understand?"

Hawk's mouth changed, hard lines flowing into a hint of softness, a promise of sensuality that was repeated in the hot brown depths of his eyes. "Yes," he murmured. "I understand."

And he did. It wasn't the motion of herring strips and water that he was talking about, though. It was the hunger making Angel's eyes a smoky green, and the visible race of the pulse beneath the soft skin of her neck. The chase was almost run. Soon the last twists and turns would be over, the last frantic burst of flight done, and she would lie panting and spent in his arms.

Hawk turned away and went out into the open stern of the boat to watch rod tips dance to the slow surge of the sea, the shine of the waves beneath the sun. But it was another type of dance he was thinking about, the slow surge of flesh against flesh, the sensual sheen of passion on smooth skin and the liquid, rhythmic waves of release.

Soon.

Braced easily against the motion of the boat, Hawk watched the rod tips against the cerulean sky. Angel looked over her shoulder, but her eyes were on the man, not on the rods. He was the most graceful man she had ever seen. The subtle adjustments of his body to the shifting boat fascinated her. Like the bird he had taken his nickname from, Hawk was fiercely quick, incredibly fluid, stunning in his completeness.

Angel forced herself to look away. Hawk had done nothing to indicate that he was attracted to her in the aching way that she was attracted to him, a fascination compounded of mind and body. All of the tactile contact between herself and Hawk could be explained by the close quarters of the boat, or by casual affection such as any friend might give her. Never had she seen from Hawk anything close to the emotion with which Grant used to watch her, love and desire intertwined until there was no room left for anything else, even breath.

Deliberately Angel recalled the rose in her mind. She needed its crimson tranquility. Five days on a boat with Hawk would be hard enough on her. She didn't need to make it worse, embarrassing both of them by running after Hawk like a lovestruck teenager. The rose came very slowly, though, single crimson petals joining and blurring like drops of blood, then sliding away, leaving her empty.

After a time she succeeded in forming the whole rose petal by petal, its color lambent with dawn, serene in its own unfolding.

It had been years since the rose had come to Angel so slowly, or she had needed it quite so much.

Trolling quietly, checking the lures from time to time, Angel floated over the area where the sea had boiled with herring and salmon, hunted and hunter. Nothing struck the lures. After several more sweeps, she had Hawk check the lines for weeds. She watched as he picked up a rod out of the holder, yanked sharply on the rod to trip the planer, and reeled in. She was envious of the power that let him so easily trip the planer, a technique that she had spent days learning to do correctly, for her arms simply weren't as strong as the normal man's, much less a man like Hawk.

When the lines were back in the water, Angel began a slow sweep up the rugged coastline that would eventually take the boat to Deepwater Bay. For a time she let the urgencies of the moment slide like light into the sunset sea. The throttled-down murmur of the engines crept into her bones and her mind, quietly freeing her. In her mind, the primal serenity of sea and forest and rock blended into radiant images crying out to be set in glass as pure as the sky.

"You awake up here?" asked Hawk, sliding into the seat opposite Angel. He faced toward the stern, where he could continue watching the rods.

"Barely." Angel smothered a yawn.

"Bored?"

She smiled and shook her head. "Just relaxed," she said softly, her hands automatically correcting the boat's course. "I love this." She looked over at him. "Are you?"

"Bored?" asked Hawk, his dark glance drifting over Angel's face. "No. This is . . . soothing."

Hawk stretched, filling the cabin with his presence. He saw Angel's eyes following the movement of his arms, saw her look at the opening of his shirt, at his neck, at his mouth. Suddenly, *soothing* was the last word that Hawk would apply to the moment. The ache of desire that had never been far below his surface became talons of need sinking into him, gripping him until he couldn't breathe. In the space of a few heartbeats he was ready for her, desire expanding thickly, hotly.

Too soon. Too fast.

With a single, powerful movement, Hawk came to his feet and walked out of the cabin. He stood with his back to Angel, watching the rods and the increasing chop of the water, watching with an intensity that made his jaw ache. Motionless but for easy adjustments to the shifting deck, Hawk fought the desire that had ambushed him. After a time he succeeded in thinking of the graceful curve of the rods instead of the inviting curve of rosy lips and of breasts arched beneath a sweater the color of the sea.

The closer the boat came to Deepwater Bay, the more small craft there were about. The *Black Moon* overtook them at a distance, heading for safe anchorage at Deepwater Bay. Hawk heard the radio behind him, heard Angel's soft reply, but he didn't turn around. It had been more than an hour since he had left the cabin. Not long enough. Too long. She was a fire beneath his skin, in his bones. He wanted her with a force that enraged him. The chase would end tonight, whether she was ready or not. He was ready. More than ready. He would take her and when he took her the lies would come like cold rain, putting out his unreasonable fire. Then he would be free of her, free to fly again, a black shadow soaring through an empty sky.

As Angel brought the boat around the point that guarded

the entrance to Deepwater Bay, she saw immediately that there were too many small boats clustered for her to take the course she usually did. Just as she began to turn the helm, she caught a motion out of the corner of her eye, a powerboat all but flying over the water toward the bay. Some weekend fisherman was so anxious to get in every bit of fishing time he could that he was ignoring the basics of good manners and safety. He was going to force her to go too close to the other sport fishermen, and his wake was going to make all of them bob wildly, probably enough to trip the planers and make everyone take in and let out the trolling lines all over again.

"Brace yourself!" called Angel, cutting the forward speed to nothing in hopes of reducing the drag on the planers.

Hawk had already seen what was going to happen. The powerboat roared past them, dragging a roostertail of churned water as tall as a man. Hawk was ready, his legs spread and his hand fastened to the door frame of the cabin. The boat rocked wildly, bucking like an unruly horse. The other small craft were no better off. There were more than a few curses and rude gestures aimed at the disappearing powerboat.

Angel eased back up to trolling speed and set a course that would take her farther from the clustered boats. Then she looked back at the stern. One rod was standing straight, unmoving. The other was bent over in a hard arc. Hawk lifted the rod and pulled sharply. Nothing gave. The rod tip moved with tiny, springy motions. Line peeled off the reel while the brake made a long, high scream. Normally that sound would signal the strike and flight of a big fish. Today it meant something a good deal less exciting. Sixty feet away Angel saw one of the men in a small blue boat stand

and wave widely to get her attention. His partner was struggling to reel in his line. There was so much tension on the man's rod that he could barely hold it.

"We've fouled his line," said Angel, cutting the throttle and putting the gear into neutral. "Let him reel in and untangle it."

Hawk stopped trying to bring in the line. Even so, the joined lines popped above water between the two boats. In the rich sunset light the lines shone like thin silver cables, fairly humming with tension. The current was making the two boats drift apart, held together only by the slender, surprisingly strong fishing line and the two hooks snagged one through the other. The man in the blue boat fumbled with the humming line for a moment, but it was far too tightly drawn. He tugged, trying to bring the joined hooks within reach. The current forcing the boats apart was too strong. He leaned out until he nearly fell into the water. He was inches too short. He shrugged, pulled a knife, and cut the line just above his hook.

Angel watched the knife descend in horror, knowing that once the tension was released, the line would come shooting back like a released rubber band; and the deadly hook would be flying behind, a weapon aimed at Hawk, who was holding the rod. There was no time to explain, to warn Hawk. Angel reached the back of the boat in two running leaps and threw herself at Hawk's head, protecting his eyes from the hook that was slashing back through the water.

"What the hell!" said Hawk, automatically grabbing Angel and bracing both of them.

"The hook—" Angel began as she pulled Hawk's face down against her breasts, and then pain took her breath away.

Instantly Hawk realized what had happened. Angel's hands loosened, releasing him. He held her tightly as he looked over her shoulder. Part of the hook's steel curve was buried in her sweater. The rest was in her flesh, just next to her shoulder blade. As he watched, a single drop of crimson welled silently, staining the soft green sweater.

Chapter 7

SWEARING SAVAGELY, HAWK PULLED A JACKKNIFE FROM his pocket. He looped the fishing line over his fist and cut through without putting the least pressure on the hook embedded in Angel's back. As soon as she was free, she headed back toward the wheel.

"Don't move," said Hawk curtly.

"We're drifting."

"I'll take care of it," he said, lowering Angel into a seat at the stern of the boat.

Hawk moved with frightening speed. Rather than take the time to reel in the two remaining lines, he cut them. Then he vanished into the cockpit and lifted the big boat into roaring life. Within minutes he had brought the boat into a sheltered anchorage on the northeast side of Deepwater Bay. In another man such speed would have been reckless; in Hawk, it was as controlled as the swoop of a raptor.

In a few strides he was back at the stern of the boat, lowering the anchor.

"Are you all right?" asked Hawk, looking at the lines of strain around Angel's mouth.

She started to shrug. Her face tightened as the motion of her shoulders made the hook's sharp point dig deeper. "I'll live," she said, drawing a slow, careful breath.

Hawk muttered a vicious curse.

"It's just pain," said Angel, her voice low. She closed her eyes for a moment, using her mind to draw tension from her body. She had learned that fighting pain only increased it. If you accepted pain, you could begin to control your response to it. Once Angel had learned that, she had found the courage to live without drugs and walk without a cane.

When Angel's eyes opened, they were clear, unafraid of pain. "Let's see what the damage is," she said quietly. "Unless you mind?" she asked, seeing Hawk's eyes narrow. "If it bothers you, I can call Carlson off the *Black Moon*," she added, looking toward the troller that was anchored a few hundred feet away.

Hawk stared at Angel's tranquil face, hardly able to believe what he was seeing. If he hadn't seen blood well beneath her sweater, he wouldn't have known from her actions that there was a hook buried in her satin flesh. Grimly, Hawk acknowledged that Angel was an actress worthy of any stage in the world.

"I've seen worse injuries," said Hawk.

He followed Angel into the cabin and switched on all the cabin lights. When he turned around, Angel was sitting with her back presented to the strongest source of light. Hawk knelt. His mouth thinned to a harsh line when he saw the blood seeping through the soft green yarn of Angel's sweater. With exquisite gentleness, he eased the sweater over the steel curve and straight shank of the hook, managing not to exert any pressure on the hook itself. When Hawk saw beneath the sweater, he said a single, violent word under his breath. The hook was almost as long as his thumb. He could see neither the hook's glittering tip nor the barb that was designed to sink into flesh and stay there.

"It's in past the barb, isn't it," said Angel. Only the slightest quiver in her voice showed how much the hook hurt her.

"Yes." Then, when she would have moved to take off her sweater, "Don't, Angel. I can see enough."

"If the entry angle isn't too steep, you can push the barb through, cut it off, and then remove the hook. Otherwise you'll have to pull it out the same way it went in."

Angel's matter-of-fact words exactly paralleled Hawk's thoughts. "Either way, it will hurt like hell," he said bluntly.

"Then you'll get to hear your fishing guide scream and swear and otherwise make a fool of herself." When Hawk didn't answer, Angel turned just enough to look into his eyes. "It's only pain, Hawk. It passes."

"I could take you to a doctor."

"Why? You have quicker hands than any doctor who ever treated me." Angel looked away. "There are pliers and a wire cutter in the tackle box. If you don't want to do it, call Carlson. He's seen me scream before."

Hawk hesitated, wanting to ask when and why Carlson had seen Angel scream. It was the wrong time for questions, though. With another soft, vicious curse, Hawk went to the tackle box. He found two pairs of needlenose pliers and the wire cutter. He brought them back, doused them in alcohol, and went to where Angel waited.

"Ready?" asked Hawk, his voice flat.

"A moment," said Angel quietly. She closed her eyes

and reached for the cascading colors. They poured through her mind, colors too beautiful to describe, too pure to be real. "Now," she murmured, and began naming the fantastic colors.

Using the pliers for grip and leverage on the steel shank, Hawk forced the hook to complete its shallow curve through Angel's flesh. He cut off the barb cleanly, then pulled out what remained of the hook in a swift, smooth motion. Angel gasped and made a low sound of pain. Hawk dropped the bloody, broken hook into the tackle box and wrapped his hands around Angel's arms, bracing her and looking at the twin wounds on her golden skin.

"It's done," said Hawk, his voice harsh.

"Thank you," Angel said, her voice trembling. She let out a long, ragged sigh.

"When was your last tetanus shot?"

"I don't fish with rusty hooks," said Angel indignantly, breathing more deeply now that the hook didn't dig into her with each breath. "Anyway, my shots are current. There's some antibiotic salve in a kit in the tackle box. That should take care of infection."

Hawk hesitated. "Can you move your shoulder blades, twist around a bit?"

"Why?"

"You've only bled about six drops. That's not enough to clean out the deepest part of the wound."

Angel rotated her shoulder blades slowly. Her sweater slipped down her back. She gathered the soft folds and pulled them over her head. Hawk's breath shortened at the satin sheen and movement of her skin. She wore no more on her back than a wisp of apricot bra and two bright drops of blood, one on each wound left by the hook as it stitched through her flesh. Despite her movements, no more blood came.

"This will hurt," said Hawk.

It was his only warning. One arm slid around Angel's waist, the other crossed just above her breasts as he bent his mouth to her back. He sucked hard on first one wound, then the other. The force of his suction drew blood, which naturally cleansed her flesh. After an initial, sharp breath, Angel neither moved nor protested. The intimacy of his hard arms and lips held her motionless. His mouth should have hurt her, but all she felt was his heat and strength.

For an instant before Hawk lifted his head, Angel thought she felt his mouth soften and caress her. When she turned to look at him, she saw a drop of her blood on his lips.

"Are you all right?" asked Hawk, his voice husky in the odd, breathless silence that had closed around the cabin.

Angel nodded. Her fingertip slowly came up to Hawk's mouth. Before she could touch the crimson trembling on his lip, his tongue moved, absorbing the drop. His eyes darkened almost to black as the salt-sweet taste of her spread through him. Slowly he stood and pulled Angel to her feet.

"You're pale," he said softly. "Lie down on the forward bunk. I'll bring in the salve and bandages."

Angel swayed slightly. She felt weak, almost dizzy—and foolish. It was Hawk's closeness, not pain, that was affecting her so strongly. Hawk opened the small door on the far side of the cockpit and helped Angel onto the triangular bed that filled the space beneath the bow. She lay face down, listening to him move about the cabin behind her. There was enough room for her to sit up in the bow, but she didn't. She was content just to lie quietly, waiting for Hawk to come to her.

Angel heard Hawk's smooth step, felt the mattress give as he sat next to her, and then the sudden, breathtaking release of the catch on her bra. A warm washcloth moved gently down Angel's back, bathing away the last of the blood.

"Hurt?" asked Hawk, his voice gritty.

"No." Angel's answer was barely a breath.

For a few moments there was only the soft sound of a damp cloth moving over skin. A pause, then Hawk's fingers replaced the cloth.

"Such beautiful skin," murmured Hawk. "Smooth, golden." He bent down. His mustache brushed over Angel's shoulder. "You smell like summer."

Angel's breath stopped. Chills moved visibly over her, a helpless response to the silky touch of Hawk.

"This may sting," he said, sitting up as though nothing had happened.

The salve was cool, as smooth as Hawk's voice and fingers caressing her. Angel sighed, breathing again, her arms bent and her hands tucked beneath her chin. Hawk pressed a bandage lightly into place over the twin puncture wounds. He gathered up the ends of Angel's bra as though to fasten it in place again. Then he let the lacy material slide from his fingers as he smoothed aside her braid and bent to kiss the nape of her neck.

Angel felt the heat of Hawk's breath, his mouth, his chest rubbing lightly over her as he caressed the sensitive skin at the base of her neck. She shivered and would have turned over to face him, but Hawk put his hands on her shoulders, chaining her. His mouth caressed her neck, her hairline, the curve of her skull; and then his hard tongue teased her ears. She moaned and moved reflexively, slowly, arching like a cat to increase the pressure of Hawk's mouth.

Hawk murmured thickly as he slid the bra straps off Angel's shoulders with a single swift motion of his hands. His tongue and teeth traced the graceful line of her back down to the sensitive hollow hidden beneath her black

jeans. His hands caressed her calves, her thighs, the taut
curve of her hips, the heat between her thighs, and all the
while his mouth devoured her delicately, ravenously, a
sensual assault that was like nothing she had ever experienced.

Only when Angel was twisting helplessly beneath
Hawk's knowing touch did he allow her to roll over. He
pulled the bra free as she moved and threw it aside. His eyes
blazed darkly, pupils dilated until there was little color,
only desire. She was more beautiful than he had expected.
She was more beautiful than anything he had ever seen.
Flawless gold skin swelling into nipples flushed deepest
rose, her eyes a soft green fire watching him, wanting him.

When he bent his mouth to her breasts, she tried to speak.

''Hawk—''

''Hush,'' he said, his voice gritty, wanting only silence
and her beauty, her body's heat surrounding him. It was too
soon for the cold rain of lies to begin.

Hawk's mouth closed over Angel's breast, pulling the
nipple deeply into his mouth. The words Angel had been
going to say scattered in the explosion of sensations
radiating through her. She moaned and twisted slowly
against Hawk's caressing mouth in a feminine demand that
was as old as desire. It was new to Angel, though. Grant
had never taken her into his mouth, had never scraped his
teeth gently, savagely, over her until she wanted to scream,
had never stroked her with his tongue until she shivered and
cried out. Grant had been cautious of the passion that
consumed him each time he touched Angel.

Hawk was not. He let the hot currents of desire take both
of them to the heights of need. And then his hands moved
quickly over Angel, taking her clothes, leaving her naked to
his touch. His fingers tangled in the golden mound of hair
below her navel, testing lightly the heat and hunger of her,

rubbing over her, teasing her until she shuddered with the tension building in her, consuming her.

"Hawk—"

His hand moved skillfully, heat showering, words stopping in Angel's throat. But not for long.

"Hawk—I'm not—experienced."

The words came between shudders of sensual tension that racked Angel's body, teaching her more than she had ever thought to know about need and pleasure. She didn't see the cold curl at the corner of Hawk's mouth or the narrowing of his eyes, his savage anger that the lies had started so soon. When Angel opened her eyes again, Hawk was naked, swooping down on her, covering her with his body like a raptor mantling its prey. She had no time to speak or think or conceal the cry of pain that came when he took her.

Hawk froze, astonishment and hunger struggling for control of his body until his emotions imploded into a searing rage. "You can't be a virgin!"

But even as Hawk spoke, he knew that Angel wasn't lying. The shock of Angel's truth went through him, shaking his certainties as nothing had since he was eighteen and his world had been shattered by a woman's lies. Like a cornered animal, Hawk fought to protect himself by attacking Angel.

"Hawk—" Angel moved reflexively, trying to ease the pressure of him inside her.

"Damn you!" he snarled, shuddering, raging against the release that was taking him whether he willed it or not. *"Damn you to hell!"* With a final shudder he rolled aside, freeing her. He fought to control himself again, to absorb the terrible knowledge that Angel had not lied to him about being inexperienced. He didn't understand what had happened. He didn't understand her. And he must understand or his world would be utterly destroyed.

Angel lay without moving, feeling Hawk's condemnation sink into her more deeply than steel talons. A tangle of emotions swept over her—frustration, bafflement, pain, and finally anger, a fury so deep that it frightened her. She had felt rage like this before; it had almost burned out all that was human in her. Silently she fought for self-control, fought not to scream, fought not to curse a life that seemed to hold out the hope of happiness only to take it away, leaving her broken and struggling to survive.

"Why?" said Angel, not hearing her own anguish, not even hearing the single word that had pierced her control.

"That's my line!" retorted Hawk, his voice as savage as his eyes. He grabbed her shoulders, forcing her to look at him. "Why didn't you tell me?"

"I tried," said Angel numbly, speaking without thinking, reduced to reflex and pain. "And then I thought you already knew."

"How in Christ's name would I know?" demanded Hawk, his hands biting into her shoulders. "I thought you were sleeping with Derry and Carlson. You sure as hell didn't respond like a virgin. You were as hot as anyone I've ever crawled into bed with."

"Sleeping with Derry? Sleeping with Carlson?" Angel repeated the words without comprehending them. "But I told you. Derry's like my brother and Carlson is a friend."

"Women lie all the time."

Silence and knowledge sinking in, talons turning in Angel, tearing her apart. "You think I'm a liar and a slut."

Angel shuddered as the knowledge went through her, breaking her as the automobile accident had once broken her. Then the habits of self-control learned at such cost closed around her, holding her emotions suspended, sealing them away. She would deal with them later, when she had the strength. Right now it was enough that she didn't shred into destructive hysteria. The car wreck had been beyond her control. This wasn't. She was alive, physically whole. She had made a mistake, a terrible, irretrievable mistake. She wasn't strong enough to reach through Hawk's cruelty to the hurt and hunger and human needs beneath.

Assuming that he had such needs. She was no longer sure of that.

"You proved that you were half right, didn't you?" said Angel, her voice quiet, as empty as her eyes watching him.

The change in Angel made Hawk deeply uneasy. He had expected hysterics, cursing, screaming, sweet lies and pleading, all the usual tricks of women. He had expected anything but the eerie, porcelain calm of Angel's face and the bleakness of her eyes.

"What does that mean?" said Hawk warily, loosening his grip on Angel's shoulders.

She slid off the bed, gathering her clothes as she went. "It means that I feel like a slut."

"What do you expect when you sleep with a man for pay?" demanded Hawk, giving vent to the rage that had come when he realized that Angel had sold her virginity to a man who didn't want it. "Cut the act, Angel baby," he said harshly, grabbing her wrist. "You want your quarter of the land sale and decided to ensure it in the oldest possible way. Your choice. If you'd asked, I'd have told you that it was useless. Nothing's going to make me buy Eagle Head but the land itself."

"I don't want Eagle Head sold," said Angel distinctly, her voice without emotion or depth. "Derry does." She met Hawk's eyes. There was nothing in her look but a color that was too dark to be called green. "I owe Derry more than a man like you could understand. When Eagle Head is sold, the money will go to Derry. All of it. But you can't believe that, can you? Your choice, Hawk." Angel looked down at the hand holding her wrist. When she spoke, her voice was calm, empty, final. "Let go of me."

Hawk stared at Angel for a moment before he released her. When she left, shutting the cockpit door behind her, he found himself wanting to follow her, hold her, take the emptiness from her eyes and voice. He realized in that instant that he wanted to believe her, wanted to believe that she had had no hidden reason for smiling at him, talking to him, being with him, burning for him.

Then Hawk cursed himself more savagely than he had cursed anything else in a long time. He had learned all there was to know about women by his eighteenth birthday. The lesson had been reinforced numerous times since then. Surely he wasn't stupid enough to need a complete refresher course at the age of thirty-five. The fact that Angel hadn't lied about her virginity didn't mean that the rest of her was pure truth.

He rolled over, reaching for his clothes, and saw Angel's blood still bright on his body. Emotion tore through Hawk in the instant before he controlled it, hating himself for even that fraction of weakness. Virginity meant nothing. All women began that way. It had just taken Angel longer than most to decide on her price.

But when Hawk asked himself what that price was, he had no answer. The question sank into him like a hook, digging into him with each heartbeat, scoring him each time he tried to turn away from it. If not money, what? What had Angel said about Derry? Something about owing. . . .

The words came back in a rush: *I owe Derry more than a man like you could understand.*

Her virginity, for instance? A small swap for a big land sale?

Hawk's mouth lifted in a small, cold curl. Angel underestimated him if she thought he didn't understand. He understood very well. She was the same as the others. Nothing new after all. And if the thought made him a little sick and very angry, that was his problem. He was old enough to know better. Old enough not to be taken in by a sweet-faced actress with sad green eyes.

The shaken pieces of Hawk's certainty settled back into place, reassuring him. Then the sound of the engines coming to life surprised Hawk. He finished dressing quickly. He opened the cockpit door, stepped out, and confronted Angel.

"A little late for fishing, isn't it?" Hawk said sardonically, gesturing toward the stars visible through the portholes.

"Yes."

Angel checked to see that the running lights were on and threaded her way between the large and small boats anchored in the bay. Once she was free of the bay, she picked up speed, although she kept it below what she would have done in the daylight, well below what she wanted to do. Fly. Flee. Vanish. But those were emotions. The reality was more difficult. She had to make the trip to Campbell River, then to the house, then to her room.

The thought nearly overwhelmed Angel. Silently she fought the emotions that were tearing her apart. One minute at a time. This minute. Just this one.

"Cutting short our little trip?" asked Hawk.

"Yes."

"What about Derry's land sale?" Hawk saw the instant of emotion flicker beneath the pale surface of Angel's face. Having guessed correctly about her price made Hawk even more angry. "What about all that you *owe* Derry?"

"You'll either buy Eagle Head or you won't."

"No guide, no deal, remember?"

"There are other guides," said Angel. Her lips changed suddenly, lifting at the left corner in a sardonic curl that exactly echoed Hawk. "Like Carlson."

Hawk's eyes narrowed. He knew that if Angel told Carlson what had happened, the big Indian would do his best to give Hawk a guided tour of hell. At the moment the thought of an explosive brawl tantalized Hawk, promising him an outlet for the unreasonable rage that still gripped him; his certainties had nearly been shattered by a woman. Again. "What are you going to tell Derry?" demanded Hawk.

"That we rub each other the wrong way."

"I thought you liked the way I rubbed you," said Hawk cruelly.

Angel looked at Hawk for a long moment. Humiliation and fury made her want to deny having enjoyed his touch. But she didn't give in to the temptation. She had the rest of her life to live. She didn't want to live it a liar as well as a slut.

"Everyone makes at least one bad mistake on the way to growing up," said Angel quietly. "You were mine."

Hawk's eyes became almost black. He asked no more questions. He was discovering that Angel's truths could be far more painful than other women's lies. And then he realized that she was doing it again, truth not lies, shattering truth.

The rest of the trip to Campbell River was completed in silence, as was the ride to the Ramsey house. Derry was asleep when they arrived. Grateful for that small comfort, Angel went quickly to the north wing, where her suite was. She neither looked at nor spoke to Hawk. He had ceased to exist for her. Nothing existed but a stained glass rose the color of blood. She held it in her mind the way a mountain peak holds light long after the rest of the world is in darkness.

Angel stripped off her clothes, dropping them in a trail that led to the shower. She stood under the hot spray for long minutes, washing herself and rinsing and washing again until her skin should have been painful to the touch. She felt nothing, allowed nothing to reach her. She knew that the blessed numbness was only temporary. She knew that the time would come when she would have to sort out her emotions, sort out hope from truth, error from pain. A learning time. But not yet. Just now it was enough that she get through this minute, and the next, and the next.

She didn't get out of the shower until the supply of hot water was exhausted. Even then she lingered until the water became unpleasantly cold. She dried herself quickly, rubbing her hair until her fingers ached. Only then did she realize that she was crying silently, had been crying since she closed the bedroom door behind her. She scrubbed her face viciously. Tears came anyway, a silent, transparent welling of emotion that she could not control.

Abruptly Angel threw aside the towel. She dressed in her work clothes, jeans and a blue cotton shirt. Both were faded almost white. She pulled on moccasins, combed back her damp hair, and went through the connecting door to her studio. The north wall of glass was as black as the center of Hawk's eyes. For a moment Angel stood without moving, wondering if she had the strength to keep going.

You don't live all your minutes at once, Angel reminded herself silently. *You just live the one you're in. You can make it through one minute. You don't have to be strong for that. Just one minute. One minute at a time.*

The familiar litany helped to loosen the talons digging into Angel. Her hand went out slowly. Wall switches

clicked and lights came on, bringing a hard white radiance
in place of darkness. She walked in, drawn to the silent
colors of glass scattered about the room. No matter what
happened she had this, a wealth of colors surrounding her, a
constructive outlet for emotions that would otherwise
destroy her.

One minute. Just one.

Angel took a long, deep breath and walked into her
studio.

There were several worktables lined up beneath the
fluorescent lights. Two of the tables were normal except for
the thick, short-piled carpet on their surface. The third table
had a translucent top. Light radiated beneath the surface,
illuminating the pattern and the pieces of glass laid out on
top.

Angel went to the table. The pattern she had been
working on was deceptively simple—three jars of jelly that
appeared to be sitting on a rustic window frame. Across the
top of the window, like a jeweled fringe, were runners of
blackberry and raspberry bushes heavy with fruit. The
"window" itself was a very pale gold muff, a glass the
exact color of late afternoon sunlight. Angel could have
used ordinary window glass, but she had not. She never
used glass that had no color. Seeing splinters and shards of
colorless glass glittering beneath hard white light brought
back too many memories of the accident, of pain, of death.

Most of the glass pieces had been cut already. She had
only to shape the bunches of berries that hung lushly from
the top of the window. The branches would be the lead
beading itself. The leaves were cut from a piece of green
muff. The natural variations in the glass provided a subtlety
of shading that recalled a living bush. The veins on the
leaves had been painted in. She would bake on the paint in
the kiln, a process that permanently combined paint and

glass. Although Angel could have achieved a similar effect by etching the leaf-lines onto flashed glass, she had chosen to use the varied texture and color shading of muff instead.

Angel turned on the kiln, drew on supple suede gloves, and went back to the light table. She picked up a simple glass cutter. The hard steel wheel and its pencil-like holder fit readily against the calluses of her right hand. She adjusted a piece of textured, raspberry-colored glass over the heavy paper pattern she had fastened onto the light table. The light shining through the paper and glass clearly showed the black cutting lines she would follow.

The wheel made a high humming sound as Angel drew the steel over glass, leaving behind a very fine trail of powdered glass. As soon as the first, major line had been drawn, Angel put down the cutter. Gently, firmly, she bent the glass until it separated at the fine line left by the wheel. Despite its name, a glass cutter didn't really cut glass; it merely set up a weakness in the peculiar molecular structure of glass. In many ways glass responded more as a fluid than a solid. Like a fluid, glass "healed" itself. Unless Angel divided the glass within minutes of cutting, glass molecules would begin flowing back together. Then the break would be ragged and almost random rather than clean and precise.

As Angel cut each piece, she ran the fresh edges of glass over each other, dulling them from razor to merely sharp. The curves of the berries were too deep to cut all at once. After the initial shallow curves had been made, Angel picked up special pliers and nipped at the glass until the desired curves were achieved. It was work that demanded care and concentration. She welcomed both, drawing them around her like a balm, minutes flickering by, uncounted.

Beneath the concentration, the deepest levels of Angel's mind continued to seethe toward some kind of resolution, some dynamic balance that would eventually allow her to live more than a minute at a time. Working with glass brought a kind of peace, a breathing space, to her. It had helped her deal with all the small disappointments of her childhood—and with the devastating death of her parents and Grant and Derry's mother in the flaming wreck. It would help her deal with Hawk. Her work would let her live in each minute as it came, nothing beyond this minute, this instant of brilliant glass taking shape beneath her fingers.

Working in silence but for the tiny, high song of glass shearing away, Angel finished cutting the pieces for Mrs. Carey's gift. When the kiln was hot, the leaves went in. While they baked she continued cutting, working this time on the piece of pale muff. It was a large piece, irregularly shaped yet oddly graceful. She cut with confidence, years of experience showing in each elegant stroke, each sure motion. She rarely had to cut a piece of glass twice.

Angel went to the bead stretcher, a simple vise that held one end of a length of soft, H-shaped lead beading while she pulled on the other, taking out any kinks. She used the thinnest possible bead that was consistent with the structural integrity of the finished piece. After the lead beading was pulled and a piece had been tamped into the rustic frame, she began to assemble the glass, beginning in the bottom right-hand corner of the frame.

As she selected each piece of glass, she polished it until she could see nothing but the beauty of the glass itself. Piece after piece, color after color, a fragile jigsaw puzzle held together by black lead stretched into suppleness. The sounds of small nails being tacked down replaced the tiny cry of glass. Nails held the beading in place while she added more pieces of the puzzle.

Angel worked through the darkest hours of the night, pausing only to wipe away the tears that came without warning, a transparent upwelling from a wound too recent to be healed. She noticed the tears only at a distance, a blurring of sight that prevented her from seeing clearly the jeweled shards of color slowly becoming whole beneath her hands. Fragments of the past forged into a new pattern, beauty where only breakage and loss had been, sanity rebuilt piece by piece.

Ebony night paled to pewter dawn. Crimson flushed the studio. Angel didn't notice the light any more than she noticed that her back muscles were burning and knotted or that the shoulders of her blouse were dark from the tears she had wiped away. She was focused wholly on the puzzle she had just completed. She mixed the cement that would be the final touch, the last assurance that the puzzle would not come undone in an hour or a year.

With a stiff brush, she worked the thick cement over both sides of the finished stained glass piece until there was no more space between glass and beading and frame. She poured sawdust over the finished surfaces, absorbing the excess cement. Then, before the cement dried, she took a pointed wooden tool and began to go over each join of lead and glass, picking up extra cement, making sure that the lines of her creation would be as clean and elegant as the glass itself.

Crimson faded into the softer colors of day. Angel didn't notice. There was no sound but that of wood squeaking over glass until Derry came in, rubbing sleep from his eyes.

"Angie? What's wrong? Why aren't you out fishing?"

Chapter 8

ANGEL LOOKED UP, SURPRISED TO FIND THAT SO MANY minutes had passed. It was morning. A little of the tension in her eased; the first night was the hardest. Blinking slowly, she focused for the first time in hours on something that was farther away than the surface of a worktable.

"Angie?" Derry came closer, swinging easily between the crutches. "How long have you been working?"

"A while," said Angel evasively, returning her attention to the stained glass. "I'm almost finished." Actually she had been finished an hour ago. She was simply using the wooden scraper to retrace the lines of what she had created. She enjoyed the colors and shapes, the wholeness where only dreams and fragments had been.

Derry frowned. "You must have been at it all night."

She made a neutral sound.

"Angie?"

She sighed and put the wooden scraper aside, knowing

she couldn't evade the issue of why she was home rather than out guiding Hawk. "Yes, I worked all night."

"You haven't done that for a long time."

"Yes."

"Angie," Derry said softly, "what's wrong? Is it because last night was the night of the wreck? Four years . . ."

Angel hesitated. It would be easier to let Derry believe that she was mourning the past. Easier, but hardly the whole truth.

"That's part of it," said Angel, looking up and meeting Derry's eyes for the first time. "But most of it is that your Mr. Hawkins and I don't get along worth a damn," said Angel, meeting Derry's eyes.

Blue eyes widened in surprise. "What happened?" Then Derry's eyes narrowed. "He didn't make a pass at you, did he?" demanded Derry, his voice suddenly hard, much older.

"A pass?" Angel's mouth turned down at one corner, sardonic echo of the man called Hawk. "Nothing that personal. There isn't a personal bone in Hawk's body."

Angel's voice carried conviction, for she didn't feel that she was lying. A pass implied unwanted attentions. Hawk's touch hadn't been unwanted, not at first. Nor had there been anything personal between them, not in the deepest sense of the word. They didn't know each other well enough to be personal. They had proved it when they had so badly misjudged each other.

Derry relaxed slowly. "Then what happened?"

"We don't speak the same language," said Angel succinctly.

Puzzled, Derry waited. When Angel said no more, he persisted. "What do you mean?"

"Does the word *misogynist* ring any bells?" asked Angel, fiddling absently with the wooden scraper.

"It's too early in the morning for dictionary games," retorted Derry, the hour and the lack of coffee finally cutting through his normal good nature.

"Mr. Miles Hawkins is a misogynist. He distrusts and hates women. I am a woman. Therefore, he distrusts and hates me. That," said Angel quietly, looking up at Derry with dark green eyes, "makes it very uncomfortable for me to be around him. He feels as unhappy to be around me."

There was a shocked silence for a moment as Derry tried to imagine anyone hating and distrusting the pale, tired woman who stood before him, her eyes haunted by too many sad memories.

"I can't believe that," said Derry.

"I can." Angel set aside the scraper with a weary gesture. "Call Carlson on the radio phone. When we ran into him at Brown's Bay, he offered to take Hawk fishing."

"He did? They must have gotten along great."

"Why shouldn't they? Carlson's all man." Angel heard the bitterness in her own voice and fought a short, silent struggle for control of her emotions. She felt tears hot at the back of her eyes, tears filling her throat. "If not Carlson, some other man," she said tightly, turning away from Derry.

Angel stopped turning so suddenly that her hair lifted and then fell about her face in soft veils. Hawk was standing in the doorway between her studio and her bedroom. His thick black eyebrows hooded his eyes, concealing them, making his face a pattern of black lines and harsh brown planes unrelieved by any light. He looked hard, tight, tired. She hadn't heard him come in. He had made no more noise than a raptor soaring on transparent currents of wind.

The intensity of Hawk's look didn't vary, even when Derry cursed at the realization that his conversation with Angel had been overheard.

"I don't dislike being around you, Angel," said Hawk, his voice deep, matter-of-fact.

"Then you must enjoy hating more than I enjoy being hated," said Angel. "Excuse me," she murmured, brushing by Hawk without looking at him again. "I'm going to get some sleep."

Quietly, she shut the connecting door behind Hawk, forcing him into the studio. The sound of the door closing seemed unnaturally loud. Angel leaned against the wall for the space of a long, shaky breath. Tears spilled again but she didn't care. She had no strength left for caring. She kicked off her moccasins and stretched out face down on the bed. She was asleep before she took another breath.

When Angel awakened it was afternoon. Clear yellow light filled the room, turning random motes of dust into tiny flashes of gold. She stretched, wincing as her right shoulder blade moved, disturbing the small wounds left by the hook. The lance of pain reminded her of all that had happened. Her lips flattened as the memories returned, slicing her like freshly cut glass. For a moment she lay very still, not fighting her thoughts, letting them lacerate her. She knew from experience that she was most vulnerable when she had just awakened, whether it was in the middle of the night or the afternoon. When she was neither asleep nor yet awake, her emotions ruled her. Fighting it only made it worse.

Mercifully the moment passed, leaving Angel hurting but fully awake and capable of controlling her thoughts again. She pushed aside the summer-weight quilt that was covering her. Her hand paused as she realized that the cover hadn't been on the bed when she fell asleep. It wasn't even her quilt. It was from one of the guest rooms. The thought of Derry struggling up the hallway on his crutches, dragging a quilt to cover her with, made Angel's mouth soften. Derry had been so careful of her, so gentle with her since the accident. No matter what she said or did, he still supported her.

Derry's thoughtfulness brought a small center of peace to Angel's emotions, a stillness that spread outward, giving her strength. A long shower increased her feeling of tranquility. She dressed in a soft rose caftan that floated in swirls around her ankles. Tiny silver bells were sewn into the bodice of the dress. Matching pure silver bells were fastened in a gleaming double chain to her right ankle and left wrist, bells shivering sweetly with each movement of her body. Matching earrings murmured and chimed sweetly beneath her hair.

Angel had bought the dress and jewelry two years ago, when the silence of her Seattle home had threatened to overwhelm her. As she brushed her hair, the bells shivered musically, a soothing counterpoint to the whisper of hair shimmering around her face in a silky, sun-streaked mass.

For a moment Angel hesitated, watching herself in the mirror. She was tempted to put on makeup to hide the pallor of her skin, the lavender shadows beneath her eyes, the near-transparency of her lips. Then she shrugged and turned away from the mirror. It didn't matter. Derry knew her too well to be fooled by makeup. As for Hawk . . . Hawk was what he was, a man who hated women.

And she was what she was, a woman who had loved the wrong man.

Quietly Angel went down the hall, her bare feet making no noise, silver bells singing so softly that only she could hear them. From the guest wing came the deep tones of

Hawk, on the phone as usual. Automatically Angel glanced at the clock. Three. They would miss the tide if they didn't hurry.

The thought died as quickly as it had come. She and Hawk had missed many tides, every tide, everything.

Derry was out on the patio, studying a book that was more formulas than words, a book as thick as the cast on his leg. A gentle wind had tousled his blond curls, making him look about seventeen. Frowning, he underlined a section of the book with a bright yellow marker. Angel moved around the kitchen discreetly, not wanting to disturb Derry. She scrambled eggs and made toast, then poured herself a cup of the lethal-looking coffee that was Derry's constant companion while he studied. She ate standing at the counter, eating more because of habit than appetite, habit and the knowledge that she would need the strength that food gave her.

This time Hawk's silent arrival did not take Angel wholly unaware. Though her back was turned to the door, she sensed his presence as clearly as if he had spoken to her. She ate the last bite of egg, turned, and rinsed the plate under the faucet. Because she wanted very much to avoid Hawk, she turned and faced him. The past had taught her that the more she avoided something, the more she came to fear it. Only when she faced a problem could she begin to accept it, live with it.

"When is Carlson meeting you?" asked Angel, her voice calm and her eyes direct, empty.

"He isn't." Hawk's fierce, clear eyes searched Angel's expression. He hadn't expected this calm stranger looking at him out of Angel's blue-green eyes. "By the time Derry was patched through to the *Black Moon*, Carlson was halfway to Alaska. There's a run on, apparently."

Angel's long eyelashes swept down, emphasizing the

darkness beneath her eyes. "That's too bad. You would have enjoyed Carlson. Who did Derry get to guide you?"

"No one."

Angel lifted her head so suddenly that her silver earrings swayed and chimed, hidden beneath the luxurious fall of her hair. Hawk's eyes dilated at the unexpected sound. He leaned toward her for an instant. She stepped back, another sudden motion that set other bells to quivering. Hawk's dark eyes searched over her, finding and counting each tiny bell, silver shivering and sighing with each breath she took.

The sound of Derry's crutches thumping on the wood deck was almost shocking. Gratefully Angel turned toward the unmusical noise, freed from the dark intensity of Hawk's eyes.

"You look a lot better," said Derry. "How are you feeling?"

"Fine." The answer sounded too abrupt, too cool to be a decent response to Derry's concern. "Thanks for bringing in the quilt."

"Quilt?" said Derry.

Angel looked at Hawk, but he said nothing, did nothing, simply watched her with the intensity of a hungry bird of prey.

"Nothing," said Angel, feeling the tiny pool of peace inside her fragment into sharp confusion. Apparently Hawk had a human feeling after all. Guilt, perhaps. God knows he'd earned it. "How goes the studying?"

Derry grimaced. "It goes slowly." He hesitated. His eyes searched hers, concern and affection apparent in his expression. "Angie?"

Angel braced herself, knowing what was coming. "Yes?"

"Carlson can't guide Hawk."

"I know."

"The other guides have their hands full for at least a week, and even then . . ."

Angel waited. Derry said nothing. And then she knew that he wouldn't ask her despite the need and hope burning behind his eyes. She didn't have to condemn herself to four weeks of Hawk's contempt. All she had to do was live a lifetime knowing that she hadn't been strong enough to help Derry gain a foothold on his dream. Derry, who had given her life itself and asked for nothing in return. Not one thing.

Four weeks of Hawk's contempt against a lifetime of self-contempt if she refused. Not a hard choice after all.

"It's all right, Derry," said Angel calmly. "I'll take care of it."

Derry couldn't conceal the relief that made him sag slightly against the crutches. Nor could he conceal the concern that came when he saw the pallor of Angel's face. He swung his powerful body across the room until he was close enough to touch her. He put his hand on her forehead.

"You sure, Angie?" asked Derry. "You look pale and there's some kind of flu going around. . . ." Again he didn't finish. He wouldn't ask her to do something that benefited only him.

For a moment Angel closed her eyes and let her forehead rest on Derry's large palm, drawing strength from him. Her eyes opened, blue-green and calm. "I'm sure."

Hawk sensed the currents of concern and affection flowing back and forth between Angel and Derry, and was both intrigued and irritated. He wondered what hold the charming Derry had on Angel that could compel her to shut herself up on a boat for four weeks with a man she hated. Abruptly Hawk decided that he was going to have some answers from Angel. He hadn't misjudged a woman so badly since he was eighteen. He wanted—*needed*—to know what had gone wrong, how he had been misled. He was no longer enraged, simply very certain that he must have Angel's truths. If Derry was the only way to flush Angel out of hiding, then Derry was what Hawk would use.

"You haven't asked if it's all right with me," pointed out Hawk, his voice cool.

Startled, Derry looked away from Angel. "But you said you wouldn't mind."

"Angel and I are going to have a talk. At the end of it, either one of us may change our mind." He lifted his eyebrow and looked at her with eyes as hard and brilliant as a hawk's. "Right, Angel baby?"

It was the first time Derry had gotten even a hint of the whiplike quality Hawk's voice could hold. Derry looked at Angel. She touched his arm gently, telling him without words that it wasn't the first time for her. But unlike Hawk, she couldn't back out. She loved Derry too much to destroy his dream. "Wrong, Hawk. Just like you've been wrong about everything else."

Angel turned and walked quickly out the door. The sound of tiny silver bells and her words floated back after her. "We'll talk on the beach."

Quickly Angel scuffed into the beach walkers she always kept by the back door, gathered gauzy folds of cloth in one hand, and went down the trail with a speed that came from years of familiarity. The trail clung precariously to the face of the cliff. She didn't notice the narrowness or the gaps where the railing had fallen away and not been rebuilt. The trail wasn't actually dangerous, unless it was slippery or very windy. It wasn't a place for children, though, or clumsy people of any age. There was a better trail farther over on Eagle Head. Neither Angel nor Derry ever used it, having grown up with the precipitous path snaking out of the back yard of the Ramsey house.

Even if the trail had been dangerous, Angel would have taken it. She desperately wanted to get Hawk to a place where Derry could neither see nor hear the conversation. Derry, like Carlson, was very protective of her. It was as though having saved her life, Derry felt directly responsible for any further pain Angel suffered. He knew that it was impossible for him to protect her from life's bitter surprises, but the impulse was still there, buried beneath layers of rationality. She blamed herself for that impulse; once she had accused Derry of selfishly forcing her to live just so that he wouldn't be alone.

A cruel accusation, but it had been a cruel time. Angel regretted her hateful words. Now she, like Derry, had a need to protect. Once Angel was down on the beach, the need would be satisfied. Whatever she and Hawk said to each other could not be overheard.

The day was unusually hot for Vancouver Island. By the time Angel reached the bottom of the trail she was perspiring lightly. She let go of the hem of her dress. The breeze picked it up and pressed the supple cloth against her legs, outlining their slender length in soft rose. Folds of cloth billowed lightly behind her, creating graceful shadows over the sand.

Almost immediately Hawk crossed the beach and stood beside Angel, watching her. It didn't surprise Angel that Hawk had come down the trail with a speed to equal hers. He had the reflexes of a predator. She turned to face him.

Her movement and the wind sent folds of cloth licking over him and brought to his keen ears the tiny cries of silver bells. Hunger raced through Hawk, hunger and something more, something that threatened every certainty he had left.

And so Hawk did what he had always done when cornered. He attacked.

"What does Derry have on you? You'd as soon kill me as look at me, but you'll shut yourself up on a boat with me for a month because Derry asks you to. Hell, he didn't even have to ask, did he?"

"No. I hope that Derry will never have to ask me for anything that I can give him. And he doesn't have anything on me, either," said Angel, her voice flat.

"Then what's his hold on you? Money?"

Angel's mouth curled at one corner, a cold gesture that couldn't be called a smile. "No."

"Then what?"

"Something you wouldn't understand."

Hawk's hand fastened on her arm. The softness of cotton and her flesh only infuriated him. "What is it, damn you!"

"Love."

There was an instant of silence. "Love," said Hawk. The word was a curse. His voice vibrated with disgust. "That's a woman's word for sex, and you sure as blazes weren't getting that from Derry. Which is the lie, Angel baby—love or that you don't want sex with Derry?"

Angel simply stared.

Hawk shook her impatiently. Bells quivered and cried. "What's Derry's hold on you? Talk, damn you! Let me hear all your lies!"

"Have you ever loved anyone?" asked Angel quietly.

"Your mother? Your father? A brother? Sister? Child? *Anyone?*"

"Are you saying that Derry is your brother?"

"Close," she said, meeting Hawk's cold eyes.

"How close is close?" he demanded.

"Twenty-four hours."

Hawk hesitated. Angel had spoken with such conviction that he felt he should know what her answer meant. "I don't understand," he said finally, loosening his grip on her arm.

"I know. There's a lot about people—and me—that you don't understand."

"Don't push me, Angel," said Hawk, anger tightening the already harsh lines of his face, "or I'll go ask Derry my questions and then tell him some things he really doesn't want to know."

Angel closed her eyes, knowing Hawk would kill Derry's dreams as casually as he had killed hers. "Derry came within twenty-four hours of being my brother-in-law," she said, her voice empty.

Hawk's eyes narrowed. "Grant," he said. "That was his name, wasn't it? Grant?"

"Yes."

"What happpened?"

"Grant died."

"When."

The word was flat, the demand unavoidable. Angel had known it would come to this, and prepared herself for it every step of the way down the cliff. Perhaps if she told Hawk, he would find enough human compassion in himself not to make her life hell for the next four weeks. Perhaps there could be a truce.

The thought gave Angel the strength to take a slow

breath, to reach for the colors cascading through her mind, to make of those colors a single rose unfolding.

"Grant—" Angel's voice thinned into hoarse silence. She rarely spoke Grant's name aloud. The hurt of hearing it surprised her. When she spoke again, her voice was without emotion or music. "Grant died four years ago last night, the night before our wedding. His mother died then, too. So did my father and my mother."

Hawk went absolutely still. He had no doubt that he was hearing the truth. He would rather have heard lies. Lies can be disregarded, discarded, ignored. Truth could not. It hurt too much; like Angel, hurting. He could sense the intensity of her emotions breaking over him in waves of rage and helplessness and pain. Her voice didn't show any of it, though, nor did her face. Only her eyes, haunted by shadows, the color of the sea torn apart by hidden rocks. Yet her words continued calmly, relentlessly, and her eyes were dry. The tiny bells she wore shivered and cried with inhuman beauty, inhuman pain.

"I would have died, too," continued Angel, "if Derry hadn't dragged me out of the wreckage as it burned. I was badly injured. He came to me in the hospital, fought for my life harder than I did. And then he took care of me until I could walk again."

"Then why the hell didn't you sleep with *him*," snarled Hawk, angered by the deep emotion he sensed beneath Angel's calm words.

"That's not the kind of love we feel for each other." Angel's eyes focused on Hawk. "I don't know if I can make you understand. Derry is the only person on earth who shares my memories of growing up, of my parents and Grant and summer picnics on the beach, laughter and firelight and the heartbreaking beauty of falling in love for the first time. Derry is the only one who remembers the night Grant and I announced our engagement, the words and the—''

''Why don't the two of you build a goddamn shrine,'' said Hawk coldly, not questioning the unreasonable rage that coiled within him at the thought of Angel loving anyone, even a dead man.

For an instant, fury tore at Angel like steel talons. With an effort that made her tremble, she kept her voice even. ''You are well named. Hawk. Bird of prey. I was very easy prey, wasn't I?''

''Is that why you raced home last night? Were you afraid you'd end up in bed with me again?''

The harsh expression on Hawk's face steadied Angel as nothing else could have done.

''No,'' said Angel quietly. ''I'm not afraid of ending up in bed with you again. I've learned the meaning of the old saying about casting pearls before swine.''

''Is that how you thought of your virginity—a real pearl?'' asked Hawk sardonically.

''No. But you made up for it. You were a real swine.''

There was a moment of savage silence.

Then Hawk said softly, dangerously, ''Why did you give yourself to me, Angel? Because you did. I didn't take you. Or is that the lie you're consoling yourself with this morning? Poor little Angel,'' he said mockingly, ''done in by an experienced Hawk.''

Suddenly Angel was glad for the tears that she had cried last night. It made it possible not to cry now. Deep inside herself the silent, tearing question changed from *Why?* to *How? How had she so badly misjudged the man who stood in front of her?*

When the answer came to her, she spoke it aloud without thinking, without caring. ''I thought I loved you. That was very stupid of me,'' said Angel, her eyes focusing on

Hawk. "I confused desire with love—and ended up with neither."

Hawk's pupils dilated, then narrowed to ebony points in brown eyes that were deep and clear. He said nothing, for he was too surprised to speak. She had said *love* with the same mocking tone that he habitually used when he spoke the word; and in doing so, she had told him that he had hurt her as badly as he had once been hurt. The thought sank like a hook deep in his gut, twisting with each breath he took. He had never meant to hurt her like that. He hadn't even believed it was possible. To be hurt like that, you must first love.

But Hawk hadn't believed in love since he was eighteen. Not for him. Not for anyone.

"No more questions?" asked Angel, her voice even. "Good. Let's go fishing."

The controlled chill of her words rocked Hawk, angering him. His mouth tightened. "Cold as the sea, aren't you?"

"The sea isn't cold," said Angel, looking out over the shimmering, cloud-shadowed expanse in front of her. "It teems with life. I'm as cold as a bird of prey. Death, not life. Do you want to go fishing this afternoon?"

"I'd like to break your neck."

"That would be a pity," said Angel, her voice indifferent as she turned to face Hawk once again. "It's about the only part of me that hasn't been broken."

Hawk's voice changed as he leaned toward her. "Including your heart?" he asked softly.

"My heart was broken long before I met you."

"Angel . . ." Hawk's voice was a warmth brushing over her temples.

"Don't call me that," said Angel tightly, feeling emotions twist, trying to elude her control.

"Why?" asked Hawk, standing so close that he could smell the delicate perfume Angel used. "Because he called you Angel?"

"He?"

"The boy you loved. Derry's brother."

Angel turned away, hating the treacherous warmth that radiated from Hawk through the filmy caftan. "We'll miss the tide change unless we hurry."

"Answer me."

Angel turned back so quickly that tiny bells trembled and cried. But her voice was soft, almost too soft for Hawk to hear though he stood only inches from her.

"He called me Angie, darling, sweetheart, honey. He called me his own special sunrise, his hidden heart, his—"

"But you didn't sleep with him," interrupted Hawk roughly, not wanting to hear any more.

"No. It's the only thing I regret about my love for him," said Angel. She tried to stop, but her voice went on softly, relentlessly. She was unable to stop the words even though they were shattering the peace she had so carefully rebuilt from the fragments of the past. "My God, how I regret it! Especially now!"

Hawk's breath came in sharply, knowing that Angel was remembering her unhappy initiation at his hands. But she was still speaking softly, so softly that he had to concentrate to hear every word, feel every hook sinking into him, barbs tearing through a lifetime of scars to the vulnerable flesh beneath.

"If I had known he was going to die, I would have made love with him." Angel's voice shook with intensity. "But I was young. I thought we had time. A lifetime. And Grant—" Her voice broke over his name and then re-formed, empty again, controlled. "Grant wanted the first time to be perfect for me. Our own home, our own bed, every right in the world to make slow, beautiful love to each other.''

Hawk closed his eyes for an instant, remembering the moment when he had taken Angel with equal parts of lust and anger. But that moment was in the past, as irretrievable as childhood. It was futile to shred himself over what could not be changed. All that could be changed, all that was left, was the future—an angel with torn wings and green eyes that had seen hell, and a hawk that hadn't known heaven when he had pierced its warm surface with angry black talons.

Hawk put the past behind him, knowing he couldn't touch it, change it, heal it. He could learn, though. That was how living things survived. Learning from mistakes. ''You haven't answered my question,'' he said, his voice uninflected. ''Why do you get angry when I call you Angel?''

''Everybody calls me Angie. There's nothing special between us. Why should you call me anything but Angie?''

''The fact that you gave your virginity to me isn't special?'' asked Hawk.

''It should have been,'' agreed Angel in sardonic tones that echoed his. ''But it ended up about as special as a skinned knee.''

''Keep pushing me. You'll find the limit,'' promised Hawk, meaning every word.

Angel's eyes narrowed. She smiled a tiny, cold smile, liking the idea. ''So what? Never argue with someone like me, Hawk. I've got nothing left to lose. It gives me an edge.''

''What about Derry?'' asked Hawk smoothly, watching her.

Abruptly Angel curbed the cruelty that had snaked out of

her own pain. She had forgotten how easy—and how terribly satisfying—it could be to turn agony into cruelty and then watch the rest of the world bleed with each razor cut of her tongue. But cruelty only bred more cruelty, maiming the people around her, corroding her soul, cruelty a downward spiral of self-destruction that wouldn't end short of death.

The realization that she hadn't learned her lesson well enough in the past was like getting an open-handed blow across the mouth. Angel paled until her haunted eyes were the only color in her face. She would try very hard not to destroy herself over Hawk. She would die rather than destroy Derry.

"Angel is the name I called myself after the accident, when I finally decided to live," she said. Her voice was soft, controlled, emotionless. "An angel is something alive that once was dead. Like me. Alive and then dead and then alive again. Angel."

Hawk fought the desire to take Angel in his arms. All that kept his hands at his side was the knowledge that she would turn on him like a cornered animal. He didn't blame her. He had hurt her cruelly, and he had no experience in healing. He had nothing to give her but emptiness and a ravenous, soul-deep curiosity about the fragile, elusive, tenacious complex of emotions known as love. A lifetime of questions waiting to be answered.

"Would you sleep with me again, for Derry?" asked Hawk.

Angel heard curiosity rather than desire in Hawk's question. "You don't want me, so the question doesn't arise."

"What makes you think I don't want you?"

The harsh sound that came from Angel's lips could hardly be called laughter. "You didn't enjoy that fiasco on the boat any more than I did.'' She glanced up at Hawk, her eyes as hard as jade. ''So don't worry, Hawk. I won't trip you and beat you to the floor. No more amateur hour for either one of us. That's a promise.''

Angel tilted her head so that she could see the face of Hawk's gold watch. ''The tide changes in twenty minutes,'' she said matter-of-factly. ''Which will it be, Hawk? Fish or cut bait.''

''Oh, I'll fish. Always.'' Then Hawk bent down until he could feel Angel's warmth seeping through the soft cotton of her dress. Close, very close, but not touching her. ''Did you really think you loved me, Angel?''

The stained glass rose Angel had held in her mind exploded into a thousand cutting shards. She retreated sharply, unable to bear being close to Hawk any longer. She turned away and began to run up the cliff trail. Each movement brought silver cries from the bells she wore. The sweet sounds went into Hawk like tiny blows too small to dodge, tiny wounds opening, tiny hooks teaching him how to bleed.

Hawk ran after Angel, afraid that she would slip on the narrow trail, afraid that she would fall because her wings had been torn and she could no longer fly. Even when he caught up with her and his hard hand held her to a more sensible pace, she ignored him, refusing in pale silence to answer his question about love.

Hawk did not ask again. He had learned that Angel's truths were as painful for her as they were for him.

Chapter 9

"LET ME TAKE THAT," SAID HAWK, LIFTING THE HEAVY, two-foot-square stained glass panel from Angel's hands.

Angel didn't object. It would have done no good, anyway. Hawk's speed and strength were superior to hers. She watched as his glance skimmed indifferently over Mrs. Carey's gift. The light in the hall was dim, more twilight than day. The pieces of glass were subdued, almost dull, as ordinary as crayon colors on cheap paper.

Then Hawk walked into the sunlight pouring over the front steps. The panel in his hands leaped into radiance, colors flashing and expanding in a silent explosion of beauty. He stopped, unable to move, consumed by colors. Silence stretched into one minute, two, three, but he didn't notice. He tilted the panel first one way and then the other, caught wholly in the fantastic sensual wealth of colors pooling in his hands. Finally he looked up and saw Angel watching him.

"That's why I love stained glass," said Angel, looking at the brilliance shimmering in Hawk's grasp. "It's like life. Everything depends on the light you view it in."

The words had no more than left Angel's lips when she realized that what she had said had more than one level of meaning. Silently she closed the door behind Hawk, hoping that he hadn't noticed.

"Are you trying to tell me that my point of view on life is too dark?" asked Hawk.

His question told Angel that he had not only noticed, he had understood all the subtle ramifications. She should have expected it. He was the quickest, most intelligent man she had ever met.

"No," said Angel, walking toward her car, not looking at Hawk. She had carefully avoided anything that smacked of personal topics in the three days since she and Hawk had talked on the beach. "I was merely making an observation on the nature of stained glass and light."

"Nothing personal, is that it?" asked Hawk with a black lift of his eyebrow.

"As you say. Nothing personal."

Angel opened the trunk of her car, shook out an old quilt, and gestured for Hawk to put the panel on the quilt.

"How much is a piece like this worth?" asked Hawk.

She watched as he handled the awkward panel with an ease she envied. Powerful, supple, hard, his body moved with a male grace that surprised her anew each time she saw it. Like stained glass, he kept changing with each angle, each moment, each shift of illumination.

And like glass, he could cut her to the bone in the first instant of her carelessness.

"A smaller panel, like this, would bring between ten and twelve hundred dollars," said Angel, wrapping the stained glass with deft motions. "Minus the gallery commission, of course, and the cost of materials. Good glass is very expensive.'' She closed the trunk lid.

''How many pieces did you have in the show in Vancouver?'' persisted Hawk.

''Thirty-two.'' Angel opened her purse and rummaged for her keys.

''Did they sell?''

She looked up, only to find herself impaled on eyes as brown and clear as crystal. ''All but three. Why?''

''How many shows do you do a year?''

Angel pulled her keys out of her purse and faced Hawk, wondering why he cared. It was easier to answer than to argue, however. And it didn't really matter. Money was a safe topic. It wasn't personal, like emotions. ''Three this year. One in Seattle, one in Portland, and one in Vancouver.''

''Did they all go well?''

''Yes.''

''You really don't need the money from Eagle Head, do you?'' asked Hawk.

''No.''

''But Derry does.''

''Yes.''

''Why?''

Angel hesitated, then shrugged. Hawk could always ask Derry. It was hardly a secret in any case. ''Derry wants to be a surgeon. That means between six and ten more years of advanced training. He's been accepted at Harvard, but no scholarship was offered because, technically, Derry is wealthy.''

''Eagle Head,'' murmured Hawk.

''Yes.''

''I see.''

''Do you?'' asked Angel, looking swiftly at Hawk. ''For

once, let me be sure there's enough *light* on the subject. This isn't a boyish whim on Derry's part." She took a swift breath, steeling herself for the words to come. "My parents were killed instantly in the wreck. Derry's mother wasn't. His brother wasn't. Derry dragged them free—and then watched them bleed to death because he didn't know enough to save their lives."

Hawk's face was expressionless, utterly still, his eyes almost black. There was a question he wanted to ask but he didn't know how to word it without watching ghosts darken Angel's eyes. "And you," he asked softly, "were you conscious after Derry pulled you out of the wreckage?"

"Yes. I couldn't help Derry." Angel's eyes were open, but they weren't focused on anything except the past. She heard the question that Hawk hadn't quite known how to ask. She knew how to answer it, though. "My collarbone was smashed, my ribs were broken, I had multiple fractures of both legs. Derry's mother was unconscious. His brother wasn't that lucky. So I lay there, I couldn't move, and I listened to Grant—" Her voice stopped. When the words resumed, they were like powdered glass, no color, just sharp edges abrading everything they touched. "When it was over, Derry wept and beat his fists against the road until there was no skin, only blood. I could do nothing about that, either."

"Angel," said Hawk softly, touching her cheek with gentle fingertips, regretting his question and her pain.

Angel stepped away from the touch. "Derry swore then to become a doctor, saving lives to replace the lives he hadn't know how to save. It's his way to make peace with a life that was cruel enough to leave him uninjured so that he could watch his mother bleed to death and his brother die in agony."

She looked up and her breath caught. She had seen

enough sadness and pain to recognize it in Hawk's dark features. "You really do like Derry, don't you?" she murmured, surprised that Hawk could feel that much emotion. "He likes you, too. God knows why," she added absently, frowning. She had never understood Derry's smiling acceptance of Hawk's razor tongue.

Hawk's face became expressionless again. "Maybe I remind Derry of Grant," suggested Hawk.

"You're nothing like Derry's brother."

"Oh?"

The black arc of eyebrow irritated Angel. "Grant was capable of love," she said coolly.

"Then he must have been loved," shot back Hawk.

"What do you mean?"

"Grant's mother loved him. Derry loved him. You loved him."

"Yes."

"That must have been nice," said Hawk. His voice was flat. His words were simple statement rather than ironic mockery: It must have been nice to be loved. "And you were loved, weren't you, Angel. Your parents, Grant, Derry, even Carlson. In their own way, they all loved you."

"Yes," whispered Angel. "And I loved them."

"Love linking to love. A bright, magic, closed circle." Hawk's face changed, memories like talons in his mind.

"But your parents—" began Angel, only to stop. Hawk's harsh laughter overrode her, laughter tearing through her. "Hawk," she said, holding her hand out as though to touch him, "don't—"

Hawk spoke, and his words were worse than his laughter. "My mother was six months' pregnant with me when she married my father. Only he wasn't my father. He didn't know it then, though. She told him when I was six. She told him by pinning a note to my shirt just before she ran off with a traveling man.'' Hawk's smile was sardonic. "Nice touch, that. Dump a kid on a man and tell him it isn't his.''

With a shrug, Hawk continued. "Dad kept me. I never could figure out why. It sure as hell wasn't out of love. His mother came to live with us. There wasn't any love in her, either. Oh, they were kind enough, so far as that goes. I had a change of clothes and a pair of shoes. I didn't starve. They never used anything worse than a belt on me no matter how drunk they were.''

Angel flinched, remembering when Hawk had told her that he had taken his dad's spinning gear without permission and been soundly beaten for it.

"I had already learned how to work when my mother took off,'' continued Hawk. "I grew vegetables, raised chickens, delivered papers, whatever. The money went to them, to pay for room and board.''

"But you were only a child,'' said Angel, hardly able to comprehend.

"I ate their food. I wore clothes they found for me. I slept in a blanket they gave me.'' Hawk shrugged again, dismissing the subject of material wealth. Being poor hadn't bothered him. Being unloved had. "They weren't fattening themselves at my expense. Our farm was a joke. Five hundred acres, and not enough water to irrigate more than ten. It's dry in west Texas. Real dry. Only thing that land is good for is raising dust and hell.'' He smiled sardonically. "It's more fun to raise hell than dust.''

With a sudden movement, Hawk went to the far side of Angel's car, opened the door, and slid into the passenger seat. Angel stood without moving, still caught in the words illuminating an aspect of Hawk that she had never suspected. Hawk's past, as harsh as the land he had described. She wanted to ask questions, many questions, sensing that there was more to be told. Other boys had been abandoned by mothers and yet had learned to love and trust women. Carlson, for one. His childhood had been no less harsh than Hawk's, and he had borne the stigma of being an Indian, having to fight for room to live and work in white society. Yet Carlson knew how to love.

Hawk leaned over and opened the driver's door, silently inviting Angel to get into her own car. She slid behind the wheel. With a hand that trembled slightly, she turned the key and started her car. She glanced swiftly at Hawk. He didn't notice. Other than opening the door for her, he seemed unaware of her existence. She wondered what he was thinking, what fragments of the past he was looking at, what their colors were . . . and how many edges they had, how deeply they cut him. She asked no more, though. She was still assimilating the first instants when Hawk's words had illuminated him. The colors he had shown her were dark, almost brutal, yet their intensity was compelling.

Silently Angel drove to Mrs. Carey's house. As she parked in front, she looked questioningly at Hawk. She hadn't expected him to come with her. She didn't know whether he wanted to go inside or wait in the car until she was finished.

Hawk looked at Angel. "I take it we're here, wherever that is."

"Mrs. Carey's house."

Hawk encouraged Angel with a look.

"She broke her hip a while ago," said Angel. "I'm bringing her groceries and taking her to the doctor until she can drive herself again."

Black brows came together as Hawk turned the name over in his mind. "Mrs. Carey. I've heard that name."

"Jams and jellies," said Angel, opening her door.

Hawk got out and joined her at the trunk. "As in this

glass?'' he asked, lifting the quilt-wrapped panel out of the trunk.

"As on our breakfast croissants.''

Hawk made an appreciative sound and licked his lips. "Now I remember the name. Are we going to buy some more jam today?''

"Mrs. Carey would sic her cat on me if I even suggested it. I've eaten her wonderful jams all my life. Gifts. Every last bite.''

"And all the sweeter because of it,'' murmured Hawk.

Again Hawk had surprised Angel. She hadn't expected him to understand. "Yes.''

"Don't look so shocked, Angel. I know what gifts mean. I used to wait in an agony of hope every birthday, every Christmas. I learned not to hope after a while.'' Hawk paused, remembering. "And then my third-grade teacher gave me a small candy cane with a green ribbon on it. I kept that candy cane until Christmas morning, when I knew that other kids would be opening their presents. Then I walked out into the fields until I was alone. I can still feel the crinkly wrapping, smell the freshness of the mint, see the bright green ribbon and the clean red and white of the cane. It was the sweetest, most beautiful thing I've ever tasted. I carried the ribbon in my pocket until nothing was left but a few green threads.''

Hawk shook his head, almost baffled by the bittersweet shaft of memory. "I haven't thought about that for a long, long time.''

Angel found herself fighting tears as she compared her own Christmases and birthdays heaped with gifts and laughter and love. She had lost so much four years ago, but at least she had had something to lose. Years of memories, years of love. Hawk had nothing but rare moments, the fading taste of mint, and a ribbon worn to shreds in a boy's pocket.

Quietly Angel shut the trunk and followed Hawk to the front door of the house. She rang the bell and waited. Hawk noted her silence and drawn face, saw the tiny indentations where she had bitten her lower lip. He didn't know what had upset her. All he knew was that he wanted to soothe the marks away with the tip of his tongue. Like the memory of mint, the impulse surprised him. He wanted to comfort rather than to seduce Angel. He wanted to see her smile because he had brought pleasure to her. He wanted—

Mrs. Carey opened the door. Her gray head barely came to Hawk's breastbone. She adjusted her glasses as she looked up at the tall, dark man who stood so unexpectedly on her doorstep.

"Good morning, Mrs. Carey," said Angel, her voice soft, still shaken by Hawk's memories. "I'd like you to meet Miles Hawkins. Hawk, this is Mrs. Carey."

"Mr. Hawkins," said the old woman, nodding her head.

"Call me Hawk," he murmured, slanting a sideways look at Angel. He shifted the quilt-wrapped stained glass panel to his other arm as he took the old woman's cool, dry hand in his. "Everyone else in Canada does."

Mrs. Carey's shrewd black eyes measured the man in front of her. Then she nodded once, abruptly. "Not many men could carry that name. Come in, Hawk." Then, dryly, "You too, Angie. Tea's brewing."

The big orange tomcat wove in and out of Mrs. Carey's walker with a breathtaking disregard for safety as she led the way to the kitchen. Finally Angel could stand the suspense no longer. She bent down and lifted the heavy cat into her arms.

"Tiger, you have no sense," she scolded softly, rubbing

the cat with her chin as she followed Mrs. Carey into the kitchen.

The tom watched Angel with wise orange eyes, touched his nose to hers, and flowed out of her arms. At least Mrs. Carey was sitting down now, no longer in danger of becoming tangled in her cat's furry little feet.

"Pour for me, would you?" asked Mrs. Carey. "I must have slept on my hands wrong last night. They're kind of slow waking up this morning."

Angel looked quickly at Mrs. Carey. "Have you called Dr. McKay?"

The old woman laughed dryly. "I'm seventy-nine, Angie. I've earned a few slow mornings, don't you think?"

"I'm driving Derry over to see Dr. McKay later this morning," said Angel. "I'll pick you up and—"

"Nonsense. Pour the tea, Angie. There's nothing the doctor can do for me that a cup of tea can't do better. Sit down, Hawk. You can set whatever you're carrying on the counter."

Angie poured tea and passed the plate of shortbread biscuits around. "About the doctor," she began firmly. "I think—"

"I remember a time a few years ago," interrupted Mrs. Carey with equal firmness. "Derry came flying over here all in a snit because he found you asleep on your studio floor. Seems you'd been working too long, or something. Dr. McKay went to the house, thumped and poked and listened, and you never woke up. He told Derry nothing was wrong with you that a lot of sleep wouldn't cure." Mrs. Carey put her teacup down with a firm motion. China clicked lightly. "Well, Angie, there's nothing wrong with me that being young again wouldn't cure. The day the doctor can turn back time is the day I'll call him and tell him I feel tired in the morning."

Angel sighed and gave up. The phone rang.

"I'll get it," said Angel, moving quickly toward the living room.

Mrs. Carey followed much more slowly. Angel answered, exchanged a few words with the person on the line, and then gave the phone to Mrs. Carey. The instant Angel walked back into the kitchen she felt the intensity of Hawk's stare.

"Do you do that often?" he asked, watching her.

"Answer the phone?" she asked, sitting down.

"Work yourself into exhaustion," he said bluntly.

Angel shrugged, trying to dismiss the subject. "No."

"Just when you're upset?" he asked, his voice too soft for Mrs. Carey to hear.

Angel sipped her tea.

"How long has it been?" said Hawk.

"Since what?" asked Angel.

"Since you worked until you couldn't think, couldn't feel, until your body just shut down and dumped you on the floor."

For a moment Angel thought of refusing to answer. Then she realized that it didn't matter. Hawk would just ask Derry. And there was the fact that she wanted to tell Hawk. There would be a certain almost cruel pleasure in revealing to him just how badly he had misjudged her.

"It was more than three years ago," said Angel, sipping her tea. "It was the night Carlson finally convinced me that the man I loved was dead and I was alive and there wasn't one damn thing I could do about it except crawl into the grave and die with him."

"But you didn't."

"Carlson wouldn't let me."

Angel's eyes darkened, remembering Carlson's cruelty. But it had been cruelty with a purpose, cruelty that forced her to accept that she was alive and Grant was not. Carlson had paid, too, more than she knew at the time. She hadn't forgiven him for a year, hadn't spoken to him, had refused even to look at him or the letters he sent. She hadn't known then that Carlson loved her as a man loved a woman. By the time she realized it, it was too late. He was inextricably bound up in her mind with Grant's life and death. She could no more be Carlson's lover than she could be Derry's.

"Carlson loved you," said Hawk flatly.

"Yes. Even before Grant did. But I never loved him, not that way."

"Because he's Indian?"

Angel smiled sadly. "Because he wasn't Grant."

"But after Grant was dead?" persisted Hawk.

With a weary gesture, Angel pushed tendrils of hair out of her eyes. "Carlson still wasn't Grant. I couldn't forgive him for that. I couldn't forgive Derry. I couldn't forgive any man." She saw another question form on Hawk's lips. Abruptly she felt that whatever she had hoped to do to Hawk, she was being hurt worse by her words than he was. Memories punished her, memories she hadn't allowed herself to review for years. "No more, Hawk, please," she said, her voice low, ragged. "Or do you enjoy torturing me with the past?"

Hawk closed his eyes, shutting out the confusion and anger in Angel's face. "No," he said very softly.

"Then why do you do it?"

"Because I have to know about you," said Hawk. His eyes opened clear and calm, as deep as night. "I have to."

"Why?" said Angel, desperation fraying the edges of her control.

"I've never known a woman who loved anything but herself."

Hawk's quiet admission destroyed Angel's protests. If

her pain could teach Hawk something, she wouldn't fight each question, each answer. She had learned so much from Derry's pain, and from Carlson's. She couldn't refuse another person an equal chance to learn.

In the sudden silence, the sound of Mrs. Carey's walker squeaking down the hall toward them was very loud.

"That was Karen," said Mrs. Carey. "She told me that the raspberries on the old homestead are coming on thick this year." The old woman looked at Angel. "I can't pick them but I can still make jam."

"We'll be glad to pick as many berries as you want," said Hawk before Angel could speak.

Mrs. Carey smiled. "A hawk in a raspberry patch." She laughed with a sound like fallen leaves rustling. "That was worth getting up for."

The corner of Hawk's mouth lifted. He looked at Angel, then at the kitchen counter where the stained glass panel lay, then back at Angel. She nodded. He stood in a lithe motion and went over to the counter.

"This," said Hawk, lifting the quilt-wrapped panel, "is worth living a hundred years for."

Hawk went to the window that overlooked the breakfast table. Sun poured through, bathing the table in warmth. Shielding the panel from Mrs. Carey's view, he unwrapped the quilt. Then he stepped aside quickly, holding the panel to the light. Colors blazed out, filling the kitchen.

Mrs. Carey leaned against her walker's support and looked at the glass transforming her kitchen into a fantasy of dancing colors. "That is the prettiest thing I have ever seen," she said slowly. "Just look at those colors. Why, I'd swear that you could eat that jelly."

"I'm glad you like it," said Angel, smiling widely, enjoying Mrs. Carey's pleasure. "It's yours."

The old woman turned and looked at Angel. "But it's too

much, Angie. I can't take it. Why, you must have spent a lot of time—''

''I've eaten your jam all my life, Mrs. Carey,'' Angel interrupted gently. ''You've spent years in the kitchen cooking for other people. Please. I want you to have the panel. I made it just for you.''

Tears sparkled in Mrs. Carey's eyes. She pulled a lavender-scented handkerchief from the pocket of her housedress and dabbed at her eyes. Then she held her hand out to Angel. Angel stood and hugged Mrs. Carey gently. When Angel stepped away, she saw Hawk watching, his eyes as intense as the sunlight pouring into the kitchen. It was as though he were memorizing each instant of affection, each nuance of giving and receiving between the two women.

''Where would you like this hung?'' asked Hawk, switching his attention to Mrs. Carey.

''Right there, where I'll see it every morning. When you're my age, you need something to look forward to when you get out of bed.''

''You need that at any age,'' said Hawk, glancing quickly at Angel.

While Hawk hung the panel so that it would take full advantage of the sunlight, Angel and Mrs. Carey worked on a list of what she would need for the upcoming canning season.

''Will you want these right away?'' asked Hawk, taking the finished list from Angel and skimming it.

''Oh no. Not for a week or more.''

''Good. Angel is going to take me fishing for a few days. Our last trip was . . . delayed.''

Angel wanted to object but knew she couldn't. When she had agreed to take up guide duties again, she had known that those duties would probably include the fishing trip.

Two days ago the thought hadn't frightened her. But it did now, for now when she looked at Hawk she saw more than his harsh, predatory features. She saw the shadow of a boy who had carried a green ribbon in his pocket until there was nothing left but a few bright threads.

It was an unusually quiet Angel who followed Hawk out to the car. She hadn't thought to be vulnerable to him again, not like this.

"I'll stock the boat while you take Derry to the doctor," said Hawk, watching Angel's profile.

She nodded without looking at Hawk. "Do you have any calls to make?"

"No. The second part of the deal is launched. There will be one more crunch before it either all comes together or falls into a million pieces."

The indifference in Hawk's voice intrigued Angel. "You sound like you don't care," she said.

"One way I'm rich. One way I'm not." He shrugged. "I've made and lost several fortunes since I quit racing cars. Either way, the adrenaline flows. Money is just a way of keeping score."

Angel thought about Hawk's words while she drove home. She was still thinking about them while she waited for Derry to be finished at the doctor's office. Even when she and Hawk walked down the wharf to his boat, she was still turning his words over and over in her mind, like pieces of glass that she couldn't quite fit into the overall design.

There was a wind blowing out of the north. Hawk's black hair lifted and rippled thickly. The motion of his hair and the light sliding through it were distinctly uncivilized. Angel glanced at Hawk's profile, then quickly away. It was his watch she needed to see, not the untamed gleam of his eyes.

Angel frowned as she read the face of the watch. North

winds usually blew up trouble. She had hoped to fish the tide turn at Indian Head, nearly three-quarters of the way up to Needle Bay, their destination. But if a good blow was coming up, she would be lucky to make Needle Bay by dark. If the wind came too hard, they would have to shelter somewhere else along the way. Despite the protection of mountains and islands, the Inside Passage was treacherous to small craft in a storm.

Angel took the boat out of the marina as quickly as the law allowed. Without a backward look, she left Campbell River behind, ignoring the boats bobbing on Frenchman's Pool and the log rafts floating along the shore. The wind stayed constant, just hard enough to make some whitecaps and set up a distinct chop. She turned up the volume on the radio, listening to fishermen coming down from the north. From what she heard, the wind was no worse up there than it was here. Reassured, she settled in for the long ride.

After a few hours, Hawk gave up his exposed position in one of the boat's padded stern seats. At first he had stayed out of the cabin deliberately, not wanting to make Angel nervous with his presence. Finally the sustained roar of the engines, the tangled white ribbon of the wake, the mountains rising green and gray from the sea, had all combined to relax him. The wind and spray, however, were getting to the point that he would be first chilled, then wet, unless he moved into the cabin.

Angel looked up, sensing Hawk's presence. "Getting rough out there?"

"A little." Hawk looked through the windshield and over the bow. In a gap between islands, solid ranks of whitecaps marched across the blue-black surface of the sea. "Not as rough as it's going to get, from the looks of that."

"That should be the worst of it," said Angel, measuring the amount of rough water to cross. "We'll duck into the narrow channel between those two islands and cut over to another route north. It will take longer, but it's more protected.''

Hawk braced himself along the padded bench seat that ran around three sides of the table. Without talking, he watched Angel handle the powerful boat. The stretch of wind-whipped water surrounded them, shook them playfully, pummeled the sleek white hull, then let the boat slide into the lee of an island where gulls wheeled and cried.

''Look,'' said Hawk, touching Angel's arm and pointing to her right.

Fifty yards away, along the sheer face of a cliff, gulls dove from the rocks into a seething ball of herring. Protected from the wind, the sea was green and slick, showing each bubble, each darting silver body. Angel checked the angle of the sun, measured it against the amount of water yet to travel, and shook her head.

''I'd love to throw a few lines into that,'' she said longingly.

''But?'' asked Hawk, accurately reading Angel's negative decision.

''This can be a nasty stretch of water when the tide is running full. We have four days to fish. I'd rather not be caught in these currents after dark.''

Only then did Hawk notice the subtle gradations of green in the water, the sinuous drift of debris marking boundaries of competing currents.

''Isn't this slack tide?'' he asked.

''Close.''

Hawk eyed the seething water with respect. If it was this lively at the slack tide, he could imagine what it was like when the tide was running at the full—unthinkable masses of water racing between islands, shouldering against rocky channels, heaping into froth and silent, violent whirlpools.

The Inside Passage had unraveled into a multitude of tiny openings winding among a maze of islands. Into that maze poured the power of the Pacific, a power that was constricted by rocks and narrows, currents and counter-currents.

Some of the islands were large, some were no bigger than boulders fringed with rock reefs. Even with a navigational map, Hawk knew that he would have difficulty picking his way through the obstacle course of rock and sea in full daylight at slack tide. With darkness and the tide coming on, piloting the boat would be as demanding as racing a car with a broken wrist.

Hawk had done that once, when he was young and hadn't cared whether he lived or died. It wasn't an experience that he was eager to repeat. Angel, however, seemed well in control of the situation. She reminded Hawk of himself during a race, alert and coordinated, hands firm on the wheel without clenching, eyes picking out the safest course. He sat back and enjoyed her skill, pleased with his guide through the unexpected beauties and dangers of the Inside Passage.

The pressure of Hawk's attention finally became too great to ignore. Angel glanced sideways quickly, wondering what lay behind the enigmatic, very male lines of his face.

"You're very good," said Hawk distinctly.

Angel's eyes widened with surprise. "Thank you."

"Did Grant teach you?"

Dark lashes closed for an instant, concealing the blue-green color of Angel's eyes. Then, clearly, "Yes."

Angel waited, but no more questions came.

Chapter 10

HAWK EASED OUT OF THE TRIANGULAR BED THAT FILLED the bow of the boat. It was absolutely black in the bow except for a lighter patch of darkness where the vent was. Carefully he opened the door to the cockpit cabin, trying to make no noise. His rubber-soled moccasins moved silently across the runner of indoor-outdoor carpeting. The cabin was empty. As he had suspected, Angel had chosen to sleep in the stern of the boat, as far away from him as she could get without sleeping on the rocks that lined Needle Bay's shore. The seats and the raised platform covering the engines combined to form an area the size of a double bed. Custom-made pads ensured that the bed was comfortable.

It was a chilly bed, though. The predawn air had a definite bite. Angel had slid down into her sleeping bag until no more than a pale cloud of hair showed. Hawk crossed to the stern and touched her hair very gently, taking

173

care not to wake her. Away from her face her hair was cool,
almost cold, yet oddly alive. It gathered light like a pearl,
shimmering and shifting with each touch of his hand. He
remembered how her hair had looked a few days ago when
he had laid her down on the dark quilt in the bow of the
boat. The pale fire of her hair and skin had made him want
to bury himself in her like a warm pool.

She had been so beautiful, and he had been so cruel.

The lines on Hawk's face deepened as he gently wound a
strand of Angel's hair around his finger. He knew so little
about her, and so much. She had given to him what she had
given to no other man. He had taken, unknowing, giving
her nothing in return, not even pleasure. Then he had raged
at her for destroying his world, for taking his certainties
about life and love and women and smashing each one of
them. He had thought she was aware of what she had done
to him, that she had done it deliberately.

Today Hawk knew that wasn't true. Angel had no more
known the depth of his cynicism than he had known the
depth of her innocence. He knew now, however. She had
taught him that there was a woman without lies. And he had
taught her that there was a man without love. Her eyes
darkened when she looked at him. She walked around tables
to avoid being close to him. All that touched her were his
questions, questions like talons sinking into her, making her
writhe with pain. Yet he had to ask, had to know. He had
never in his life found anything more compelling to him
than the truths spoken by her soft lips.

As gently as Hawk had gathered it, he released the pale
ribbon of Angel's hair that he had wound around his finger.
His skin suddenly felt chilled, missing the warmth of her
silky hair. He touched the blond softness once more, sliding
his fingertip down until he felt only the cold material of the
sleeping bag. Then he turned and went back into the cabin,

making no more noise than the sunrise staining the eastern horizon.

Angel woke to the smell of coffee and fried bacon. She sat up quickly, her heart pounding, her mind disoriented in the instant before awakening. The cold air and multicolored sky told her that she was outside at dawn. Then she felt the subtle motions of the boat and remembered. Hawk. The first day of their fishing trip.

"How many eggs?" asked Hawk, opening the cabin door and watching her tousled emergence into awareness.

"Fried or scrambled?"

"I'll know as soon as I crack the shells," said Hawk, returning to the stove.

A smile curled the corners of Angel's mouth. She unzipped the sleeping bag, shivered, and walked quickly to the cabin door, closing it behind her to keep in the heat from the galley stove.

"Do you want me to make omelettes?" she asked, hesitating. The cabin seemed very small. Hawk's height and wide shoulders all but filled the area.

Hawk looked over his shoulder, sensing Angel's sudden unease. "That's all right. I enjoy cooking breakfast once in a while."

Angel stood just inside the doorway. Her hair was rumpled, her shirttails showed beneath the hem of her dove-gray pullover sweater, and her stocking feet looked oddly vulnerable. Obviously she had changed her clothes last night and then crawled into her sleeping bag.

"I'll have to try your method tonight," said Hawk, turning away from Angel. He cracked eggs into the frying pan with a deftness that suggested he cooked eggs more than once in a while.

"My method?"

"Putting on clean clothes before getting in bed," explained Hawk. "I'd forgotten how cold clothes get when they're left out all night."

"Especially when you're all warm from bed," agreed Angel.

"Fried," said Hawk.

"What?" asked Angel, off balance. "Oh, you didn't break the yolks. Congratulations. I'll have two."

Angel watched in fascination as the corner of Hawk's mouth curled upward. She was close enough to see that the corners of his eyes crinkled slightly too. She held her breath, hoping to see him really smile. When he didn't, she sighed quietly. Maybe when he caught a salmon. . . .

The thought made her start guiltily. "We should be out on the water. I overslept."

"I don't think it matters."

"Why?"

"Wind," said Hawk succinctly. He gestured with the spatula toward the bow windows. "Whitecaps until hell won't have it."

Angel eased past Hawk. The aisle was so narrow that she couldn't prevent her body from brushing over his, couldn't help but notice the width of his shoulders and the narrowness of his hips, the muscular lines of his body beneath jeans and wool shirt. She took a deep breath to steady herself. It only made things worse. The smell of soap and clean after-shave, wool and male warmth, assailed her.

Abruptly Angel hurried to the bow. She had known that the mornings would be the worst for her. They always were. Her mind woke up several beats behind her senses. With a man like Hawk around, that could be dangerous. Or would it? He hadn't crowded her with anything but questions since their disastrous attempt at making love.

The sight of wind-churned water took Angel's mind off Hawk's male presence. The ocean beyond Needle Bay's protective cliffs was a seething mass of whitecaps and spray torn off by the wind. Fishing of any kind was out of the question. She wouldn't go out in that wild water unless a life was at stake.

"Do these winds usually last long?" asked Hawk, looking beyond Angel to the violence of wind and sea.

"Anywhere from an hour to a week," said Angel. "Nothing was predicted, though. It should blow over by evening."

"If it doesn't?"

Angel sighed. "Do you know how to play cribbage?"

Again the corner of Hawk's mouth curved up. "I'm willing to learn."

Angel listened to his deep, gritty voice and found herself wondering if cribbage was all that Hawk was willing to learn from her. She was still haunted by the feeling that beneath Hawk's harshness there was a capacity for love as great as his capacity for cynicism and hate. It had been that way with her. Her rage and hatred at life had been as deep as her love for Grant. She had survived both, though, the love and the violent rage. What would it have been like if she had known only violence, only rage, only cruelty? What it would be like never to have known love?

Love linking to love. A beautiful closed circle.

And Hawk, always on the outside. How long could a man live on the outside before he lost the ability to love?

"Your eggs are getting cold."

Hawk's matter-of-fact voice cut across Angel's thoughts. She sat and ate the food that Hawk had cooked for her, drank the coffee that he had poured into a mug and handed to her. When he sat across from her to eat his own breakfast, their knees met briefly under the table. The enforced intimacy of the boat was as unsettling to her serenity as the northern wind was to the surface of the sea.

By the time she finished her breakfast, she knew that she wasn't going to spend the day on the boat with nothing between her and Hawk but a cribbage board.

"Do you like bouillabaisse?" asked Angel, getting up quickly and rinsing her dishes in the small galley sink.

"Yes," said Hawk, watching her with narrowed eyes. He had sensed Angel flinching away from even the most casual kind of physical contact with him. The fact that he had earned her fear didn't make it any more pleasant to take.

"What I have in mind is closer to beachcomber's stew," she admitted. "I wish I'd thought to bring a crab trap."

"Try in there," said Hawk, gesturing toward the lower row of cupboards that lined the hull. "First door to the left."

Angel bent and opened the cupboard door. A coil of yellow plastic rope and a bright, collapsible metal mesh basket met her eager fingers. She stood and smiled at Hawk, holding the new trap triumphantly. "How did you know?"

"Derry said you loved to eat crabs. The man at the bait store said that trap would be fine for casual crabbing."

For a moment Angel simply stared at Hawk, realizing that he had gone out of his way to find something that would please her. "Thank you, Hawk," she said slowly. "You didn't have to."

"I know." His voice was soft, as deep as the color of his eyes. "That's why I enjoyed doing it."

Angel's hands tightened on the trap as she looked into Hawk's clear brown eyes. She had never thought of brown as a warm color before. But it was. Deep and warm with flecks of gold like laughter suspended, waiting only for the right moment to be set free.

"First," said Angel, turning away quickly, wondering why she felt as though she couldn't breathe, "clams."

"Clams?"

"Clams," she repeated firmly. "And a bucket."

"Third cupboard from the end." Then, amusement rippling beneath his words, "The bucket, not the clams."

Hawk saw Angel's eyes widen with understanding. He stretched out his leg and hooked the cupboard open with his foot. "Buckets, diggers, and beach shoes."

"You thought of everything."

"No," softly, "but I'm trying to learn."

Angel's hands tightened painfully in the wire mesh. She knew that Hawk wasn't referring to beachcombing.

"Don't look so frightened, Angel," said Hawk, his tone low, almost harsh. "I'm not asking you to do anything except be yourself." Then, his voice rich with shades of curiosity and regret, he added, "Is that too much to ask?"

Angel's breath came out shakily. "No," she whispered. "That's not too much to ask. But—"

Angel's voice broke. She closed her eyes and rebuilt a rose in her mind, petal by scarlet petal, until her pulse was steady and her throat was no longer tight. Hawk watched her, knowing what she was remembering, a hook and a hawk buried in her, making her bleed. He felt an almost overwhelming need to hold her, to protect her from sadness and hurt, to replace pain with pleasure. The intensity of the feeling shook him. He had felt nothing like it before in his life. All that restrained him from gathering Angel into his arms was the certainty that she would fight him, and then they both would lose.

Quickly Angel gathered everything she and Hawk would need on the beach. The tide was out, revealing a small sandbar at the mouth of the creek that drained into Needle Bay. As the name implied, the bay was long and narrow, more a notch in the mountains than a true bay. Several hundred yards deep and less than eighty feet wide where it

opened into the Inside Passage, Needle Bay was walled by
cliffs and steep-sided hills bristling with rock and cedars.
Where Needle Creek came in, the cliffs gave way to a
narrow ravine. The beach was tiny, filled with coarse sand
and small pebbles. As it blended into the cliffs, the beach
became more rocky. There clams burrowed and oysters
clung stubbornly to gray rocks.

With great care and gentle nudges of the throttle, Angel
lightly beached the bow of the boat on the sandbar. Hawk
vaulted over the bow and landed with the lithe grace she had
come to expect from him. She handed equipment to Hawk,
then backed the boat off a few feet to allow for the ebbing of
the tide. She anchored, peeled off her jeans, and prepared to
wade ashore.

Hawk had beaten her to it. He was waiting for her by the
bow. Like Angel, he had taken off his jeans to reveal a
swimsuit beneath. His red wool shirt looked incongruous
above the black trunks. A few inches of tanned, powerful
thigh showed above the chilly water. The result was
startling in its sensual contrast, the heavy shirt and muscular bare legs with a sheen of black hair slicked into small
curves by water dripping down. Hawk's face was as
impassive as the sea as he watched Angel hesitate. He held
his arms up to carry her to dry land as though she were just
one more parcel of equipment.

If it had been Carlson or Derry, Angel would have
stepped off the bow without a second thought. But this was
Hawk. She paused, then remembered what he had said
about being herself.

"How did you know that I hate cold water?" asked
Angel lightly.

Hawk's face relaxed into something close to a smile. His
eyes warmed. "A lucky guess," he said, lifting her off the
bow.

Angel held on to her jeans with one hand and Hawk with the other. When she felt the heat of his hand on her bare leg, something uncomfortably like fear shot through her. She couldn't help the stiffening of her body. Nor could Hawk help feeling it. In silence he waded the short distance to the beach. He set Angel on her feet immediately, not prolonging the moment of intimacy.

"Thank you," said Angel, grateful as much for being released quickly as for being carried above the chilly sea.

"No trouble," Hawk said with a shrug. "Angels don't weigh much."

He turned away and began to pull on his jeans. He concentrated on the stubborn fabric clinging to his wet legs, on the cold rivulets of water running down to his ankles, on the coarse sand caught between the soles of his feet and the rubber beach sandals he wore. He concentrated on everything except the tactile memory of Angel's smooth flesh burning into his hand . . . and then her withdrawal, a reflex as involuntary as breathing. It took a great amount of pain to instill such a reflex after only one lesson.

With every moment Hawk was close to Angel, he was learning how deeply he had wounded her. He hadn't thought it was possible for a woman to feel that much emotion, that much pain. Nor had he thought it possible to share another's hurt the way he was coming to share hers. The complexity of the emotions flowing between him and Angel was as baffling, difficult, and compelling to him as the truths she gave to him so painfully, not knowing that each truth was a separate talon rending the certainties of Hawk's past.

Angel pulled on her own jeans, rolled them to her knees, and helped Hawk carry everything up beyond the high-tide mark. There was a small patch of grass near the stream. They put everything but the clam buckets and digging tools there. Angel led the way to the beach. The sky was absolutely clear, as deep and cold as time. The ocean reflected every shade of blue, except along the cliffs. There the water became green, reflecting the color of cedar branches sweeping low over the sea. Small fragments of wind found their way into the bay, barely enough to ruffle the sun-struck surface. It was silent but for the distant song of wind and the tiny, liquid sounds of water nibbling at the rocky shore.

"Ever dug for clams?" asked Angel, her eyes on the line of beach revealed by the ebbing tide.

"Not too many clams in west Texas," said Hawk.

Angel smiled slightly. "No, I guess not." She sat on her heels near a stretch of mixed rock and sand beach that was just above the water. "They're easy to get at low tide. You only have to go down a few inches. If you find one, you'll find more nearby."

Hawk sat on his heels near Angel, watching her rake through the sand and rock with a digging tool. It wasn't a true clamming fork. There were too many rocks for that. It was a three-pronged, hand-held garden tool that was sturdy enough to survive abuse. With a triumphant sound, Angel held her sandy hand out to Hawk. Several clams were in her palm. At least, Hawk assumed that the lumps were clams; they were so covered with sand that he couldn't tell. She rinsed off the clams, filled the bucket halfway with salt-water, and chucked in the clams.

"Actually," said Angel, scrounging happily in the sand and occasional patches of sea slime that covered the intertidal zone, "we should wait at least a day before we eat the clams. Gives them a chance to get the sand out of their systems. But I haven't had bouillabaisse since last summer and I can't wait. Do you mind?"

Hawk's expression softened into something very like a smile. "No," he said, "I don't mind."

Caught by the unexpected gentleness in Hawk's voice, Angel looked up. Hawk was very close, his leg all but brushing hers as he began to dig in the sand with another tool. She looked down quickly, disturbed. Her fault, not his. He was only following her lead, digging through cold sand in search of succulent bits of flesh.

"I never asked," said Angel, struck by a sudden thought. "Do you like clams?"

"I'll find out tonight."

For a time there was only silence and the low sounds of steel grating over rocks and sand. Hawk set aside his digger and probed through the sand he had raked up. His sensitive fingertips quickly learned to distinguish between the random rough surface of rocks and the curved, gently ribbed surface of clam shells.

"I'll be damned," he murmured as he pulled out a handful of clams. "You're quite a teacher, Angel."

Angel looked up into Hawk's dark features and smiled almost shyly. "Clamming is easy to learn," she murmured.

Hawk and Angel dug clams in a companionable silence that reminded her of the time she and Hawk had spent before the fishhook had gone into her back. The wounds were still there, more sore today than yesterday or the day before. She had meant to have Derry check her back but every time she had thought of it, he had been immersed in formulas as long as his cast. She had tried cleaning the wounds herself and had given up in disgust. It would take a contortionist to effectively treat that particular area.

"That should do it," said Angel after they had pursued the ebbing tide to a line of bedrock. She stood and stretched, wincing slightly as the motion pulled against the sore spot near her shoulder blade. Then she put the pain out of her mind as she had learned to do when she forced herself to walk again. As Carlson had pointed out, what can't be cured must be endured. "Twenty for you and twenty for me," said Angel, lifting the clam bucket.

"What if I don't like them?" asked Hawk, his voice amused.

Angel licked her lips with delicate greed. "I'll think of something."

Hawk's black eyebrow lifted.

"They're not very big," said Angel reasonably.

A strong hand wrapped around the bucket handle, lifting it from Angel's grasp. Under her watchful green eyes, Hawk rinsed the clams, scrubbed them with a stiff brush, then rinsed them again. He filled the bucket with clams and saltwater and turned to Angel.

"Now what?" he asked.

"Put the bucket in the shade and let nature take its course. We," she said triumphantly, "are going crabbing."

Angel went over to the grass, retrieved the crab trap and a chunk of bacon, and returned to Hawk. "This is a little trickier than clamming."

"Crabs are faster?" suggested Hawk dryly.

She smiled. "Much." She led him to a shelf of rock that slanted out into the bay. The shelf ended in a deep green shaft of water. Deftly Angel wired the hunk of bacon to the bottom of the trap. "Now," she said, lowering the metal mesh into the water, "the crabs get a whiff of bacon and come running."

"There's no top on that thing," Hawk pointed out. The trap consisted of little more than concentric mesh rings of graduated sizes, rather like a blunt funnel. "What keeps the little beasties from getting out the same way they got in?"

"That's the tricky part," admitted Angel. "You have to be faster than they are."

The trap hit bottom, invisible beneath the green sea. Angel counted beneath her breath. When she got to one hundred, she began to pull up the trap hand over hand, hauling as fast as she could. Just as she pulled the mesh above the surface, a crab flipped over the edge and back into the sea.

"Damn!" said Angel. "And he was keeper size, too!" She sighed. "Good thing they're stupid. Sooner or later, he'll be back for more."

Hawk watched while Angel repeatedly lowered the trap and counted beneath her breath, raised it quickly, and looked with varying degrees of disappointment at the contents of the trap. The crabs were either too small or of the wrong kind. After twenty minutes, Angel and the bait were looking equally frayed.

"May I?" asked Hawk, holding out a hand for the trap.

Without a word, Angel handed over the bright yellow rope. She peeled off her sweater and tied it around her neck. Sun reflected off the rocks and water, heating the air. Despite the wind beyond the bay, it was warm within the sheltering cliffs.

Hawk lowered the trap, counted, then pulled. The basket came up empty, not so much as one tiny crab. He looked at Angel.

"I forgot to tell you," she said, blowing wisps of hair off her hot forehead. "You have to pull straight up. If the basket tips over—"

"The crabs fall out," finished Hawk.

After a few more tries, Hawk got the feel of it. Angel sat on the slanting shelf and watched him work. His powerful arms brought the basket up so quickly that whatever was inside was all but flattened. He seemed tireless, raising and lowering the trap with the same ease after twenty tries as after two. Angel put her head on her knees and memorized the grace and power of Hawk's body, designing a stained glass panel in her mind, the man and the rock and the sea.

Then Angel realized that Hawk had snagged a huge crab and was casually reaching in to take it out of the trap.

"No!" said Angel, lunging for Hawk's wrist, yanking his fingers out of the mesh.

Startled, Hawk looked from the slender hand wrapped around his wrist to the blue-green eyes only inches from his.

"Those pincers can hurt," explained Angel.

Cautiously, she approached the large crab from the rear, slid her thumb underneath and her fingers on top, and lifted the crab out of the trap. The crab was a male, more than eight inches across the shell. Its pincers waved and clicked angrily. Hawk looked at the thick claws and realized that once again Angel had put herself between him and possible injury.

"First the hook, now the crab," Hawk said softly. His fingers touched Angel's cheek for an instant. "Thanks. For both."

His hands were cool from the ocean and Angel's cheeks were flushed with sun. The contrast only increased the sensual impact of his touch. Angel looked at Hawk for a moment, too surprised to move. Then she turned her head away.

"I should have warned you about the crab," she said, her voice even.

Hawk's hand returned to the cold yellow rope. "How many crabs do we need?"

"This should do it."

Hawk looked dubious. "I suppose I can always swap my clams for your half of the crab."

"Not a chance," said Angel quickly.

The corner of Hawk's mouth lifted as he bent over and lowered the trap into the sea again. While he counted, he watched Angel walk across the narrow beach and drop the crab into the clam bucket. The faded jeans she wore fitted softly, firmly, to every curve of her hips and legs. Her hair had been gathered at the nape of her neck, but time and exertion had loosened the clip. Bright wisps burned around her face and across the gray sweater. She walked confidently despite the uneven surface and the rubber beach sandals snapping at her heels with each step. Watching her grace, Hawk found it hard to believe that she had ever been broken and in pain, doomed but for Derry's strength pulling her from the twisted wreckage of her dreams.

Hawk realized that his hands were aching from the force with which he was holding the yellow rope. The thought of Angel lying helpless was unbearable to him. He had known too many women who had no truth. He had come too close to never knowing a woman who had no lies.

"Are you giving the crabs a free lunch?" asked Angel lightly, walking down the slanting rock shelf until she was beside Hawk. Then his bleak expression and the coiled intensity of his body struck her. "Hawk?"

A tremor went through him. When he turned and looked at Angel, hunger and hope and loneliness radiated from him. She stood transfixed while all the colors of his emotions poured through her, illuminating man and woman alike. The force of the moment overwhelmed her. Nothing in her life had prepared her for a man like Hawk.

Hawk saw Angel tremble and step back reflexively even as her hand reached toward him.

"Hawk?"

"It's all right, Angel," he said quietly. He turned away and pulled up the trap with swift, powerful movements. "I was just thinking."

"About what?" she asked. Then, quickly, "I'm sorry, it's none of my business."

"I was thinking about women and lies," said Hawk. "And about truth and angels."

Angel tried not to ask, but found it impossible. She had to know what had made Hawk turn his back on emotion, on love. "There's more to it than your mother abandoning you, isn't there?"

"More to what?"

"Your hatred of women."

Hawk pulled up the trap. It was empty. He lowered the trap again. "I don't hate all women," he said finally. "Not anymore."

"It isn't easy, is it?"

"What isn't?"

"Not hating me."

Stillness went through Hawk, her truth sinking into him. Angel was right. It went against every reflex he had acquired during a lifetime of surviving in a harsh world. Yet it was impossible to hate Angel. She had the aching purity of one of her stained glass creations, all the colors of life distilled into a woman with haunted eyes and a mouth still willing to smile.

"It's frighteningly easy not to hate you," said Hawk, watching Angel with eyes that consumed her gently, utterly.

Angel's breath wedged in her throat. *Frightening*.

Yes, it was all of that and then some to have your personal verities shattered in a single instant. It had happened to her twice. Once with Hawk, when she had learned to distrust her own judgment. And once in the wreck, when she had learned to distrust life. It had been very hard to crawl out of the wreckage of her world and learn to walk again in a new world, a world that never could be as secure as the old had been. Love had given her strength. Derry's love. Carlson's love. And finally, painfully, her own memories of Grant had been allowed to return, healing much of the regret and all of the bitterness.

How much worse it must be for Hawk to stand naked and alone amid the shards of past certainties. Hawk, who had never known love.

The sound of the trap being pulled from the sea's green embrace startled Angel. She saw the dark, angular shape clinging to the mesh and came quickly to her feet, drawn again into the world she had chosen, the world she loved.

"You've got one!" she said, standing on tiptoe and peering over Hawk's arm. "It's keeper size too! Just look at that beauty!"

Hawk's eyebrow climbed at Angel's enthusiasm. "I am. Looks mean as hell to me," he added, eyeing the black-eyed crab that was crouched against the trap, waving serrated pincers around.

"The harder the shell, the sweeter the meat," said Angel.

"That's not the way I remember that particular bit of folk wisdom," Hawk said, lips curving just short of a smile.

"New world, new saying," Angel retorted blithely, shaking the trap.

With a sure, rapid motion, Angel grabbed the distracted crab and headed back up the beach. Hawk coiled the yellow rope, hefted the trap, and followed, wondering with each step how something as soft and silky as Angel had survived a world where teeth and claws were the rule. Then he remembered her deft capture of the wicked-looking crab. The corners of Hawk's mouth lifted. Maybe the better question would be how teeth and claws could survive in the presence of an angel.

Chapter 11

HAWK WADED BACK FROM THE BOAT TO WHERE ANGEL waited, stretched out on her stomach on an old quilt. Her chin was propped on her hands as she watched huge, sleek bumblebees go from blossom to blossom among the scattered wildflowers.

"Feeling sorry for the flowers?"

"Hmmm?" murmured Angel, absently holding out her hand for the soft drink that Hawk had brought from the boat. "Why should I do that?"

"The bee goes from flower to flower to flower, sipping honey and then flying on without a backward look."

"That's the bee's point of view," said Angel, her lips curving upward in a small, secret smile.

Hawk saw the smile as Angel rolled over gracefully and sat up to take a drink from the can. "What other point of view is there?" he asked, popping open his beer.

"The flower's."

"Which is?" prompted Hawk, enjoying the very feminine smile on Angel's lips.

"The flower gets bee after bee after bee."

The corners of Hawk's mouth shifted beneath the midnight mustache. There was a flash of white teeth and then the soft, rough-edged sound of male laughter. Angel watched, riveted by Hawk's transformation. The hard planes of his face gentled, making his expression younger, more open, a face both experienced and warm. She had thought him harshly handsome before; when he laughed, he was more beautiful than a pagan god.

When Hawk turned and smiled at Angel, she felt as though she had been handed the sun after years of darkness.

"Bee after bee after bee," he murmured, shaking his head, his mouth still curved in a smile. "Angel, you're . . . special."

"So are you," she said, her blue-green eyes drinking in every instant of Hawk's transformation. "And when you smile," she added huskily, "you're incredible."

Surprise changed Hawk's face again. Eyes that had lit with laughter changed to a soft blaze of brown as he saw that Angel, as always, was telling the truth. "I'll have to smile more often," said Hawk quietly, searching her eyes and seeing only pleasure, no shadows of fear or unease.

"Yes," Angel said, meeting Hawk's eyes. "That would be . . . special," she added, echoing his intensity.

Hawk's lean brown hand reached slowly toward Angel. His fingertips traced the burnished curve of her eyebrow, the straight line of her nose, and the hollow beneath her high, slanted cheekbone. He wanted very much to lower his mouth and taste her very gently, feel the warmth of her skin beneath his lips. Instead, he smiled at her again and felt her own smile go through him, transforming everything it touched into radiant colors. Slowly, he withdrew his touch before the pleasure glowing in her eyes became shadowed by fear.

"What else do we have to do for our dinner?" Hawk asked as he began to gather up the debris of their impromptu picnic.

Angel heard the faint huskiness beneath Hawk's impersonal words and realized that she had been sitting motionless while his fingers memorized her face. She felt a tremor move through her as she remembered what being intimate with Hawk had been like. Gentle at first and then fierce, hurtful.

"Fish," she said, then cleared her throat and tried again. "Fish."

Hawk looked out beyond the narrow neck of the bay. Wind and whitecaps claimed the Inside Passage. "Maybe we should settle for crabs and clams," he said dubiously.

"In the bay," added Angel. "For cod. Maybe even a halibut if we're lucky."

"Salmon?"

Angel sighed. "Doubt it. But anything's possible." *Even,* she added silently, *a smile from a hawk.*

Together they bundled up all the equipment. Angel waded in the bay this time. The heat of the day made the water feel merely bracing rather than punishing. When she got to the boat, the water was just up to the curve of her hips. The boat's railing was at eye level, and there was no sea ladder at the stern. Climbing back onto the boat would be awkward.

"Now comes the hard part," she said, shifting her grip on the bucket.

Hawk unceremoniously dumped everything he held onto

the deck. He grabbed the railing and pulled himself out of the water and into the boat with a single, surging movement that left Angel staring in disbelief.

"What hard part?" asked Hawk, leaning over and plucking the bucket out of Angel's hand. "Cleaning the crabs?"

Angel realized that he wasn't teasing her. He really didn't know what she had meant. She threw a glance at the sky, silently asking why life distributed physical gifts so unfairly.

"Getting into the blasted boat," she said, her voice rich with disgust. "At least for some of us mere mortals, it's the hard part."

Hawk looked startled for a moment, then understood. His mustache shifted and glimmered with dark lights as he fought not to smile. Keeping his head down and taking his time about it, he braced the bucket so that it wouldn't be kicked over in a careless moment.

"Go ahead," said Angel, smiling despite her disgust at her own limitations. "Smile. I'll get even."

With a chuckle that sent ripples of sensation through Angel, Hawk lifted his head and leaned over the rail toward her, revealing the white flash of his smile. She noticed that both of his eye teeth were very slightly crooked, and there was a tiny scar along the upper curve of his lip. The small imperfections in his smile only made it more beautiful to her, like the flaws that made each piece of muff glass unique.

Then the smile vanished, leaving only fierce, clear brown eyes. "Let me help you," said Hawk.

"You're going to loan me your wings?" asked Angel wryly.

"Sort of." Hawk grasped Angel under her arms and lifted. He pivoted as he lifted, bringing her smoothly aboard without banging her shins against the railing. Yet he saw the wince that she tried to conceal. Very gently, Hawk set Angel down on the deck.

"Thanks," she said, relaxing her body despite the pain lancing down her back from the hook wound. Tensing against pain only made it worse. She breathed carefully and moved her shoulder.

"Did I hurt you?" asked Hawk, watching her intently.

Angel shook her head. "My back's still a bit sore."

"Let me see."

For a moment Angel hesitated, remembering the last time Hawk had washed the wounds left by the fishhook. But this time she had on a bathing suit beneath her blouse, and it was full daylight rather than the mysterious intimacy of twilight on the sea.

And this time she knew that an angel and a hawk were a bad match in bed.

"All right," said Angel, turning her back on Hawk and unbuttoning quickly. She winced again as she flexed her shoulders in order to take her arms out of the long-sleeved blouse. "I meant to have Derry check it but—"

The hiss of Hawk's indrawn breath cut off Angel's words. The twin wounds where the hook had gone in were swollen, angry, hot to the touch. Hawk's mouth flattened into a grim line as he remembered the instant when Angel had thrown herself at him, protecting his face at the cost of her own flesh.

And then he had repaid her care by making her bleed again, hurting her even more.

"When was the last time you soaked this?" asked Hawk, his words like a whip.

Angel tightened to hear the harshness back in Hawk's voice. "I haven't. It's rather hard to reach," she said, her own tone careful, neutral.

Hawk swore softly, a single violent word. Then, "I'll heat some water."

Angel started to object, then realized it would do no good. She looked at the sun. There was plenty of time left for cod fishing. A whole afternoon. And then perhaps a nap, for she hadn't slept very well last night, with every sense alert to Hawk's presence on the small boat. Not that a bigger boat would have been any better. At times, the knowledge that she and Hawk shared the same world was enough to unnerve her.

While Hawk heated the water, Angel spread the picnic quilt over the pad at the stern of the boat where she had slept the night before. Though she wore only a bathing suit, she wasn't cold as she stretched out on her stomach. The sun was directly overhead, pouring warmth and light into the tiny, sheltered bay. The boat rocked very gently, rising with the subtle movements of the tide. Random fingers of wind combed the trees, making them shiver and sigh, sounds that blended with the liquid murmur of water.

"Are you awake?" asked Hawk softly.

"Mmmmmm," Angel said, turning her face toward Hawk, too relaxed to speak.

Her eyelashes made intriguing, fringed shadows that quivered across her clear skin. Sun had brought a delicate flush to her cheeks, and peace had softened her lips into full, sensual curves. The bathing suit was the exact color of her eyes in the sun, vivid blue-green, shining softly. She had unclipped her hair and swept it aside. It shimmered white-gold in the sun, a fire burning across the dark quilt. The smooth curve of her shoulders, the tempting shadow valley of her spine, the contrast of her waist against the surprisingly ripe swell of her hips, the graceful length of her legs emphasized by the French cut of her suit; every line of Angel's body was so essentially feminine that Hawk had to look away from her for a moment in order to control the hunger that exploded through him.

Hawk sat down next to Angel and concentrated on wringing out the washcloth in the pan of gently steaming water. The sounds were liquid, sensual, like the sea and the sun and the random caress of the wind. Hunger swelled into an aching heat between Hawk's thighs. Grimly he shaped the washcloth into a pad and placed it gently on the small, angry wound.

"Tell me if it's too hot," said Hawk.

Angel's eyes closed until there was only a suggestion of blue-green glitter.

"Does it hurt?" asked Hawk softly, his voice gritty. Then, "I don't want to hurt you, Angel."

Her breath came out slowly. "It's fine, Hawk."

"I'll be back in a minute."

When Hawk returned, he was wearing jeans over his swim trunks. He rinsed out the washcloth, renewing its heat. With the gentleness that was becoming second nature when he touched Angel, Hawk placed the pad over the wound.

"All right?" he asked quietly.

Angel nodded, sending ripples of light through her hair. Hawk sat down again, looking at Angel with dark, brooding eyes. Every time he rinsed out the washcloth, the twin wounds mocked him. No one had ever gone out of the way to save him from hurt before. Angel's unselfishness was as shattering to him as her innocence.

And now he wanted her as he had never wanted a woman in his life. Yet even greater than his desire was his determination not to hurt her again. She had been hurt too much already, lost too much; there were too many ghosts in her beautiful eyes.

"You should have let the hook go into me."

Hawk didn't realize that he had spoken aloud until Angel's eyes opened, blue-green, as deep as the sea.

"I couldn't," she said simply.

"Why not? Other people would have."

Angel tried to answer, but in the end could only shrug. "I just couldn't. I knew what was happening. You didn't. You had no way to protect yourself from something you couldn't foresee."

"That's the nature of life," said Hawk sardonically. Then, softly, "I wish I had known you a long time ago. Before—"

His words stopped. He rinsed out the cloth again, replaced it very gently on her skin.

"Before what?" asked Angel, watching Hawk from beneath her long eyelashes, wondering what memories had drawn his face into cold, predatory lines. "Who was she, Hawk?"

"There was more than one." The sardonic voice and cold line of Hawk's mouth were back, yet his hands were still gentle. Then his face changed, hardening into contempt. "That's not quite true. There was only one, really. The first one. She taught me everything a woman can teach a man."

"Except love," said Angel.

"She didn't have that in her."

Angel closed her eyes against sudden tears. Hawk's bleak voice, his eyes narrowed against memories that brought only pain, the hunger and the yearning buried deep within him, reached out to Angel with compelling force. She wondered who the woman was and what she had done that had taught Hawk hatred instead of love.

Hawk left, only to return with more hot water. He sat down again, then bent over Angel and touched the skin around her wounds with exquisite care. Angel drew in a swift breath.

"Hurt?" said Hawk, lifting his fingers.

Angel shook her head. She could think of no way to tell Hawk that it was pleasure rather than pain that had made her gasp. The gentleness of his touch had radiated through her, taking away pain as surely as hot water took the inflammation from her back. The washcloth touched her again, bringing a soothing, healing heat to her flesh. Hawk felt Angel relaxing beneath his touch. The knowledge that he had brought her something besides pain eased the talons of need and regret digging into him.

The easing of Hawk's own tension taught him that there was more to his desire for Angel than simple sexual hunger. He needed to know that he was capable of more than destruction and hurt. He needed to believe that his being with Angel wouldn't be another kind of wounding for her, a deeper, more insidious inflammation that would ultimately poison her as he had been poisoned long ago.

He couldn't take back the past, wiping out his bitterness and all its consequences. He could try to explain what had happened, though, and then perhaps Angel would realize that he hadn't meant to hurt her, not really. Not the person who was Angel Lange. He had simply been doing what he had always done since he was eighteen, using women as casually and cruelly as he himself had been used.

"When I was twelve," said Hawk, rinsing out the washcloth again, his voice as calm as the soft sounds of the water, "my father died. The tractor rolled on him, crushing him."

Angel's hands curled slightly, fingernails digging into the quilt. Hawk spoke of death so calmly, a fact like sunset, just one fact among the many facts of life.

"Grandma and I couldn't handle the farm alone, but we couldn't afford to hire a man, either. She had another grandchild. A true grandchild, as she always pointed out to me. Her daughter's daughter. Jenna was eighteen when she came to live with us. She was strong, wild and cold as a north wind."

Instinctively, Angel knew that Jenna was the woman who had taught Hawk how to hate. It was there in his voice, ice and contempt.

"The three of us kept that farm alive. It was brutal work. Grandma died when I was fourteen. Jenna became my guardian." Hawk hesitated, comparing what he was about to tell Angel with her own teenage years, picnics on the beach and laughter, innocence. "She seduced me the night of Grandma's funeral."

Angel couldn't conceal the shock that went through her. "You were only fourteen!"

"I was man-sized, and I'd been woman hungry for two years without knowing it. Jenna knew, though. She knew everything about men. She was a born whore. Cold-hearted screwing was her specialty. I didn't know it then, of course. My body was a man's, but my judgment and emotions were those of a boy. I thought Jenna was the most perfect woman God ever made."

Hawk's near-silent, bitter laughter raked over Angel's nerves. "The truth was a bit different," continued Hawk. "The truth was that I was the biggest fool God ever made."

Angel made a sound of protest at the self-contempt in Hawk's voice. She rose up on her elbows, twisting in order to see him. "You were just a boy. How could you expect yourself to know about a—a—"

"Bitch?" suggested Hawk sardonically. "Whore? Slut? I've called Jenna all those names, and worse. All of them were true, especially the worst ones." His eyes narrowed to glittering brown lines. "Jenna told me we needed money, so I took to racing boats, cars, whatever I could get my hands on. I had good reflexes and a kid's belief in life everlasting. I won more than I lost. I gave the money to Jenna, and she kept the bank from closing us down during the dry years. Then we had two good years, rain and sun in just the right amounts at just the right times."

Hawk realized that the washcloth had fallen from Angel's back. "Lie down," he said quietly.

Angel hesitated, wanting to see Hawk's face while he talked. Strong hands pressed gently on her shoulders. She gave in, lying down again. But her eyes never left his face as he wrung out the washcloth in hot water. She hardly noticed when the cloth again rested on her back, held in place by the light pressure of Hawk's hand.

"I kept on racing. The money was better than anything I could make working on the farm. Then Jenna came to me with a plan—sell the farm and buy a real car for me to race. I couldn't believe my luck." Hawk's voice was lazy, but cold contempt for himself and Jenna made every word distinct, cutting. "Not only was I living with the hottest piece of tail in Texas, but she was willing to give me her half of the farm so that I could race in the big time. What more could any boy ask?"

Love, said Angel, but she said it only to herself.

"So we went to the lawyer and signed papers," continued Hawk. "The money would come to me on my eighteenth birthday, the day Jenna stopped being my guardian. We were going to get married, buy a race car, and live happily ever after."

There was a short silence. Angel tensed, sensing what was coming next.

"So I came back from a race the day of my eighteenth birthday, grinning like an idiot, a shiny plastic trophy in my hands. There was nobody in the house but a young woman. She was pregnant, and as surprised to see me as I was to see her. Then she told me that her husband had bought the farm from Jenna, paid cash, owned every damn thing except the clothes on my back.''

The silence stretched so long that Angel was afraid Hawk wouldn't speak anymore. But he did. His voice was flat, bland, as though the past no longer had the power to hurt him. It hurt Angel, though. She kept thinking of the boy who had hoarded a Christmas candy cane and still treasured the sweet memory, tangible symbol of someone caring for him, if only a little.

''Seems that I'd signed my half of the farm over to Jenna in that lawyer's office,'' continued Hawk. Contempt and amusement laced his voice. ''Seems that she'd been sleeping with that lawyer for a while. Seems that I was on my own. And Jenna? Well, Jenna was gone. Big city lights and men who didn't have Texas dirt ground into the skin of their hands.''

''What did you do?'' asked Angel, her voice soft, almost afraid. The Hawk she knew today would have hunted Jenna down. No. The Hawk she knew today wouldn't have been taken in by Jenna. The Hawk she knew today wouldn't have cared enough to hunt anyone down.

''I raced cars.''

The clipped words told Angel more than she wanted to know. She saw a younger Hawk driving like a man possessed, not caring about living or dying or anything in between.

''I had a lot of women, too,'' said Hawk. ''As long as I was winning, anyway. Too many losses, a crash, and the women went away. Start winning again, and they came back like buzzing black flies.''

Angel closed her eyes at the contempt in Hawk's voice,

contempt for the women and for himself. "You're lucky you didn't kill yourself," she said.

"It took me a while to figure that out," admitted Hawk. "At first, I was kind of disappointed by all the near misses. Then a funny thing happened. Each time I nearly died, life became that much more valuable to me. By the time I was twenty-three, I knew that racing wasn't a bright way for a grown man to make a living. It took me six months to come back from that crash, and another three years to make enough money to get out of the race game altogether."

In silence, Hawk removed the washcloth, rinsed it in the hot water, and replaced the cloth over Angel's back.

"What did you do?" asked Angel, glancing over her shoulder at him.

"Played the stock market. Bought and sold land. I had a flair for it. Like racing. And like racing, I didn't really care whether I won or lost. The adrenaline was enough."

"And now?"

Hawk's hand hesitated. Without touching Angel, he traced the smooth line of her spine. He thought of all the women he'd taken and then left, the cold emptiness of the sky and his heart, the hunt and the kill and the taste of ashes. "Now, adrenaline isn't enough. But it's better than nothing."

The bleak acceptance in Hawk's voice was a talon sliding into Angel, pain searing through her. She closed her eyes for a moment, unable to bear looking at him without touching him, giving him a simple moment of human contact, human caring. But she was still afraid of him, afraid of herself, afraid of the sensual hunger that rippled tightly through her when she remembered the initial beauty of their lovemaking. Nor had she forgotten how it had ended, pain and contempt and fury.

Hawk lifted the cloth, touched Angel's skin gently, and

reached for the antibiotic salve he had brought out when he had pulled his jeans over his swimsuit, blurring the blunt outline of his desire. He rubbed the balm into Angel's skin so carefully that she hardly felt it.

"How does your back feel now?" he asked.

"Better," she said, sitting up. "Much less sore."

Angel's words reassured Hawk, but her voice was frayed and she refused to look at him.

"Angel?"

Silently she shook her head. Her hair fell over her face, veiling her tears before Hawk could see them. He had heard them in her voice, though. Gently he smoothed back the bright fall of hair. Tears sparkled on her eyelashes.

"I'm sorry," Hawk said, afraid to touch her, to wound her again. "I never meant to hurt you, Angel. Not *you*. I didn't realize that you were different from the others."

Angel's eyes opened, releasing the glittering tears. Through them she saw the pain on Hawk's face, the regret shadowing his eyes and making his voice hoarse.

"I know that now," she whispered.

Slowly, Hawk gathered Angel into his arms, holding her lightly, murmuring words of comfort. Tears welled transparently, for she was helpless to stop them. Hawk's life had been so different from hers. She knew now why he had become harsh, merciless, predatory, a man with neither softness nor love in him. Yet he wanted love, needed it, longed for it with a fierceness that would have frightened Angel if it hadn't been so like her own hunger.

"It's all right, Hawk," she said, touching his cheek with a hand that shook very slightly. "I understand what happened now. You had never known love, and I had never known hate." Her lips curved in a sad smile. "No wonder we misjudged each other so badly. You thought I was pretending to love. That's what you called me, wasn't it? An actress?"

Hawk closed his eyes, unable to bear seeing Angel's sadness and trembling smile. "Yes."

"I'm a terrible actress," said Angel.

"Yes," he whispered, smoothing his palms over her arms, her shoulders. "I know that now."

Angel stared up at Hawk, caught by the emotion in his voice. "It wasn't your fault," she said. "Hawk, listen to me. I don't blame you for what happened."

"I do. You gave me what you had given to no other man. And I . . . I gave you what I'd given to every other woman. Your innocence shocked me. Your truth destroyed me. So I hurt you. Badly. You're still hurting." Hawk's mouth brushed over Angel's hand, her wrist, the parted lips that trembled so close to his. "Let me give you something besides pain, Angel. Let me use what I know for something besides destruction. Please," he murmured, kissing her lightly. "I won't take you. I won't touch you with more than my hands, my mouth, my breath."

Angel looked into Hawk's clear, extraordinary eyes and saw only herself reflected in them, her own need to create beauty from the shards of the past. His face was no longer cruel. It held an agony of hope suspended, waiting like a child for presents that never came, waiting for a love that was measured only by its absence, an aching emptiness as cold and blue as the sky.

Hawk felt the warmth of Angel's body beneath his hands, felt the sweet sigh of her breath against his chest, felt the tremor ripple through her as she gave herself to his keeping. He didn't need to hear Angel's whispered *yes* in order to know her answer, yet the word swept through him, a gift greater than any he had ever been given. He tried to speak, to thank her for the trust he didn't deserve, but he had no voice. His hands trembled as they caressed her hair. He held her lightly against himself and rocked slowly, eyes closed, absorbing her presence within his arms.

Lips that were warm and gentle kissed Angel's temple, her eyelids, the hollow of her cheek. Long, strong fingers eased into her hair, bringing its sun-bright warmth to Hawk's mouth. He buried his face in her silky curls, breathing in her scent until he was dizzy with her sweetness. He felt Angel smooth her cheek against the gleaming black hair on his chest and thought he would break with pleasure. His index finger tilted her face up to his. For a long moment Hawk looked at the blue-green mystery of Angel's eyes, radiance and color and almost no shadow at all. Slowly, he lowered his lips to hers.

The first touch was so sweet, so gentle, that tears formed in Angel's eyes. Her eyelashes lowered, concealing her tears. When her breath came in through parted lips, it brought with it a subtle taste of Hawk, warmth and tenderness and restraint. He kissed the corners of her mouth, outlined the curve of her smile with the moist tip of his tongue, and then brushed his mouth repeatedly over hers. His lips barely touched hers with each kiss, each gliding caress that ended almost before it began. Then he began all over again, touching her temples and eyes and smile, his tongue gentle on her lips, his mouth restrained and sweet as he worshiped her with small, exquisite caresses.

Deep inside her body, Angel felt herself come apart with a slow, liquid unraveling that brought a soft moan to her throat. Tears slid soundlessly down her cheeks, moistening Hawk's lips as his tongue had moistened hers. He felt her tears, tasted them, and lifted his head.

"Angel?" he asked softly, his voice deepening over a tremor of emotion. "What is it? What's wrong?"

"You make me feel so beautiful," she whispered, opening her eyes and looking into Hawk's. "I've never felt beautiful before. Not like this."

The words both humbled and exalted Hawk, shaking him with a fierce pleasure he had never known until this instant. "Thank you," he said, his voice husky. Then he whispered against Angel's throat, "Touching you teaches me the meaning of the word *beauty*."

Angel shivered as Hawk's lips found the sensitive rim of her ear. His tongue tip moved lightly, sensuously, warmly, spiraling down and in until he knew all the secret turns and curves of her ear. For a moment his tongue hardened, probing, and then he retreated, taking warmth with him. Angel trembled and made a small sound. Hawk lifted his head and looked at her through half-closed eyes, reading pleasure and growing passion in the taut line of her body. His hand shaped itself to her throat, savoring the softness and the pulse racing beneath his thumb.

Angel's hands reached out to Hawk, her fingers warm at his waist and the small of his back as she snuggled against him. He closed his eyes, not wanting her to see the hunger clawing through him at her innocent touch.

"You're so warm," she murmured, turning her head until she could rest her lips against Hawk's chest. The resilient pad of muscle tempted her. She rubbed her mouth against his skin, tickling her lips on the glossy black hair that curled over his chest. "And furry," she added, lifting her head, laughter and sensual pleasure making her eyes brilliant.

"I'll get my shirt," said Hawk, his eyes still closed, his voice tight with the effort it took to restrain himself. He cursed himself for not guessing that Angel wouldn't be used to a man's naked chest. If Grant had been as smooth as Derry, she probably had never felt the rough textures of a man's body hair before now.

"Don't put on your shirt," Angel said quickly. Then, softly, her fingers testing the rough silk and resilience of Hawk, "I like the way you feel. Unless you mind?" she added, lifting her hand suddenly.

Hawk's eyes opened, clear and warm. His hand captured hers and pulled it slowly across his chest. "I like it when you touch me." *Too much,* he added silently, feeling the rigid expression of his desire press harder against his jeans with each heartbeat. Yet he wouldn't have traded one instant of Angel's innocent torture for all the experienced release other women had brought him.

"Are you sure?" asked Angel, her hesitation in her eyes, her voice, her hand no longer stroking him.

"I've never been more sure of anything in my life."

Hawk lowered his head until his mouth fit perfectly over Angel's. With slow, gentle movements of his tongue, he melted her lips until they flowed apart beneath him. The tiny serrations of her teeth fascinated him. He traced their edges again and again before he allowed himself to taste the moist sweetness of her mouth with a single delicate touch of his tongue against hers.

The tremor that went through Angel was echoed deep in Hawk's body, blood pooling hotly, pressing against the restraints of cloth, demanding release. His tongue returned, learning the velvet textures of her. The hands on his back tightened, urging him closer in silent, unknowing invitation. Her tongue answered the teasing pressures of his, meeting retreat with boldness. His tongue responded with a gliding, satin roughness that drew tiny sounds from deep in Angel's throat. The kiss lasted until her heart was a wildness shaking her and her mouth opened deeply to his. Even then the kiss continued, filling her softness and moist warmth, making her tremble with each wave of pleasure sweeping over her.

The palms of Hawk's hands were almost hot as they moved from Angel's cheeks to her shoulders and then down her arms to her fingertips. He threaded his hands through hers, gently unwrapping her arms from around his waist. His hands slid inside hers slowly, rhythmically, stroking the burning skin between her fingers, and then his hands moved with ravishing seduction along the inner softness of her arms. The caress was as unbroken as his kiss, Hawk filling Angel's senses until she shivered and drank his presence, wordlessly telling him of the pleasure coursing through her, pleasure he had brought to her.

Hawk's kiss deepened even more as his palms slid over the skin revealed by the deeply cut sides of Angel's suit. He ached to let his fingers slide beneath the silky fabric and discover the softness of flesh that had never known the sun. But his hands moved on, sliding up to her ribs, brushing the firm swell of her breasts. His caress lingered there, learning the satin curves of her, seducing her nipples into a tightness that inflamed him as much as her ragged moan.

Only then did Hawk release Angel's mouth. His lips moved with slow heat across the taut skin of her neck. Head tipped back, eyes closed, Angel abandoned herself to the marvelous sensations Hawk's caressing mouth and hands gave to her. His mouth slid with exquisite care across the hollow of her throat, lingering long enough for his tongue and lips to learn the heated race of her heart. When his mouth drifted over the curve of her breast, then closed with melting gentleness over her nipple, Angel shivered and arched into the caress unselfconsciously, knowing only the pleasure Hawk gave her. Hawk's teeth rasped lightly over the outline of her nipple beneath the smooth fabric of the bathing suit, and she moaned.

The sound ripped through Hawk, pain and pleasure combined, a hunger that made him want to cry out in anguish and fierce delight. Blindly, Hawk's fingers pulled at the satin cords holding up Angel's suit. The tie parted, sliding down her shoulders. Angel held her breath, wanting nothing more than to feel the hot touch of Hawk's tongue on her naked breasts. Then she realized what she was thinking, and froze in surprise at the abandonment that Hawk's touch called from her. She had loved Grant, wanted Grant. But not like this. This was as much outside her experience as Hawk himself.

Hawk sensed the change in Angel. He held her gently away from his body, his hands restrained, his mouth no longer touching her anywhere.

"Hawk?" asked Angel, her voice soft, ragged.

"I think it's time I put a bandage on your back," said Hawk, standing and turning away in a single motion. "Lie down on your stomach and close your eyes."

The words echoed in Hawk's mind, mocking him. Angel didn't have to have her eyes closed for him to put a bandage on her, but it might prevent him from scaring her with his obvious hunger. There was no way for him to hide it from her, and no way to convince her that he would not take her no matter how hot and cruel the talons of need digging into him became.

And he had barely begun to give Angel the pleasure he wanted to.

Grimly, Hawk went into the boat's cabin. He took his time finding the first aid kit. He took even more time selecting a bandage, choosing among the varied sizes and shapes as though Angel's life depended on having just the right one.

Chapter 12

ANGEL LAY ON HER STOMACH, HER FACE TURNED AWAY from the cabin. She didn't want Hawk to see her confusion when he returned. Small tremors of desire and frustration shook her with every few breaths she took. Her body was flushed, aching, alive with nerve endings she had either forgotten or never known she had. With every heartbeat she wished that Hawk hadn't left, that he was still close to her, hands and mouth caressing her. She no longer cared that his lovemaking had brought her pain once before. She didn't believe that he would hurt her again. The Hawk who had just caressed her was not the same man who had taken her quickly, ruthlessly, a few days ago. This Hawk was a lover, not a predator.

His hands had trembled as he touched her.

Angel felt the thick pad shift as Hawk sat next to her. His warm fingers stroked lightly down the length of her spine. She shivered helplessly, wanting more.

"Are you cold?" asked Hawk, his hand poised above Angel's back. Though the sun was overhead, he knew that it was always cool on the water.

"Only when you stop touching me," said Angel.

Hawk's breath came in sharply. The sudden race of his heart made it all but impossible to unwrap the small bandage and smooth it into place on Angel's back.

"When you froze in my arms," he said softly, kissing the warm skin revealed by the crisscross of straps and the deeply cut back of Angel's bathing suit, "I thought that you didn't want me to touch you anymore."

"I was just . . . surprised," Angel said. The last word was a ragged intake of breath as she felt Hawk's tongue slide along her spine down to the sensitive small of her back. As the tip of his tongue touched her, his warm hand kneaded lightly from her ankle to the firm curves of her thigh.

"Why were you surprised?" murmured Hawk. He felt the ripple of pleasure take Angel when his teeth caressed the sensitive nerves at the base of her spine.

For a moment Angel's only answer was a moan that sounded like Hawk's name. Then, breathlessly, "I thought I knew myself, knew what it was to want someone." Her breath shivered out as she felt the heat and strength of his fingers sliding along her thigh, sending shock waves of need racing through her, melting her. "I was wrong, Hawk. Every time you touch me, I learn something new, something beautiful."

Again, without knowing it, Angel had both destroyed and created Hawk with a few words. He closed his eyes and rested his cheek in the warm hollow of her back, letting his breath pool moistly against her sweet skin. He had known nothing like her in his lifetime. She made him want to believe in things that he had long since abandoned, gentleness and generosity, human warmth, truth. She was a woman without lies, and he wanted to worship her.

Hawk's caressing palm slid down Angel's right leg again. The muscles of her leg shifted and flexed, giving back his touch. Her calf was smooth and curved, firm. There were faint scars beneath her tan ankle. His fingers stoppped, then gently found and memorized each reminder of old pain. Her skin was tight and warm, incredibly alive. He found it hard to believe that she had ever been injured, broken, an angel wounded and lost but for Derry's courage.

Hawk realized that he was holding Angel's ankle too tightly. "I'm sorry," he murmured, cradling her ankle in his hands as his lips and tongue smoothed across faded scars. "Did I hurt you?"

Angel's answer was a silent shake of her head that made sunlight gather and run through her hair. When she propped herself on her elbow and looked over her shoulder, she saw the naked intensity of Hawk's eyes and the mixture of emotions on his face as he caressed her. "Hawk?" she asked, uncertain. She had never seen him look quite like that, almost afraid.

"It's all right," he said quietly, smoothing his mustache over the arch of her foot. "I was just thinking of how much I owe Derry."

"Derry? Why?" asked Angel, searching Hawk's face with eyes as deep as the sea.

"You, sweet angel," murmured Hawk. "I owe him you. I owe him the most beautiful moments I've ever shared with anyone."

Tears magnified Angel's eyes for a moment, then hovered on the brink of release. Hawk moved swiftly, catching the tears on the tip of his tongue before they could fall. When Angel would have turned completely over, reaching for him, Hawk gently prevented her. He released the soft ties of the bathing suit that crisscrossed on her back. The suit fell away, revealing the firm curves of Angel's breasts. Where the sun had never touched her, her skin had the soft gleam of a pearl. Her nipples were taut, elegant, as pink as the tip of Hawk's tongue. He caressed each aching peak just enough to leave a sensual sheen of heat and moisture behind.

Angel was torn between passion and shyness. She had never felt so naked as she did now, not even when Hawk had undressed her completely. Then there had been the thick twilight intimacy of the bow. Now there was only sunlight and the clear brown fire of Hawk's eyes looking at her.

"You are more beautiful than I remembered," said Hawk, slowly, his voice husky as his tongue touched her again, heat and moisture making her ache, "and I remembered you as the most perfect woman I had ever seen."

"Hawk," said Angel softly, leaning against him as waves of longing took her, "you make me weak."

Her bright hair swirled across Hawk's naked stomach and the weight of her head was a sweet burning in his lap. He held his breath, knowing that Angel must have felt the hard insistence of his passion beneath her cheek. She didn't retreat. Hawk closed his eyes and knew that he would remember this moment long after every other woman had faded from his mind.

Very gently, Hawk lifted Angel in his arms. His lips moved over her face, caressing all the curves and hollows that he had already made his own. When his mouth brushed over hers, Angel moaned and threaded her fingers into his thick black hair. Her lips opened, wanting him, needing him, hungry for the sensual excitement of his mouth. Hawk's tongue slid between her teeth, thrusting slowly across her tongue, retreating, thrusting again, inciting her with the rhythms of love. Her arms tightened around him, pressing her breasts closer, and her hard nipples teased him as she twisted in his arms.

Without ending the slow movements of his tongue, Hawk moved his fingers down Angel's spine to the hollow of her back. As he slid her bathing suit down her legs, he touched for an instant the hidden, sensitive flesh within the shadow curve of her hips. Sensual fire shivered through Angel, making her moan into the heat of Hawk's mouth. His arm tightened around her waist, shifting her in his lap. When his hand returned from sliding the suit off her ankles, his fingertips caressed the smoothness of her inner legs and gently stroked the liquid heat hidden within the burnished blond curls.

Eyes closed, Angel felt herself come undone all over again, slow liquid rhythms uncoiling deep in her body. She shivered and sighed and melted over Hawk, knowing only his touch, pleasure shimmering and gathering in her. When he lifted her once more, then lay down with her on the dark quilt, Angel kissed his shoulders and the powerful muscles bunched in his arm. She felt the shiver of his response. She continued moving her lips and teeth and tongue across his chest, glorying in the throttled groan that she felt as much as heard. Then he claimed her mouth, filling her with a kiss so deep that she could only cling to him, melting again, shaping herself to the hard male lines of his body.

By the time Hawk lifted his mouth, Angel was making small sounds in her throat with each swift, shallow breath that she took. When his lips left hers, she protested with a word that became a cry of intense, unexpected pleasure when his tongue curled around her breast. His teeth raked lightly over her, feeling her response in the aching hardness of her nipple pressed against his tongue. He groaned and suckled her deeply, glorying in the passionate reflex shivering through her. When his hand touched her stomach, her breath stopped, and when his fingers found her liquid secrets she cried out in pleasure.

For long moments Hawk caressed Angel, drinking each soft cry, each hot shivering of her tender flesh. When he pressed lightly against the inside of her thigh, she shifted, revealing more of herself to him. Hawk's fingers traced each petal softness, each curve and hollow of her until Angel was twisting in slow motion, her hips blindly seeking. Very gently he deepened the caress, and was rewarded by feeling her shudder and melt and cling to his touch. He bent over her, drank her cries with hungry lips and tongue as he stroked her slowly, lost in the sweetness and intense excitement his touch called from her.

Angel moaned as muscles deep inside her body tensed and then relaxed, wildness gathering and melting through her in shimmering waves. Hawk saw surprise and pleasure equally mingled in her brilliant eyes. He knew then that he was the first man to touch Angel so deeply, to make her body melt and run like liquid fire. His lips sought her throat and he told her of her softness, the exciting beauty of her response, the warm sliding velvet of her body clinging deeply to his touch. She tried to say his name but could not form the word. Hawk had stolen the ability to speak from her lips. Slowly he made his caress less intimate.

"Am I hurting you, Angel?" asked Hawk, rubbing the words over the softness and heat of her lips.

She answered his question wordlessly, moving her hips, capturing his tantalizing touch, feeling him inside her again.

When Hawk's thumb found and teased the aching nub hidden in her softness, Angel cried out his name, trying to tell him about the incredible pleasure sweeping through her. Then his head bent and his mouth caressed her breasts, the shadow dimple of her navel, and finally the hot, honeyed secrets his touch had revealed.

The world fell away, leaving only the angel and the hawk who worshiped her, an angel's sweet cries of ecstasy filling the empty blue sky. And when she had no more breath, he gathered her along his body, sheltering her, bringing her gently back to earth.

Angel's eyes opened slowly, dazed with the extraordinary pleasure Hawk had given her. She wound her arms around him and rubbed her cheek against the heat of his chest. Strong fingers laced through her hair, bringing her even closer. She tilted her head back and looked into his clear, burning eyes. She wanted to tell him what she had felt, what she was still feeling, but she didn't know how. There were no words. With lips still flushed from Hawk's kisses, Angel gave him the only truth she knew.

"I love you, Hawk."

Angel saw the sudden darkening of Hawk's eyes, felt the shudder that ripped through his strong body.

"Angel," he said hoarsely, "I didn't mean—I didn't expect—" His breath caught. He kissed her eyelids tenderly, closing them, unable to bear the emotion shining in their blue-green depths. "I would tear out my throat rather than hurt you again," he said, his voice thick with emotion. Then, almost too softly for her to hear, "I've hated too long, Angel, hated too well. It's too late for me to love."

The hunger and regret in Hawk's voice were a pain as great as Angel's pleasure had been. Her hands went up to his face, cradling him, understanding and loving him, all of him, the hatred as well as the gentleness, the cold past as well as the shimmering present.

"It's you I love, not the idea of love itself," said Angel, kissing Hawk's lips as gently as he had first kissed hers. "You don't have to love me in return. Let me share the next

weeks with you. I won't ask for anything more. Except"—
Angel's eyes changed, shadows where brilliance had been
—"don't tell me when you're going to go. Just go. I'll
know then that it's over."

"Angel—" Hawk's voice was ragged.

"It's all right, my love," she murmured, kissing him,
her eyes brilliant again. "I'm strong enough to love you and
then set you free. Just don't deny me what you can give me.
A few weeks of flight on the wings of a hawk."

Hawk's body tightened as he resisted the gentle pressure
of the hands pulling him down to Angel's mouth. Then her
tongue teased his lips, using the gliding touches he had
taught her to unlock the warmth of his mouth.

"Please, Hawk," she whispered, "don't deny my love."

With a nearly soundless groan, Hawk opened his mouth
and drank deeply of the wild sweetness that waited for him.
For a long time he knew nothing but Angel's taste, the
supple heat of her body moving against his. The hunger that
he had kept leashed threatened to explode, tearing him
apart. His arms closed tightly around her, stilling the
sensual movements of her body.

"You don't know what you're doing," said Hawk, his
voice harsh with the cost of subduing his savage hunger.

"I'm inexperienced, not stupid," said Angel, smiling at
him with a smile as old as Eve. "I know that you gave me
everything, taking nothing for yourself. Now I want to give
you something."

"Angel, Angel," Hawk said, his voice tight and low as
he fought against himself and the sensual promise of her
body. "I want you too much. I'm afraid I'll hurt you again.
You don't know—!"

"Then show me, Hawk," she murmured, rubbing her
lips across his chest, finding and caressing his dark male

nipples with her tongue, touching him as he had touched her. "I want to be your woman."

"Are you sure?" asked Hawk, his voice so tight it vibrated with suppressed emotion. He stood swiftly, as though afraid to be touching her if she decided not to risk his passion after all.

Angel looked up at the dark, powerful man standing so close to her. She sensed that he was remembering the first time, when he had taken her casually, carelessly, hurting her. She saw the waiting and the strength coiled in his muscular body, and the hunger straining against the worn fabric of his jeans. Deliberately she lifted her hand over him. At the first touch of her fingers, he tightened like a drawn bow.

"'I'm sure," Angel said, enjoying the dark blaze of passion that leaped in Hawk's eyes as her hand moved over him. "You'll have to teach me what you want, though. Will you mind that?"

Hawk's laugh was thick, short. His hips moved sinuously, increasing the pressure of Angel's hand caressing him. Angel's fingernails raked lightly down, a fierce yet gentle touch she had learned from him. Hawk's hands closed over hers. For an instant he held her hard against the rigid ache of his desire, then he lifted her hand, biting her palm and the soft pads of her fingers.

"How do you know how to touch me?" he asked, his voice husky, his body hot with desire.

"You told me," Angel whispered, capturing one of Hawk's hands, biting him with the same leashed wildness he had just shown to her. "Like that."

Hawk thought of the other ways he had caressed Angel, the intimate taste of her, the soft cries and liquid fire of her pleasure. She had been inexperienced, yet she had responded to him with an abandon that had all but destroyed his control. Innocent, generous, and sensual beyond his dreams.

"Angel," he said thickly, taking her mouth with a hot, deep kiss, "you deserve a better man than me."

"There is no better man," she said simply, certainty and love in every word.

"There's a world full of them," said Hawk, his voice almost harsh.

"Not for me."

Each word was clear, distinct. Hawk closed his eyes, knowing that Angel was neither foolish nor insincere, knowing that she loved him whether he deserved it or not, whether he loved her or not. He knew also that he should step back, fly away, leave her to find the man she deserved to have.

"There's nothing I can teach you but pain," said Hawk, his voice almost desperate.

"Hawk," Angel said softly, "there's nothing you can teach me *about* pain. Everything of me that can be broken, has been. Mind, body, heart. Don't be afraid of hurting me. Don't hate yourself for making love to me. I'm not a child. I'm a woman. Your woman, for as long as you want me."

Slowly Angel's hands moved to the fastening of Hawk's jeans. Emotion seethed in her, something more than the sensual hunger that he had just taught her. She ached with a need to bring him pleasure, to know that she could touch him as deeply as he had touched her. The force of her emotions made her hands tremble so badly that her normally quick fingers were unresponsive.

Hawk watched Angel with dark, hooded eyes, afraid to believe. He made no move to either help or stop her as her fingers fumbled at the buckle of his belt, trying to work the familiar object from a totally unfamiliar angle. By the time the belt was finally unfastened, Angel felt clumsy and inadequate, remembering the smooth skill with which Hawk had undressed her. The metal buttons on his jeans were even worse than the buckle. It was like trying to cut her hair in a mirror. Every move she made was opposite of the one she should have made.

And then Angel realized that there were many ways to say no. Hawk had already tried most of them. He was a skilled lover. She was not. Perhaps that was what he had been trying to say kindly. He was hungry, yes. Any man would have been in his position. Arousal wasn't love, though. It wasn't even caring. It was a simple biological reflex that inevitably resulted from a certain level of stimulation. There was nothing really personal about it. He had hurt her and felt guilty about it. So he had taken away her memory of pain and left in its place memories of pleasure. But she had mistaken his intention, seeing more in his touch than there had been. Again.

Angel's hands dropped to her lap as she abandoned her futile efforts. She turned and stretched out on her stomach on the dark quilt. As she lay down, she caught a corner of the quilt, covering her nakedness.

"I'm sorry, Hawk," she said quietly. "I misunderstood. Again."

Though Angel wasn't facing him, her words were clear, as clear as the shadows that Hawk had seen in her eyes in the instant before she turned away.

"What did you misunderstand?" asked Hawk.

Angel lay quietly, building a stained glass rose in her mind, scarlet petals curving against a radiant sun.

"Angel?" murmured Hawk, touching her bare shoulder with hesitant fingertips.

The rose trembled and shattered into crimson fragments.

Angel's fingernails dug her palms. She took in a deep

breath and let it out slowly. She spoke without looking at Hawk, seeing nothing at all.

"I didn't realize that you were simply feeling sorry for me," said Angel, her voice almost even.

Almost, but not quite. It was the difference that tore at Hawk. "Angel," he said softly, stroking the warm smoothness of her shoulder. "That's not—"

"Please, don't," she interrupted with aching calm. "It's all right, Hawk. You don't have to feel sorry for me anymore. As you told me, it's a poor substitute for passion."

"I told you?" Hawk's hand hesitated. "What are you talking about?"

"You. Just now, when you let me find out for myself how inept a lover I am." Angel's laugh was tight, almost choked. "I don't blame you for wanting a woman who can at least unbutton a damned pair of jeans!"

Hawk tugged the quilt out of Angel's hand, leaving her naked again. When she rolled over and reached blindly to retrieve the cover, he caught her hand beneath his. Gently he guided her fingers over the fastenings on his jeans.

"I don't want someone who's undressed a thousand men," said Hawk, his voice husky. "I want a woman who wants me so badly that her hands shake too much to unfasten my jeans. I've never had a woman like that, Angel. I didn't even know a woman like that existed. Until now."

The last metal button slid free of its narrow hole. Hawk moved Angel's hand inside the worn blue fabric. A deep thread of sound escaped his throat when he pressed her palm against the rigid flesh beneath his bathing suit.

"That isn't pity you're feeling," said Hawk, his voice gritty and his eyes almost black with passion. "It's more need than I've ever had for a woman. And that's good," he added, pulling off his bathing suit and jeans with a single twisting motion, "because you're more woman than I've ever had."

Desire went through Angel like shock waves through glass, shattering her. Hawk was the most beautiful thing she had ever seen, his body powerful and taut and as hard as the stone cliffs lining the bay. But unlike the cliffs, he responded when she touched him. For long moments he permitted her sensual exploration, unable to conceal the tremors that shook him. Then he groaned aloud and lay down next to her, pulling her body along the hot length of his.

"No more, Angel," Hawk muttered thickly, burying his lips in her neck, "not now. I need you too much."

Hawk rolled over swiftly, pinning Angel beneath his body as he settled between her legs. His hips moved against her, telling her exactly how much he needed her. She shivered and cried out, twisting against him wildly, instinctively, running the sensitive soles of her feet up and down his flexed calves, trying to capture him inside her. His hand stroked down her body and found the liquid heat of her, a single touch that sent tiny, passionate convulsions rippling through her body.

"Now, Hawk," she pleaded.

"My sweet Angel," he whispered against her lips as his hot flesh moved slowly over her in a long, inflaming caress.

Hawk took Angel's mouth and her body with the same smooth motion, becoming a part of her, melting her around him. He moved with aching care, afraid that he would hurt her in his need. But there was no pain, no hesitation on Angel's part. He fit her perfectly, hot and very close, caressing her even when he was still. She smiled against his throat and murmured words that had no meaning, simply sounds telling him of her pleasure.

Hawk moved slowly despite the need hammering inside him. He savored each tiny motion of their bodies so perfectly matched. Angel's legs shifted, circling Hawk's hips as she sought to know more of him, wanting him even more deeply inside her. Her hungry seeking took Hawk's breath away. Reflexively, he gave her what they both wanted, holding back nothing. With each speeding motion, each instant of shaking pleasure, he knew he should withdraw slightly, not take the chance of hurting her. Then he felt the intimate pulses of her release all around him and it was too late for anything but the need he had so long denied. His body arched into her, tearing a cry of ecstasy from her and from him in the same instant. He shuddered and arched again and again, giving himself to her as deeply as she had given herself to him.

For slow, sweet minutes Hawk and Angel lay spent in each other's arms, drifting slowly back to an awareness of sunlight and sky and the soft, subtle movements of the boat beneath their joined bodies. Hawk smoothed his lips against the tangled, silky fall of Angel's hair. He kissed her temple, her cheek, the secret inner curve of her ear, the corners of her smile. Her fingers moved down his back to the powerful muscles of his buttocks and beyond, tracing his shadow curves as he had once traced hers. Hawk groaned and tightened inside her, sending sensations streaking through flesh that was still aroused, hypersensitive. Very gently, she caressed him again, learning the contours of his maleness as he had once learned her softer female curves.

"Angel," said Hawk, his low voice both husky and amused, "do you know what you're doing?" Before she could answer, he moved deeply inside her, stealing her breath. He drank Angel's choked cry from her lips as his hips moved again. "Is this what you want?" he asked thickly, feeling hunger coil deep inside him again with each hot, sliding caress of her flesh over his.

Hawk saw surprise widen Angel's blue-green eyes, felt the clinging of her body as she instinctively sought to increase the beautiful, gliding pressure of his intimate caress. Passion tightened in Hawk, but its talons were no longer painful, merely sharp, because he knew his hunger was met and matched in Angel's straining softness.

"Hawk?" she asked, her breath short already, her eyes smoky with the passion he could call out of her between one instant and the next. "I thought men couldn't—not so soon."

"A few minutes ago I would have sworn you were right," said Hawk. Then his body arched into hers, glorying in her response, the sweet clinging as she moaned and her hand closed around him, learning and caressing the tight flesh hidden within the midnight roughness of his hair, inflaming him until he could hardly breathe. "I was wrong," he said, his voice gritty with passion. "When a hawk and an angel make love, the rules change."

The tiny, electronic alarm on Hawk's watch cut through his sleep as delicately and ruthlessly as a steel cutter through glass. When Hawk moved to shut off the alarm, he realized that there was a soft, warm weight curled against him. Memories came back in a sensual flood that made him acutely aware of every sweet inch of Angel's body pressed along his. The memories sent heat and blood hammering through him until both pooled thickly between his legs, passion's sweet pressure crying for release. Hawk ached to be inside Angel again, feeling her heat and firm softness surrounding him.

The endless urgency of Hawk's need for Angel shocked

him. He had felt nothing like it with any other woman, even
when he was young and Jenna had teased him to the point of
violence.

Hawk reached up and switched on the small, battery-
powered light. Soft yellow illumination revealed the triangular bow bed. Angel's hair was a pale golden fire burning
against Hawk's dark arm. Her lashes cast long, fringed
shadows and her lips were very red, still slightly swollen
from the passionate kisses she had given and taken. When
he bent and brushed his mouth against hers, he felt her
smile and heard her gentle murmur as she snuggled sleepily
closer to his warmth. He knew that she wasn't awake; her
movement toward him was an unconscious reflex as deep
and true as her loving of him had been.

"Angel," Hawk whispered. Then, even more softly,
"My sweet, generous woman. What am I going to do with
you?"

Hawk's hand slid beneath the covers, finding and touching Angel's breast, kneading it gently as his lips nestled in
the curve of her neck. Slowly, languidly, Hawk caressed
Angel's body, calling to her wordlessly until she moved
with his touch, neither asleep nor yet awake, suspended in a
beautiful sensual dream. Her body melted, wanting him.

"Angel," said Hawk, his voice husky as he parted her
legs. "*Angel.*"

Her eyelids fluttered open in reponse to Hawk's deep-
voiced call. He waited until he knew that Angel was awake,
aware, looking into his eyes . . . and in that instant he slid
into her, taking her completely. His slow, sensual invasion
undid Angel. Her soft cries of ecstasy ripped through
Hawk, undoing him in turn. He flew with her, spiraling
quickly upward into a sky that was neither cold nor dark,
but hot and bright and infinite.

When Angel had the breath and the strength to speak

again, she whispered her love against the warmth and power of Hawk's shoulder. His answer was an exquisitely gentle movement that made her cry out and cling to him all over again.

"Hawk," she said finally, her breath uneven, "we're going to miss the tide again."

Hawk murmured something against Angel's neck.

"What?" she asked.

Reluctantly, he lifted his lips from her fragrant skin. "I set the alarm a bit early," he admitted.

Angel's eyes lit with understanding and laughter. "Such a clever hawk," she said. "I'll have to reward you."

"You already have," said Hawk, smiling.

Angel's breath stopped at the beauty of his smile. She touched his lips with fingers that trembled, measuring anew the depth of her love for this hard and gentle man.

"What are you thinking?" asked Hawk, wondering at the emotions he sensed quivering through Angel.

"How much I love you."

Hawk's eyes closed. "I shouldn't let you," he said fiercely. With a harsh sound Hawk pulled Angel against him and buried his head between her breasts. "Oh, God, what am I going to do? I can't love you and I can't let you go!"

Gently, Angel stroked Hawk's hair, trying to comfort him, to tell him that she understood. And, sadly, she did. She realized that every time she told him of her love, it brought him pain rather than pleasure. He didn't want to hurt her. She knew that as certainly as she knew that she loved him. Yet he believed himself incapable of love. And, believing that, he would hurt her as surely as she loved him. She knew that, too, and accepted it as she had learned to accept so many painful things.

With a skill won at great cost from the past, Angel

reached for the serenity of the rose. When she had achieved it, she stirred in Hawk's embrace.

"I know what you're going to do," said Angel, kissing Hawk gently, smiling against his lips. "You're going fishing. We're going to catch a beautiful dawn salmon."

Hawk lifted his head and looked at her. Tears came to Angel in a burning instant as she saw the pain and sadness and regret in Hawk's clear dark eyes.

"It's all right," she said, stroking his face. "Please, Hawk. Believe me. I know you'll do everything you can not to hurt me. I don't ask any more than that of you. Don't ask it of yourself. Please."

Hawk saw his own sadness and need not to hurt reflected in Angel's haunted eyes. And he saw something more, her certainty and her love. She understood his limitations, his lifetime beyond the closed circle of human warmth, his inability to love her as she deserved to be loved.

Yet she loved him anyway.

Hawk bowed to that, and to Angel. Very gently he kissed her palm, accepting her as she had accepted him.

Chapter 13

THE MINUTES AND HOURS, DAYS AND WEEKS WITH HAWK swept by, each with its own aching beauty. Angel didn't allow herself to count the days, to add them up and discover the end of summer coming toward her with each sunset. Loving and losing Grant had taught her not to live in the past. Loving and knowing she would lose Hawk had taught her not to live in the future. Instead she lived in each moment, loving Hawk more with each touch, each smile, each shared memory.

"Angie?"

Angel looked up, startled out of her thoughts by Derry's call. The tiny silver bells hanging from her ears rang sweetly with her sudden movement. "I'm in my studio," she answered.

Derry swung lithely into the room. He had long since overcome any awkwardness with his crutches. Nor had there been any awkwardness over Angel's changed relation-

ship with Hawk. Angel knew that Hawk had talked to
Derry, but she didn't know what had been said. Any fear
she might have had that Derry would resent Angel loving a
man other than Grant was erased when Derry had hugged
her and told her that she had never looked more beautiful.

"Where's Hawk?"

"On the—"

"Phone," Derry finished, grimacing. "Who is it this
time?"

Angel shrugged and smiled sadly. "Tokyo, I guess. He's
already talked with London, New York, Houston, L.A.,
and whoever was vacationing on Maui." In the last week
Hawk had spent more and more time on the phone. Despite
her determination not to count, Angel knew that Hawk had
already stayed past his original time limit. The complex,
interlocking business transactions that he had mentioned
when he first came to the island were coming to fruition.
"From what I've gathered," said Angel, "things are
getting to the crisis stage."

"Hawk and I will probably take the same plane off the
island," said Derry, referring to the fact that tomorrow he
would get his cast removed and fly to Harvard; for Hawk
had bought Eagle Head, paying more than Derry thought
the land was worth. Derry saw the quick flash of agony that
Angel couldn't wholly conceal. "Hey," said Derry quickly. "I'll visit you in Seattle." He didn't say anything about
Hawk visiting her, because it never occurred to Derry that
Hawk would not be in Seattle too.

Angel smiled and kissed Derry's cheek. "Summers and
holidays," she agreed. But the instant Derry could no
longer see her face, Angel's mouth turned down in a sad
curve. Yes, Derry would come back to her.

Hawk would not.

"I think I'll take my sketch pad and go up to Eagle

Head,'' said Angel. She looked at the wall clock. ''If Hawk gets off the phone before five, give him directions to the old Smith homestead. The raspberries are ripe, and he's never gone berrying.''

''He got his salmon, though,'' said Derry.

Angel smiled. Yes, Hawk had caught his dawn salmon, had known the thrilling primal power of the fish as it leaped and tail-walked across the radiant sea. The look of awe and delight on Hawk's face as he had felt the seething, silver life was something Angel would remember long after the pain of losing him had faded. If it ever faded. She had never known anyone like Hawk. She could only guess what life would feel like when he was gone.

''I still don't know why he turned that salmon loose,'' said Derry.

''It was too beautiful to kill.''

''So were the other fish he caught, but we ate them anyway, and quarreled over the last scrap.''

''They weren't the first salmon of dawn,'' said Angel simply, remembering and loving Hawk until she thought she would break.

Derry hesitated, seeing the depth of emotion that transformed Angel. ''I may have dragged you out of that wreck,'' said Derry softly, ''but it's Hawk who brought you alive. I'm so glad, Angie. There were times when I was afraid that I had condemned you to a lifetime of unhappiness.''

Angel hugged Derry a little fiercely, then grabbed her sketch pad and fled. She thought of Derry's words as she climbed the steep trail to the top of Eagle Head. The small chiming bells around her wrist and ankle kept her company with each step. She was still thinking about Derry's words as she sat on the very edge of the summit, sketch pad forgotten in her lap. Before her was the Inside Passage, the restless sea and ragged islands crowned in evergreens. Peak after peak fell away to the east, receding into a distance veiled with a blue so deep that it verged on black. Both harsh and serene, the country called to her senses as nothing had—until Hawk. He was like the land itself, a paradox of stone and warmth, midnight and noon, the enigmatic distance of the horizon and the intimate textures of the air, the salt of the sea and the sweetness of berries heavy with the promise of harvest.

"You love this land, don't you?"

Hawk's quiet question didn't startle Angel. Beneath her concentration on the view had been a growing awareness of Hawk's presence, a subtle certainty like the knowledge of her own heartbeat deep inside her body.

"More than anything except you," said Angel simply. Then she realized that she had done exactly what she had been trying so hard to avoid; she had spoken of her love for Hawk. She didn't want to hurt him with the very words that should give him pleasure. "What time is it?" she asked, speaking quickly, before there would be any silence that might seem like a demand that Hawk speak to her of love. She didn't expect that of him. She never had, once she understood what his life had been like.

"It's almost five."

"Do you have time to go berrying?" she asked.

"I made time."

Angel looked into Hawk's dark eyes and saw the future coming down on her in a soundless rush. He would be leaving soon. It was there in his eyes, in his voice, in the fact that he had made time to be with her.

"Angel—" said Hawk tightly, seeing the shadows deepen in her eyes, knowing why.

Overhead an eagle called. The high, savage whistle

descended until there was nothing left but silence and empty sky.

"We'd better hurry," said Angel, coming to her feet in a graceful surge. "We haven't much time."

As Angel moved, silver bells cried and chimed. The exquisite sounds went into Hawk like a thousand tiny knives. His arms came around Angel, lifting her off her feet. He held her with all his strength and kissed her as though he knew that the world was crumbling around them. Time stopped until Hawk finally released Angel, allowing her to lead him down the rocky path. Neither of them spoke, content to share the other's presence with simple touches, gentle smiles, swift looks, as though each feared the other had vanished between one heartbeat and the next.

The silence remained while they drove to the berry patch. It was at the end of an abandoned, rutted road. Once, a long time ago, there had been a farmhouse, neat fields, and the orderly rows of a home garden. Now the fields were nearly consumed by resurgent forest. All that remained were waist-high fieldstone fences where raspberry bushes strove and twined thickly, growing over stone and field alike. An ancient, magnificent climbing rose mantled the ruined stone chimney that was the only remainder of the farmhouse. From this bush had come the crimson rose that bloomed deep within Angel's mind, triumphant and serene. She had first seen the Smith homestead and the climbing rose as a child. She had been haunted by the rose ever since.

As though at a distance, Angel heard the car trunk close. Only then did she realize that Hawk had left the car and was standing near the rosebush, waiting for her. He had empty pails in one hand, a picnic basket in the other, and a thick quilt over his shoulder. Angel took a deep breath, letting the future slide away, taking all shadows with it. There was only this instant, Hawk waiting for her, smiling his heart-breaking smile.

Angel got out of the car and walked toward Hawk, wrapped in the sweet chiming of bells.

"A picnic," she said, looking at the basket and loving Hawk for thinking of it, smiling at him in return. "What a wonderful idea."

"I have ulterior motives," he said, his voice deep. "As much as I like Derry, I want some time just with you."

Angel's smile slipped, then steadied. She knew how Hawk felt. They were alone only when they were on the boat or late at night when the house was all darkness. There hadn't been enough time for just being together, sharing the silences and small touches that spoke so eloquently of their pleasure in each other. Not enough time.

And then Angel found herself asking silently how much time was left.

Deliberately, Angel tilted her face up to the old climbing rose. A single blossom remained, its petals soft and quivering, gathering the rich afternoon light into each luminous crimson curve. She closed her eyes and wondered if the fragile rose knew that winter was closer with each sunset.

Hawk bent and kissed Angel's lips gently. He sensed the sadness in her, knew its cause, and was helpless to ease it. The thought of how he was hurting Angel tore at Hawk, making him bleed in ways he had never imagined possible. He knew that the longer he spent with her, the greater the hurt would be each time she was brought up against his inability to love her as she should be loved.

Every day he had promised himself that he would leave her, set her free, stop hurting her. And every day he had awakened and seen an angel sheltered in the curve of his body. She would look at him, smiling, and he would know that he could not leave her. Not yet. He had to taste for a few more hours the miracle of her love.

"Where should we begin?" asked Hawk, lifting his mouth just enough to let Angel answer.

"In the center," she murmured, rubbing her lips against his. "I know a path through the center of the brambles. That's where the sweetest berries are. Surrounded by thorns."

"And mosquitoes?"

"A few," admitted Angel. "No such thing as a free lunch, remember?"

Hawk smiled. "I remember. That's why I brought insect repellent. I didn't want anything but me biting your smooth skin."

Angel felt a frisson of desire race through her. The more Hawk touched her, the more she wanted to be touched by him. She never tired of his lovemaking, of having him become a part of her.

"It's in my pocket. Would you get it?" Hawk asked.

He held out his hands to her, showing that they were fully occupied with buckets and picnic basket and couldn't be expected to pull a bottle of repellent from a tight pocket. First, Angel tried the back pockets of Hawk's jeans, which was where she carried insect repellent when she thought to bring it. Hawk's back pockets were empty. She tried his front pockets, wiggling her hands into the worn, confining cloth.

"Nothing," Angel said.

"Keep searching," said Hawk, the corners of his mouth curling in a secret smile beneath his mustache. "You'll find it."

For a few seconds Angel took Hawk at his word and

wriggled her fingers around in his pockets. Then she felt the heat and hardness of him swelling beneath his jeans. "You're teasing me," she said, trying to look angry and failing utterly.

"I would have sworn I was the one being teased," said Hawk, his voice deep and rich with hidden laughter. Then Angel's hand moved inside his pocket and his breath caught. "My *shirt* pocket, Angel."

She smiled with an innocence that was belied by the dancing light of her eyes. Slowly, very slowly, Angel removed her hands from Hawk's pockets. She found the insect repellent in the breast pocket of his cotton flannel shirt. She applied the pungent lotion to Hawk's exposed skin and to her own. Then she put the small squeeze bottle back—in his front jean pocket.

"The repellent only works against insects," said Hawk.

"That's a relief," said Angel, smiling with an invitation that made Hawk's eyes gleam.

As Angel turned and ran toward the raspberry brambles, the silver bells at her ankle and wrist shivered with music. For a moment Hawk stood and watched her graceful flight, aching with a hunger that went much deeper than the temporary urgency of desire. Then he began to run, moving lightly despite his burden. Angel was soon lost to sight in the twists and turns of the bramble patch, but the sweet silver cries of the bells called to him, telling him that she was close.

Hawk caught up to Angel in the clearing at the center of the huge raspberry patch. The air was thick with the delicate perfume of ripening fruit. Leaves shimmered and stirred lazily beneath a caressing wind. Canes laden with fruit arched richly against the cobalt sky, and the serrated green foliage quivered with golden sunlight.

"Derry was right," said Hawk, turning to Angel. "You know every beautiful place on the island. Or maybe it's simply that you bring beauty to every place you are."

"It must be you," Angel said, her voice husky. "I don't remember the homestead being like this before."

Angel took the buckets from Hawk's hand and waited while he spread the quilt and put the picnic basket in the shade. When he came back to her, she silently held out a bucket to him.

"Berrying is a cross between clamming and crabbing," said Angel, lacing her fingers through Hawk's as she led him toward the bushes heavy with fruit. "Like clams, raspberries aren't going anywhere. Like crabs, raspberry bushes will get you if you're careless."

"No free lunch?" suggested Hawk wryly.

"No free lunch," agreed Angel. "The first rule of berrying is that if the fruit were easy to pick, something would have already picked it."

Hawk smiled slightly. "Any other rules?"

"Don't eat more than one berry for every one you put in the bucket. Otherwise you'll get sick."

"Learned that the hard way, didn't you?" guessed Hawk.

"Is there another way to learn?"

Angel showed Hawk how to choose the best fruit, ripe without being mushy, tart without being green. They picked side by side, sharing a companionable silence.

"Is this one ripe?" asked Hawk finally, holding out a berry to Angel.

"Only one way to be sure," said Angel, opening her mouth slightly.

Obediently, Hawk fed Angel the berry. She made a clicking sound with her tongue.

"A bit tart," she said. She looked at a cluster of raspberries hanging from a nearby cane. Picking the most perfect berry, she turned back to Hawk. "Try this one."

Hawk sucked the raspberry from Angel's fingertips, licking her skin as he did. He closed his eyes and made a sound of pleasure. "It tastes like you," he murmured. "Incredible."

Hawk opened his mouth again in silent demand. Angel popped in another berry. He opened his mouth again, and then again, until she laughed and stood on tiptoe, kissing him. The taste of Hawk and raspberries swept over her senses. Suddenly she clung to him, kissing him as wildly as he had kissed her on Eagle Head. When the embrace finally ended, they were both breathing raggedly.

"How many more berries does Mrs. Carey need?" asked Hawk, his eyes a clear brown fire.

"Buckets and buckets."

Hawk swore softly. "Then we'd better get to it," he said, reluctantly stepping back from Angel.

They returned to picking, working quickly, watching each other with secret, sidelong glances. They filled their buckets, emptied them into a larger container, and returned to picking.

"You're eating more than you're putting in the bucket," said Angel after a time.

Hawk turned fully toward her. His mouth was stained with the rich juice of the fruit he had been sneaking like a child. "But if I get sick, I have something better than a hot water bottle to curl up with," he pointed out.

Smiling, Hawk and Angel both returned to picking. Then Angel found an extraordinary raspberry. Full, richly colored, all but bursting with sweetness, the berry glowed like a jewel in her palm. She set down her bucket and ran to Hawk.

"This is the most perfect raspberry I've ever seen," Angel said, holding it between her thumb and forefinger. "Open up."

"You found it," said Hawk, looking at the transparent red juice staining Angel's lips. "It should be for you."

"It's got your name on it."

The corners of Hawk's mouth curled up gently. He looked at the bright, unblemished berry. "I don't see my name."

"The light must be wrong for you," said Angel, letting the raspberry roll down and nestle in her palm. "See? Right there. Your name."

Hawk looked, but he saw only the love implicit in Angel's gift. Slowly he bent his head. He licked the berry from her palm, then kissed the spot where the fruit had rested. The ache he felt tearing through him had nothing to do with desire, everything to do with the angel who watched him with love in her eyes. He wanted to ask where her softness and strength had come from, to delicately touch every secret of her past and future, to know if he could ever love as she did, sweetness and fire and courage in equal measure. Yet even as he opened his mouth, he knew he couldn't ask that of her. So he asked the only question he could; and Angel heard the other question beneath it, the one Hawk couldn't ask.

"Are these wild raspberries?" asked Hawk, looking at the thicket that all but surrounded him.

"No. They're like a house cat that has gone feral," said Angel. "Bred and created by man, for man, and then abandoned to live alone. Most things that are treated like that wither and die. Some things survive . . . and in the right season the strongest of the survivors bear a sweet, wild fruit that is the most beautiful thing on earth. Like you, Hawk."

Hawk let the bucket of raspberries slip from his hand. He picked up Angel in a single, swift movement, and then he held her tightly, saying all that he could, her name a song on his lips until his mouth found hers in a kiss that left both of them shaking. He carried her to the quilt and undressed her as though it were the first time, his hands exquisitely gentle, his mouth a sweet fire consuming her. When she could bear no more he came to her, filling her mind and her body, loving her in the only way he could.

It was the same later that night, a beauty that destroyed and created Angel, death and rebirth in the arms of the man she loved. She touched Hawk equally, fire and hunger, the promise of her mouth both hot and sweet, innocent and knowing, worshiping him until he pulled her around him and was burned to his soul by an angel's ecstatic fire.

Long after Angel fell asleep in his arms, Hawk lay awake, watching the patterns of moonlight and darkness beyond Angel's windows. Then he slowly eased away from Angel, holding his breath for fear that she would wake. If she awakened, he knew that he would not have the strength to leave her. He would stay and stay, drinking from the well of her love, giving nothing in return.

If he stayed, he would destroy her.

For long, long minutes, Hawk stood beside the bed and watched his angel sleep. He bent down, aching to touch her, but did not. His hand hesitated over his pillow before he turned and walked soundlessly out of the house, into the night.

Sunlight woke Angel, sunlight spilling in golden magnificence across her pillow. She murmured sleepily and reached for Hawk. Her hand touched emptiness. She sat up quickly, looking around. And then she froze. Resting on Hawk's pillow was a small candy cane wrapped with a shiny green ribbon.

Angel put her head in her hands and wept, knowing that Hawk had gone.

"I don't have to leave for Harvard right away," said Derry, looking at Angel's wan face and determined smile. "I'll wait until Hawk wraps up whatever he had to do and comes back."

"Don't be silly," said Angel, her words calm, her eyes too dark in a face that was too pale, her skin almost transparent.

She said no more. There was no reason to disturb Derry's assumption that Hawk had left her only long enough to put his business in order. Derry had enough to worry about with moving thousands of miles and learning to walk on his leg again. He didn't need to add Angel to his list of problems. Nor was there any reason for Derry to stay with her. Not really. She needed to be alone, but she didn't think Derry would understand that.

"Do you need any help packing the last of your things?" she asked.

"No. Matt, Dave, and I got it done while you were out berrying yesterday. Hawk told me not to worry about the furniture or anything."

Emotion seethed through Angel, fighting against the serenity that she had finally imposed over her grief. It was only yesterday that she and Hawk had been together, feeding berries to each other and laughing, staining their hands and mouths with the bursting summer sweetness of ripe fruit until passion flared and they kissed each other deeply and tasted a wilder, sweeter fruit.

"All I have left here is the suitcase that I'm taking on the plane," added Derry, "and it's already packed."

A horn sounded out front. One of Derry's friends who was also going to the mainland had come to take him to the ferry. The horn sounded again. Angel looked at the clock in her studio.

"You'd better hurry," she said, bending down and picking up the small suitcase Derry had set by the door.

"Angie—"

Angel turned and walked into Derry's arms. For a long moment they hugged each other.

"I love you, Derry," said Angel, her eyes bright with tears. "I'll always be here if you need me."

"I don't feel right about leaving you," said Derry, concern showing in his voice. "I know how much you're missing Hawk."

Angel looked up and saw Derry's love and concern for her. "Get out of here before I cry all over the shirt I just ironed for you," she said softly, giving him a smile that trembled.

Derry smiled in return. He handed Angel a piece of paper. "I'll be at that number by eleven o'clock tonight. Call me, okay? I'm going to be homesick as hell."

Derry kissed Angel quickly, grabbed his suitcase, and walked down the hall, limping slightly. Angel watched him from the window until she could see nothing but her own tears. Then she went down to the beach and walked until darkness came and she could see nothing at all. She had not known how much she loved Hawk until she felt the pain of his loss. It was like breathing shattered glass, each instant a new lesson in agony.

Angel paced through the empty house until it was time to call Derry. After she called she went to her studio, turned on every light, and began to sketch. As the dark hours melted into dawn she drew and discarded design after design, seeking one that would summarize her pain and love, and in doing so, forge new beauty from the shards of the past.

By dawn Angel had found her design.

She worked all day, submerging herself in the demands of her creation. She enlarged the proportions of the sketch until it would fill a panel five feet tall and three feet wide. She traced the working drawing onto heavy paper, using a black marker as wide as the lead bead holding the glass would be. Then she pinned the working drawing to the wall and numbered each segment of paper according to the color she had chosen for it.

Choosing the glass consumed several hours. Every piece had to blend with and enhance the bronze and brown flashed glass she had chosen for the major figure. She tried several shades of gold muff glass before she found one that she liked. Then she went to her bedroom, propped the muff against the floor-to-ceiling window there, and watched light pour through. She turned the glass several times. Suddenly, she stood absolutely still. The hair on her arms stirred in primal response as she looked into the extraordinary flawed glass and saw the suggestion of a woman's awakening smile.

Quickly Angel marked out the area to be cut. Though she never cut glass piecemeal, this time she did. She pinned the pattern to the light table and cut out the golden cloud that had first emerged on her sketch pad. As soon as the cloud was cut, she broke another rule and continued working out of sequence. She took a fine brush and filled in the vision she had seen in the glass. The shadow of a smile, the suggestion of eyes slowly opening, a few elegant strokes to evoke hair rippling in the wind, and it was done.

She turned on the kiln and went back to choosing glass. She worked for hours until she realized that there was only one choice. Since the accident, she had refused to use clear glass, for to see its shards glittering was to see again wreckage and death. Yet there was no other backdrop possible for the summation she had chosen to set in glass—daggers of beveled crystal glass radiating outward from the focal point of the picture, a hawk's extended talon as the bird swooped down out of an empty sky.

Hours slipped into days as Angel worked. She ate when the demands of her stomach became too insistent to ignore and slept when her eyes refused to focus on her work. She dreaded those times, the night closing around her, her heart as empty as the echoing rooms of the house. She began to wear her silver jewelry all the time, letting the tiny cries of the bells speak for her, filling the silent void.

The hawk itself took several days, for each bronzed highlight was brought out by acid eating into different levels of the brown and bronze flashed glass. Etching was a long, patience-stretching process but Angel sought its demands eagerly. When she worked she was totally absorbed, unable to think or feel beyond the instant in which she lived. Finally she finished the hawk. More than thirty pieces of etched glass lay gleaming on her worktable, each brown feather highlighted in a fabulous network of bronze.

At last, Angel was ready to assemble the pieces. She took the polished mahogany frame she had chosen to set the glass in and fastened the frame to a large, unusual table. It was rather like a drafting table on wheels, except that it was a table within a frame consisting of two thick, metallic runners with grooves deep enough to hold both the table surface and the frame of whatever Angel was working on at the time. The table surface itself was rigged so that it could slide out and the frame could be tilted vertically, allowing light to pour through the panel while still holding it securely in place. Angel used the table to build and display stained glass panels that were too large for her to lift easily.

Angel worked steadily, disregarding midnight and noon, breaking only rarely to eat or catch a quick nap on the studio sofa. And finally she stopped sleeping at all, caught wholly in the creation coming together beneath her fingertips, glass polished and gleaming, a suggestion of a smile, a large crimson drop glowing amid the radiant gold and a subtle echo of that drop on the hawk; and all of it surrounded by the hard brilliance of beveled crystal shards. Finally the last piece was leaded, the cement worked in and then removed, each glass surface polished until it shone.

With a sigh so deep that it made her earrings swing and cry, Angel leaned against the table. She knew that her summation was finished, yet she was unable to accept it. She wasn't ready to face the emptiness ahead of her, inside her, nothing left but the numb gray of exhaustion. She pushed the special table into her bedroom. With hands that shook, she removed the plywood panel and fixed the frame in its vertical position, leaving nothing between the stained glass and the night beyond. The panel was almost colorless, as bleak as her soul, for there was no light pouring through the stained glass, only darkness.

Angel looked at the bed that she hadn't slept in since Hawk left. The small candy cane lay on the pillow, untouched, green ribbon gleaming in the light from the bedside lamp. With a silent cry, Angel picked up the candy, hearing the rustle of its clear paper wrapping. Despite the exhaustion that made her tremble, she couldn't face the thought of lying down, of sleeping, of wakening again, and again finding Hawk gone.

She returned to the studio. For the first time in weeks, she really looked at it. The studio was a shambles. Normally she cleaned up as she worked. This time she hadn't. Shards of glass covered the small worktable, colors she had tried and rejected, pieces she had broken and forgotten. She walked into the studio, hearing silence and the tiny songs of the bells she wore.

As Angel stood near the worktable that was cluttered with brilliant fragments of glass, she realized that she was dizzy. She reached for the table, trying to brace herself, but it was too late. The table tilted, shaking off Angel, sending her into darkness.

A powerful black car pulled up in front of the Ramsey house. For a long time the driver sat unmoving in the darkness, staring up at the lights in the north wing. Hawk had fought against coming back, was still fighting against being there. He hated himself for returning to Angel with no more to give her than he had had when he left.

Yet he could not stay away. Life without her was as close to death as he had ever come.

Slowly, Hawk opened the car door. The stones of the front walk gleamed palely beneath the waning moon. He moved soundlessly, more shadow than man. He paused, then tried the door. Open. He walked inside and called her.

"Angel?"

Only an echo returned.

"Angel!"

The silence was like another shade of night, another kind of death.

Abruptly, Hawk ran down the hall to Angel's studio. He saw the tilted table, the glitter of shattered glass—Angel unconscious, veiled in brilliant, lethal fragments. He called her name as he knelt beside her, and the sound of his voice was like glass breaking. His hand trembled over her neck, seeking her pulse. When he found it, he bowed his head to the weakness and relief coursing through him. Delicately Hawk removed each shard of glass covering Angel. As he picked off the last bronze fragment, he saw that Angel's hand was clenched around something. With infinite care he opened her fingers, afraid that he would find a piece of razor glass pressed against her palm. It was not glass that he found, but a candy cane wrapped in a green ribbon.

For the first time since he was a child, Hawk wept.

Angel didn't awaken when Hawk undressed her and carried her to bed. She didn't stir when Dr. McKay examined her and then told Hawk in sleepy, irritable tones what Hawk had already guessed: Angel had pushed herself too hard and her body had shut down, hurtling her into a deep, restoring sleep.

Hawk undressed and went to Angel's bed, gathering her into his arms, giving her his warmth, intense brown eyes watching her sleeping face through all the hours of night. He watched her as the strong morning sun climbed above the mountains and poured in the bedroom window, flooding the stained glass panel with life and light. Beveled crystal split sunlight into rainbows. Fantastic colored shadows crept across the room until they spilled over Angel, bathing her in beauty.

Distracted by the dancing light, Hawk looked from the rainbow shadows on Angel's face to the panel that stood in the midst of radiance. And then Hawk forgot to move, forgot to breathe, forgot everything but the stained glass so silent and yet so incredibly alive. He saw a hawk descending from a transparent sky, a single talon outstretched to pierce a golden cloud. Where the talon touched the cloud, a large crimson drop welled, glistening with light. And there was something more . . . something in the cloud itself.

Compelled by beauty, Hawk came to his feet and approached the panel, drawn by the enigma within the golden cloud. As he walked, he saw first the swirl of evocative lines that transformed part of the cloud into a

woman's hair lifted on the wind. Next he saw the slightly
tilted eyes, a blend of shadow and brightness that shifted
from moment to moment, extraordinarily alive. Her enigmatic smile could have come from agony or ecstasy or some
beautiful, terrifying combination of both. Hawk made a
muffled sound and leaned closer, staring at the blood-red
drop that welled from the point where the hawk's talon
pierced the cloud. A rose was deeply etched into the
crimson teardrop.

For a moment Hawk closed his eyes, afraid to look
further. Yet he knew he would have to. He knew he
couldn't evade the hawk, its coldness and cruelty, the talon
tearing into the defenseless golden cloud. Slowly, he
opened his eyes and confronted Angel's vision of him.

The hawk was magnificent.

Captured at the ultimate moment of its descent from the
sky, the raptor shimmered with light in every shade of
bronze and brown. Power and grace and speed were
implicit in each line of the wings and body, the talon
reaching down, the topaz eye fixed on its prey. There was
something more, too, something so tiny that it was almost
lost in the fire of the larger pieces. A crimson tear welled
from the hawk's eye.

Silently, Hawk went even closer, staring at the tiny tear.
On its surface was etched the faint, delicate outline of a
rosebud. More suggestion than reality, more hope than
certainty, the nascent rose told Hawk more than he had
believed he would ever know about love.

Hawk stared at the crimson tear until he could no longer
see it. He hadn't believed in love, yet he had held it in his
arms time and again, heard love call his name in ecstasy,
felt love hot and sweet and unafraid around him . . . and
then he had turned and walked away, afraid to risk and love

in return. He could see that now, see it as clearly as sunlight pouring through glass, shattered fragments of the past transformed into a beauty that tore at his soul mercilessly, making room for love to live and grow.

Hawk stood motionless, absorbing light and color into himself until the muted cry of bells called to him. When he turned around, he saw Angel's hand move restlessly over the empty bed as though searching for something. He went back to the bed in a silent, gliding stride and gathered Angel against him, understanding finally why he had returned, knowing that he would never leave her again. He had learned what love was. It was an angel who loved a hawk enough to offer him everything, risk everything, give everything in the hope that even a bird of prey could learn to love. He had learned, too, that the hawk was neither cold nor cruel, simply the instrument of an angel's awakening, an awakening that was both agonizing and beautiful. The hawk shared in the beauty, and in the pain.

And in the awakening.

Silver bells shivered and sighed as Angel instinctively moved closer to the naked warmth of Hawk's body. He kissed her very gently, cherishing her. Her eyes opened, shadows and brilliance focusing on him, disbelief and incredible hope combined.

Hawk bent his dark head toward the bright golden cloud of Angel's hair.

"Hawk . . . ?"

"I love you, Angel."

Hawk joined the heat and sweetness of Angel's mouth with his own, retreating only long enough to whisper his love again and again, love returned by her soft lips, words and caresses mingling until he became a part of her. With slow, sensual movements they rediscovered what they had lost, cherishing and consuming and renewing each other, words of love transformed into soft cries of ecstasy and completion.

Sounds became words again, *I love you* whispered amid the shiver of silver bells. Bathed in colored shadows, the woman who knew no lies and the man who worshiped her held each other, knowing only each other. Wrapped in one another's arms, they slept deeply, their pain transformed into peace by the surpassing beauty of love.

EYE OF THE STORM

MAURA SEGER

A powerful portrayal of the events of World War II in the Pacific, *Eye of the Storm* is a riveting story of how love triumphs over hatred. In this, the first of a three book chronicle, Army nurse Maggie Lawrence meets Marine Sgt. Anthony Gargano. Despite military regulations against fraternization, they resolve to face together whatever lies ahead.... Also known by her fans as Laurel Winslow, Sara Jennings, Anne MacNeil and Jenny Bates, Maura Seger, author of this searing novel, was named by ROMANTIC TIMES as 1984's Most Versatile Romance Author.

At your favorite bookstore in March.

EYE-B-1

If you enjoyed this book...

Thrill to 4 more
Silhouette Intimate Moments
novels (a $9.00 value)—
ABSOLUTELY FREE!

If you want more passionate sensual romance, then Silhouette Intimate Moments novels are for you!

In every 256-page book, you'll find romance that's electrifying...involving... and intense. And now, these larger-than-life romances can come into your home every month!

4 FREE books as your introduction.

Act now and we'll send you four thrilling Silhouette Intimate Moments novels. They're our gift to introduce you to our convenient home subscription service. Every month, we'll send you four new Silhouette Intimate Moments books. Look them over for 15 days. If you keep them, pay just $9.00 for all four. Or return them at no charge.

We'll mail your books to you *as soon as they are published.* Plus, with every shipment, you'll receive the Silhouette Books Newsletter absolutely free. *And Silhouette Intimate Moments is delivered free.*

Mail the coupon today and start receiving Silhouette Intimate Moments. Romance novels for women...not girls.

Silhouette Intimate Moments

Silhouette Intimate Moments™
120 Brighton Road, P.O. Box 5084, Clifton, NJ 07015-5084

☐ YES! Please send me FREE and without obligation, 4 exciting Silhouette Intimate Moments romance novels. Unless you hear from me after I receive my 4 FREE books, please send 4 new Silhouette Intimate Moments novels to preview each month. I understand that you will bill me $2.25 each for a total of $9.00 — with no additional shipping, handling or other charges. **There is no minimum number of books to buy and I may cancel anytime I wish.** The first 4 books are mine to keep, even if I never take a single additional book

☐ Mrs. ☐ Miss ☐ Ms. ☐ Mr   BMM225

Name _____ (please print)

Address _____ Apt. #

City _____ State _____ Zip

Area Code   Telephone Number

Signature (if under 18, parent or guardian must sign)

This offer, limited to one per household, expires June 30, 1985. Terms and prices subject to change. Your enrollment is subject to acceptance by Silhouette Books.

Silhouette Intimate Moments is a service mark and trademark.

MAIL THIS COUPON
and get 4 thrilling
Silhouette Desire®
novels <u>FREE</u> (a $7.80 value)

Silhouette Desire books may not be for everyone. They *are* for readers who want a sensual, provocative romance. These are modern love stories that are charged with emotion from the first page to the thrilling happy ending—about women who discover the extremes of fiery passion. Confident women who face the challenge of today's world and overcome all obstacles to attain their dreams—*and their desires*.

We believe you'll be so delighted with Silhouette Desire romance novels that you'll want to receive them regularly through our home subscription service. Your books will be *shipped to you two months before they're available anywhere else*—so you'll never miss a new title. Each month we'll send you 6 new books to look over for 15 days, without obligation. If not delighted, simply return them and owe nothing. Or keep them and pay only $1.95 each. There's no charge for postage or handling. And there's no obligation to buy anything at any time. You'll also receive a subscription to the Silhouette Books Newsletter *absolutely free!*

So don't wait. To receive your four FREE books, fill out and mail the coupon below *today!*

SILHOUETTE DESIRE and colophon are registered trademarks and a service mark.

For the woman who expects a little more out of love, get Silhouette Special Edition.

Take 4 books free – no strings attached.

If you yearn to experience more passion and pleasure in your romance reading ... to share even the most private moments of romance and sensual love between spirited heroines and their ardent lovers, then Silhouette Special Edition has everything you've been looking for.

Get 6 books each month before they are available anywhere else!

Act now and we'll send you four exciting Silhouette Special Edition romance novels. They're our gift to introduce you to our convenient home subscription service. Every month, we'll send you six new passion-filled Special Edition books. Look them over for 15 days. If you keep them, pay just $11.70 for all six. Or return them at no charge.

We'll mail your books to you *two full months before they are available* anywhere else. Plus, with every shipment, you'll receive the Silhouette Books Newsletter absolutely free. *And with Silhouette Special Edition there are never any shipping or handling charges.*

Mail the coupon today to get your four free books — and more romance than you ever bargained for.

Silhouette Special Edition is a service mark and a registered trademark.

READERS' COMMENTS ON SILHOUETTE INTIMATE MOMENTS:

"About a month ago a friend loaned me my first Silhouette. I was thoroughly surprised as well as totally addicted. Last week I read a Silhouette Intimate Moments and I was even more pleased. They are the best romance series novels I have ever read. They give much more depth to the plot, characters, and the story is fundamentally realistic. They incorporate tasteful sex scenes, which is a must, especially in the 1980's. I only hope you can publish them fast enough."

S.B.*, Lees Summit, MO

"After noticing the attractive covers on the new line of Silhouette Intimate Moments, I decided to read the inside and discovered that this new line was more in the line of books that I like to read. I do want to say I enjoyed the books because they are so realistic and a lot more truthful than so many romance books today."

J.C., Onekama, MI

"I would like to compliment you on your new line of books. I will continue to purchase all of the Silhouette Intimate Moments. They are your best line of books that I have had the pleasure of reading."

S.M., Billings, MT

*names available on request